Queens of Romance

A collection of bestselling novels by the world's leading romance writers

Much-loved author Paula Marshall has written over 45 historical romances for Mills & Boon and she has always been a very versatile author, with her novels spanning from the 15th century to the 1920s, and everything in between.

The Beckoning Dream is dedicated to the memory of Aphra Behn. A wit, poet, dramatist, novelist and secret agent, Aphra Behn lived the life of a free woman in the mid-seventeenth century which was no mean achievement.

THE BECKONING DREAM

BY

PAULA MARSHALL

All the characters in this book have no existence outside the imagination of the author, and have no relation whatsoever to anyone bearing the same name or names. They are not even distantly inspired by any individual known or unknown to the author, and all the incidents are pure invention.

First Published in Great Britain 1997
Large Print Edition 2008
Harlequin Mills & Boon Limited,
Eton House, 18-24 Paradise Road,
Richmond, Surrey TW9 1SR

ISBN: 978 0 263 20690 6

Set in Times Roman 15½ on 17 pt.
82-1108-74827

Printed and bound in Great Britain
by Antony Rowe Ltd, Chippenham, Wiltshire

Author's Note to the Reader

This novel, like all of mine, is firmly based on fact, and is dedicated to the memory of Aphra Behn, wit, poet, dramatist, novelist and secret agent, who lived the life of a free woman in the mid-seventeenth century—no mean achievement. It has taken three hundred years for her reputation to be revived and her many talents to be properly appreciated.

One of her greatest achievements as an agent in Holland was to warn the British Government in 1667 that the Dutch Navy was about to launch a major attack on the naval bases of Sheerness and Chatham on the River Medway. Her warning was ignored, as she recorded in her autobiography, and for three hundred years her biographers and critics mocked her for having claimed that, had the Government heeded her report, a major disaster for the British Navy would have been avoided.

Three hundred years later, Aphra's claim was vindicated when her letter, giving details of the proposed attack, was discovered in the State Papers. In the same way, her right to be seen as the mother of the English novel and as the writer of a number of witty and actable plays was also derided until the Sixties of the present century when her work was looked at with fresh eyes.

Prologue

"True love is a beckoning dream."
Old saying

Two men from the court of King Charles II at Whitehall sat on the side of the stage of the Duke of York's Theatre in the early spring of 1667. One of them was short and plump and was wearing a monstrous black-curled wig. The other was tall and muscular; his wig was blond, and his hooded eyes were blue. Both of them were magnificently dressed and were wearing half-masks so that it was impossible to detect their true identity.

They were watching a play called *The Braggart, or, Lackwit in Love,* which had just reached the scene where, as the script had it, the following ensued:

Enter to LACKWIT, BELINDA BELLAMOUR, disguised as a youth, one LUCIUS.

LACKWIT Ho, there, sirrah! Art thou Mistress Belinda Bellamour's boy?
BELINDA Nay, sir.
LACKWIT How "Nay, sir'? What answer is that? Art thou not but just come from her quarters?
BELINDA Aye, sir, but nay, sir. Aye, sir, I have come from her quarters. Nay, sir, I am not her boy—my mother was of quite a different kidney! So, aye, sir, nay, sir!
LACKWIT Insolent child! (Makes to strike her with his cane.)
BELINDA (Twisting away.) What is the world coming to when a man may be beaten for speaking the truth!
LACKWIT Man! Man! Thy mother's milk is still on thy lips!
BELINDA Aye, sir—but it is not Belinda's!

By now the audience—which was in on the joke of Belinda's sex—was roaring its approval as Belinda defied Lackwit by jumping about the stage to dodge his cane, showing a fine pair of legs as she did so.

Master Blond Wig drawled at his dark friend, "Now that she has chosen to show them, her legs are better than her breasts—and they, when visible, were sublime. A new star for the stage."

He took in the pleasing sight that the actress playing Belinda presented to the world in boy's clothes; lustrous raven hair, deep violet eyes, a kissable mouth and a body to stiffen a man's desire simply by looking at it!

"Aye," agreed Black Wig, who was also appreciating Belinda. "And a new playwright, too. The bills proclaim that he is one Will Wagstaffe."

"Will Wagstaffe!" Blond Wig began to laugh. "You jest, Hal."

"Nay, Stair, for that is what the playbill saith. And the doxy who affects the boy is none other than Mistress Cleone Dubois, who made a hit, a very hit, as Clarinda in *Love's Last Jest* by that same Wagstaffe whilst thou were out of town."

"Did she so? I do not believe in Will Wagstaffe, and nor should you," exclaimed Blond Wig. "But I have a mind to play a jest of my own."

The action of the play had come close to them whilst they spoke, as Belinda and Lackwit sparred. Blond Wig picked a fruit from the basket that the orange girl had left before them, and threw it straight at Belinda, whom nothing daunted, either as Belinda playing a boy on the stage or in her true nature when not an actress. On seeing the orange coming, she caught it neatly and flung it back at Blond Wig as hard as she could.

He retaliated by rolling it across the stage towards her as though it were a bowling ball. Mr Betterton, the doyen of all Restoration actors, who was playing Lackwit, jumped dexterously over it, so that it arrived at Belinda's feet.

She bent down, picked it up, and examined it before beginning to peel and eat it, segment by segment, exclaiming as she did so, "Why, Sir Lackwit, I do believe that the fruit thou hast refused is better than the wit. For that is dry, and this orange is juicy. I shall tell my Mistress Belinda that whilst you may have pith and self-importance, you lack the true Olympian oil which the Gods bestow on their favourites.

"But for the orange peel, this," and she threw the shards of the peel straight at Blond Wig, who was on his feet applauding her improvisation, as were the rest of the audience.

"The doxy is wittier than the man who writes her lines," exclaimed Blond Wig after bowing to the audience, who applauded him as heartily as they had rewarded Belinda. "And if you and the audience cannot see the jest in a man who writes plays calling himself Will Wagstaffe why, then, you and they are duller than I thought."

"Enough of this," whispered Betterton to Cleone as they grappled together in a mock and comic wrestling match. "Improvisation is well enough, and one of Rochester's Merry Gang interfering with the action on stage may have to be endured, but you need not encourage him."

"Need I not? But the audience, who is our master, approved."

"Aye so, but we risk every fool in town wanting to be part of the play." He turned himself back into Lackwit again in order to declaim in the direction of the pit, *"Why, I vow thou art as soft as a very girl, Master Lucius. You need some lessons in hardening thyself."*

"Dost think that thou are the man to give me them, Sir Lackwit?"

The pit roared again. Some of the bolder members threw pennies on to the stage at Belinda's feet. Blond Wig had produced a fan and waved it languidly in her direction.

"I vow and declare, Hal," he whispered to Black Wig, "Master Wagstaffe is as bawdily witty as his master, the other Will."

"And what Will is that, Stair?"

"Why, Shakespeare, man. Will Shakespeare. He who wags the staff. Is all the world as thick as a London fog in winter, these days?"

Black Wig couldn't think of a witty answer to that. He might be Henry Bennett, m'lord Arlington, King Charles II's Secretary of State who ruled England, but his wit was long term, carefully thought out, unlike that of his friend Blond Wig, otherwise Sir Alastair Cameron. Stair Cameron was known for his cutting tongue as well as his reputation for courage and contempt for everything and everybody. He was also known for his success with women.

And now, if Lord Arlington knew his man, his latest female target would be the pretty doxy on the stage who was back in skirts again, teasing and tempting Lackwit—as well as every red-blooded man in the audience. Her charms were such that she might even attract the attention of the King himself.

The pretty doxy on the stage was well aware that Blond Wig was making a dead set at her, as the saying went. At the end of the first Act, he bought a posy from a flower girl and tossed it to her as she left the stage.

She tossed it back at him.

In the second Act, he kissed his hand to her whenever the action on stage brought her near him.

Halfway through the third Act, Belinda pretended to woo Lackwit, and to allow him to woo her, her true lover, Giovanni Amoroso, being concealed behind a hedge to enjoy the fun. At the point when Lackwit had worked himself into a lather of desire, Blond Wig drew off one of his perfumed gloves and slung that in Belinda's direction at the very climax of her scene with Lackwit.

"Why, what have we here?" she extemporised, holding up the glove. "What hath Dan Cupid sent me as a love token?" She sniffed at it. "Fie upon him, it hath a vile stink. He may have it back."

And she slung it back at Blond Wig, who rose and bowed to her.

M'lord Arlington applauded him vigorously, whispering to his friend as he did so, "The wench will serve us well, will she not? Old Gower hath the right of it again. A pretty wit and a quick one. As quick as thine, Stair, I do declare."

"But shallow, like all women's wit, I dare swear. But I agree, she will do as well as another—and better than some. And mayhap she will tell me who Will Wagstaffe is, and where I may find the fellow."

"Hipped on Wagstaffe, Stair?"

"Aye, hipped on any pretty wit—particularly one of whom I do not know."

"Make the doxy thine, friend Stair, and she will tell thee all. Look, Lackwit hath learned that he truly lacks wit, and that Amoroso and Belinda are about to sing their love duet to signify that the play is over, and that he was cuckolded before he even wed his Mistress and made her wife!"

The play was, indeed, ending. Belinda was reciting the Epilogue, a poem in which she averred that she had followed the beckoning dream which led towards true love, and might now marry Amoroso.

"Truly a dream, that," Stair whispered to Arlington. "But not the kind one of which the lady speaks. I can think of no nightmare more troubling than that which ends in marriage."

The Epilogue over, Mistress Dubois, Betterton, and the pretty boy who played Amoroso linked hands and were bowing to the audience, which was on its feet again, applauding the actors. Blond Wig was shouting huzzahs at Belinda, who refused to look at him.

"To the devil with him," hissed Belinda, or rather Mistress Cleone Dubois, to Betterton. "He tried to ruin all my best scenes. Another courtier come to entertain himself by destroying us."

"He got no change from you, Cleone, my pretty dear. On the contrary, your quick wits had them laughing at him as much as you."

"And who the devil is he? I know his friend, Sir Hal Bennett, late made Lord Arlington, but not the human gadfly in the blond wig."

Betterton smiled and bowed, his head almost touching his knees before he led the company offstage, before saying, "Sir Alastair, known as Stair Cameron, Baronet. Rochester's friend—everybody's friend, aye, and enemy, too, gossip hath it. Avoid him like the plague that hath just left us. He would be no friend of thine, Cleone—or of any woman's. Mark me this, he will be in the Green Room this evening, to pursue you further."

"May God forbid," Cleone shuddered. She trusted no man, least of all those who infested Charles's court. "I want naught of him."

But he wasn't in the Green Room. Sam Pepys was there, and Lord Arlington, who bowed at Cleone and said in a butter-melting voice, "My felicitations, Mistress Dubois. You have grown since I last saw thee at Sir Thomas Gower's when you were Mistress Wood. A very child, were you not?"

He tittered a little behind a fine white handkerchief edged with lace. "You look about you, mistress. Is it my friend you seek?"

The violet eyes were hard upon him. "Nay, m'lord. Unless it is to teach him manners—if indeed it were possible to teach him anything."

Sam Pepys, standing by them, gave a jolly guffaw. "Come, come, mistress, you are too harsh. Stair Cameron is a right good fellow."

Cleone rounded on him, shaking her fan in his direction, Belinda's fan. She knew who Sam Pepys was. The Secretary to the Navy, a womaniser and a gossip—but there was no harm in him.

"Fie upon you, too, sir. What, I wonder, would you say, if Stair Cameron entered your office and upset the contents of your inkpot on your newly written letter to your master, the King, ruining it? Would you think the destruction of your work a jolly jest to be applauded? For such were the offences he committed against me!"

Lord Arlington clapped his hands together, and even Sam himself joined in the joke. "Why, madam," m'lord offered, "you are as spirited a lady as you were a lass. I should introduce you to Sir Stair. How the fur and the feathers would fly, for I vow that in spirit you are well matched."

Cleone stared at him, nothing daunted by his name or his position, something that pleased the man before her mightily. Oh, he had plans for Mistress Wood, also named Mistress Dubois, great plans. And now he could go to Sir Thomas Gower, his spymaster supreme, to tell him that Cleone Dubois was a lass of spirit who would serve them well.

What she said next had him laughing again behind his lace-gloved hand. "For," smiled Cleone, "it would please me greatly never to see Sir Stair Cameron again, either on stage, or off it. Unless it were to hand him such a *congé* from a woman as he has never received before. But enough of him. To talk of him wearies me. What thought you of the play, m'lord?"

Graciously, m'lord Arlington told the lady that he had enjoyed it, his smooth face even smoother than usual.

And all the time he was laughing to himself as he thought of the delightful possibility that the spirited lady and her tormentor might soon meet again—and wondered which of them would come off the best, as the fur and the feathers would inevitably fly like the orange, the posy and the perfumed glove!

Chapter One

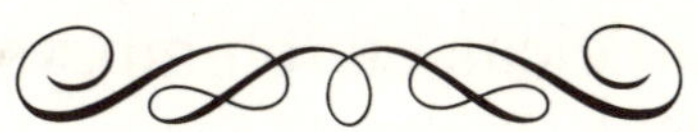

1667

"Who the devil can that be at this hour, Catherine?"

Rob Wood had just carved himself a large chunk of cold bacon for his breakfast to go with the buttered slice of bread that his sister, whom he always insisted on calling by her true name, had cut for him.

He had no sooner transferred the bacon to his pewter plate than a vile hammering had begun on the door of their small house in Cob's Lane, London, not far from the Inns of Court where Rob was studying to be a lawyer. Or was supposed to be studying.

Rob was as idle as his sister was diligent. The only hard work he did was to write pamphlets attacking the rule of King Charles II and praising that of the late usurper and regicide, Cromwell. This was a particularly foolish act since England was at present at war with the Netherlanders—

fighting them in order to prevent them from seizing the major share of the world's trade. Opposition to the king was thus bound to be seen as treason.

Catherine, who was busy buttering a slice of loaf for herself, said crossly, "Answer the door, Rob. Don't stand there yammering. It's probably Jem Hollins come to clean our chimneys."

Grumbling, Rob rose to do as he was bid. Although he was living entirely on his sister's earnings in the theatre, he resented that fact rather than being grateful for it. Their father, once a rich country gentleman, had supported Cromwell in the late Civil War. Charles II's Restoration had seen his estates confiscated; he had died penniless, leaving his two children to make their own way in the world.

Rob thought of himself as a dispossessed Crown Prince and behaved accordingly.

He never reached the door. Tired of trying to attract their attention, the Woods' importunate visitors ceased their knocking abruptly.

Shouting "Ho, there, take heed and attend to us," they knocked down the house door with iron-tipped staves of wood, before rushing in, seizing Rob and throwing him to the floor.

A third man, carrying a large piece of parchment importantly before him, put one foot on the struggling Rob, whilst a fourth placed himself between

Catherine and her brother in case she tried to come to his assistance.

"By what authority—?" she began, using all the power of her stage voice to try to overawe them.

"By the authority vested in me by his most noble majesty, King Charles II, I hereby arrest Robert Wood for the crime of high treason, and detain his sister Catherine Wood, also known as Cleone Dubois, actress and whore, for questioning as to his activities."

"My sister's no whore," shouted Rob as he was hauled to his feet, his hands pinioned behind his back, "and I know of no law which says that a man may not speak or write freely of his opinions—unless you have just invented one."

If only Rob would learn to keep silent when challenged he would not find life so difficult, mourned Catherine as the leading tipstaff struck her brother across the mouth, bellowing, "That should silence your lying tongue, you treacherous rogue."

He and two of his fellows began to drag Rob outside. The fourth seized Catherine roughly by the arm with one hand, while running the other across her breasts.

Hissing at him, "No need of that, I have no desire either to have you fondle me, or to escape," Catherine brought her high-heeled shoe down hard on his instep. The tipstaff let out a shrill cry before striking her across the face with such force that she was thrown against the wall.

"Had I the time, you insolent bonaroba, you whore, I'd serve you as a man should serve a whore—later, perhaps," he roared at her as she tried to recover her balance.

And who am I to criticise poor Rob for not keeping his tongue under guard when I can't keep mine shut, either? Catherine thought as she walked painfully into the street. Outside a small crowd had gathered to watch the two Woods dragged away. She looked around her; where are they taking us? To prison? To Newgate? Or to the Tower of London itself?

She was destined for none of them, it seemed. She and Rob were half-walked, half-dragged to the nearest wharf on the Thames where two wherries were waiting. Rob was shoved into one, and she into the other.

The last she saw of him was his wherry making for the Tower, whilst she was rowed off in the opposite direction. To the Palace of Whitehall, no less, the King's home in London, and consequently, the seat of government. Catherine's mounting curiosity almost overcame her fear for herself, even as she worried over poor Rob's ultimate fate.

No time for that, though. She was bustled along Whitehall's gravelled walks towards one of the many buildings that made up the Palace precincts.

The tipstaffs waved their staves, doors were opened for them, and presently, after traversing a number of long corridors, they came to a pair of double doors, on whose panels the tipstaffs knocked more subserviently than they had done in Cob's Lane.

Beyond the doors was a largish room, one wall of which consisted almost entirely of latticed windows looking out on a garden. A number of finely dressed gentlemen were standing about, but they left the room even as Catherine entered it.

At the opposite end from the doors was a long table, where a man whom she immediately recognised sat in state. Behind him, covering the whole wall, hung a huge tapestry showing the Greeks pouring out of the Wooden Horse to capture and destroy Troy.

Catherine had no time to admire wall hangings. She was too busy staring at Sir Thomas Gower. Sir Thomas had taken her father, Rob and herself into his household for a short time after King Charles's Restoration had made them homeless. He had been as kind to her father as his position as a powerful Royalist had permitted him to be.

Why had she been brought here? She was soon to find out.

"Come here, Mistress Wood," Sir Thomas bade her, and then, "Bring the lady a chair, she seems distressed. Place it before me. Sit, sit," he commanded her as she walked slowly forward, rubbing her arm, bruised where the tipstaff had seized it.

Now that she was near to Sir Thomas, Catherine could plainly tell that he had aged since she had last seen him. His face was lined with over sixty years of life, but he still possessed the calm gravity that had been so different from her father's impotent rage at what had happened to his pleasant life.

She could also see that level with herself, and in front of Sir Thomas's grand oak table on which books, ledgers and parchments stood at one end, was an armchair in which a man lounged. A man who was staring at her, not with Sir Thomas's kind and paternal stare, but hungrily, almost ferally, his blue eyes cruel.

Bewildered, but still retaining the steady calm for which her fellow actors admired her, Catherine returned Sir Thomas's grave look. She must not show her fear, but must keep her head so that Rob might not lose his, and pray that there might be a way out of the dire situation in which he had placed them.

"My dear Catherine," said Sir Thomas, kindness itself, "I fear that your condition—or perhaps I should say, your brother's condition—is a sad one. Treason!" He shook his grey head helplessly. "An ugly word, my dear. Nevertheless, God willing, we might find a way through the wood for you."

What wood was he speaking of? The good old man,

Catherine thought dazedly, was being so tactful that she hardly knew what he was saying. The lounging fellow on her right, whose eyes were still so hard on her that she could feel them when she could no longer see them, grunted "Ahem' in a meaningful tone—although his meaning escaped Catherine!

But apparently not Sir Thomas, for he threw a sideways glance at his unmannerly aide, and said smoothly. "Ah, yes, Mistress Wood. I must be plain. We are not engaged in one of Master Wagstaffe's comedies, are we?"

"No, indeed," agreed Catherine.

"Whoever Master Wagstaffe is," drawled the lounging man. "Another mystery."

"No matter." Sir Thomas was a little brisk. "I put it to you, Mistress Wood, that you do not share your brother's Republican views."

"I doubt—" and now Catherine was dry "—that he shares them himself. Rob is a weathercock. An attack of the megrims and he is all for the late usurper. If the weather is fine, and there is good food on the table, then it is 'God save King Charles II'."

Sir Thomas was suave. "All the more reprehensible of him, then, mistress, to put his life in jeopardy by writing treason. You, I understand, are a good and loyal subject of the King?"

Since his question seemed to invite the answer "Yes", Catherine gave it to him.

"Oh, excellent," smiled Sir Thomas. "So you would be willing to do the state some service. You speak Dutch, mistress, do you not? Your late mother being a Netherlander, as I remember."

This seemed neither here nor there, and its relevance to poor Rob seemed questionable, but doubtless there was some point to this that escaped her. The lounging man was fidgeting again.

Sir Thomas gave him a benevolent stare. "Patience, Tom Trenchard, patience. We are almost at the heart of the matter."

"Oh, excellent," drawled Tom Trenchard, mocking Sir Thomas's earlier remark. "I had thought that we were trapped in the outworks for ever."

This time Catherine favoured him with a close examination, particularly since Sir Thomas was allowing him more freedom than was usually given to an underling. The principal thing about him was that he was big, much bigger than any of the men in Betterton's company.

His shoulders were broad, his hands large, and he appeared to be at least six feet in height. His hair, his own, was of a burning red gold—more gold than red. It was neither long like the wigs of the King's courtiers, nor cropped short like one of Cromwell's Roundheads, but somewhere in between. It was neither straight nor curly, but again, was also somewhere in between, waving slightly.

His clothes were rough and serviceable. His shirt had been washed until it was yellow, and the weary lace at his throat and wrists was darned. His boots were the best thing about him, but even they were not those of a court gallant. Neither was his harsh and craggy face.

She already knew that he was mannerless, and he gave off the ineffable aura of all the soldiers whom she had ever met, being wild, but contained. Or almost contained. He saw her looking at him, and nodded thoughtfully. "You will know me again, mistress, I see."

"Do I need to?" Catherine countered, and then to Sir Thomas, "Forgive me, sir, for allowing my attention to stray," for she knew that the great ones of this world required all attention to be on them, and not on such lowly creatures as she judged herself and the lounging man to be.

He forgave her immediately. "Nay, mistress, you do well to inspect Master Trenchard. You will have much to do with him. As you have not denied either your loyalty, or your knowledge of Dutch, I am putting it to you, mistress, that you might oblige us by accompanying him to the Netherlands, there to use your skills as a linguist and as an actress. You will join him in an enterprise to persuade one William Grahame, who has done the state some service in the past, to bring off one final coup on our behalf.

"William Grahame has indicated to us that he is in a position to give us information about the disposition of the Dutch army and their fleet. He has also said that he will only do so to an emissary of my office who will meet him in the Low Countries at a place of his choosing. Once he has passed this information to us, and not before, your final task will be to bring him safely home to England again. He is weary of living abroad."

He beamed at her as he finished speaking. Tom Trenchard grunted, mannerless again, "And so we reach the point—at long last."

"Tom's grasp of diplomacy is poor, I fear," explained Sir Thomas needlessly. Catherine had already gathered that. She was already gathering something else, something which might help Rob, even before Sir Thomas mentally ticked off his next point.

"You must also understand, mistress, that success in this delicate matter—if you agree to undertake it—would prove most beneficial when the case of Master Robert Wood comes to trial—*if* it comes to trial, that is. The likelihood is that, with your kind co-operation, it will not."

"And if I refuse?" returned Catherine.

"Why then, alas, Master Robert Wood will pay the price for his folly on the headsman's block on Tower Hill."

"And if I accept, but fail, what then?" asked Catherine.

"Why then, you all fail. Master Tom Trenchard, Mistress Catherine Wood and Master Robert Wood. Such may—or may not be—God's will. Only He proposes and disposes."

"Although Sir Thomas Gower makes a good fist of imitating Him," drawled Tom Trenchard. "Particularly since it will not be his head on the plate handed to King Herod, whatever happens."

So there it was. The price of Rob's freedom was that she undertake a dangerous enterprise—and succeed in it.

"I have agreed with Master Betterton—" Catherine began, but Sir Thomas did not allow her to finish.

"Nay, mistress. I understand that Master Wagstaffe's masterpiece has its last showing tonight—at which you will, of course, be present to play Belinda.

"Moreover, Master Betterton would not, if asked by those who have the power to do so, refuse to release you for as long as is necessary. Particularly on the understanding that, when you return, you shall be the heroine of Master Wagstaffe's proposed new play—*The Braggart Returns, or, Lackwit Married.* I look forward to seeing it."

This time the look Sir Thomas gave her was that of a fellow conspirator in a plot that had nothing to do with his bully, Trenchard, or with William Grahame in the Netherlands. Unwillingly, Catherine nodded.

"To save Rob, I will agree to your demands." She had been left with no choice, for Sir Thomas had not one hold over her but two. The greater, of course, was his use of Rob to blackmail her. The lesser was his knowledge of who Will Wagstaffe really was.

And it was also most likely sadly true that the only reason why the authorities—or rather Sir Thomas Gower—had ordered poor Rob to be arrested was to compel her to be their agent and their interpreter.

"That is most wise of you, Mistress Wood. Your loyalty to King Charles II does you great credit."

To which Catherine made no answer, for she could not say, Be damned to King Charles II, I do but agree to save Rob's neck. Tom Trenchard saw her mutinous expression and read it correctly.

"What, silent, mistress?" he drawled. "No grand pronouncements of your devotion to your King?"

"Quiet—but for the moment. And I have nothing to say to *you.* Tell me, Sir Thomas, in what capacity will I accompany Master Trenchard here?"

"Why, as his wife, who fortunately speaks Dutch—and French. You are an actress, mistress. Playing the wife should present you with no difficulties."

"Playing the husband will offer me none," interjected Tom meaningfully.

"And *that* is what I fear," returned Catherine robustly. "I will not play the whore in order to play the wife. You understand me, sir, I am sure."

"I concede that you have a ready tongue and have made a witty answer," drawled Tom. "And I can only reply alas, yes, I understand you! Which may not be witty, but has the merit of being truthful."

"Come now," ordered Sir Thomas, "you are to be comrades, as well as loving husband and wife. Moreover, once in the Low Countries you are both to be noisily agreed in supporting the Republicans who wish to replace the King with a Cromwellian successor. Master Trenchard will claim to be a member of that family which followed the late Oliver so faithfully.

"And you, being half-Dutch, will acknowledge the Grand Pensionary, John De Witt, to be your man, not King Charles's nephew, the powerless Stadtholder." He paused.

"As a dutiful wife," remarked Catherine demurely, "I shall be only too happy to echo the opinions of my husband."

Tom Trenchard's chuckle was a rich one. "Well said, mistress. I shall remind of you that—frequently."

Sir Thomas smiled benevolently on the pair of them. "I shall inform you both of the details of your journey. You will travel by packet boat to Ostend and from thence to Antwerp in Flanders where you may hope to find Grahame—if he has not already made for Amsterdam, where I gather he has a reliable informer.

"You will, of course, follow him to Amsterdam, if necessary. You will send your despatches—in code—to my agent here, James Halsall, the King's Cupbearer. He will pass them on to me.

"You will pose as merchants buying goods who are sympathetic towards those unregenerate Republicans who still hold fast against our gracious King. To bend William Grahame to our will is your main aim—because like all such creatures he plays a double game. Why, last year he sold all the Stadtholder's agents in England to us, and now word hath it that the Stadtholder hath rewarded him with a pension—doubtless for selling *our* agents to *him.*

"Natheless, he is too valuable for us to carp at his dubious morals, and if gold and a pardon for his past sins brings him home to us with all his information—then so be it, whether there be blood on his hands, or no."

Sir Thomas was, for once, Catherine guessed, dropping his pretence of being a benevolent uncle, and doing so deliberately in order to impress on her the serious nature of her mission. She heard Tom Trenchard clapping his hands and laughing at Sir Thomas's unwonted cynicism.

She turned to stare at him. He was now slouched down in his chair, his feral eyes alight, one large hand slapping his coarse brown breeches above his spotless boots. The thought of spending much time in the Netherlands alone with him was enough to eat away at her normal self-control.

"It seems that only a trifle is needed to amuse you, Master Trenchard. I hope that you take heed of what I told you. I go to Holland as your supposed wife, not as your true whore. Remember that!"

"So long as you do, mistress, so long as you do."

The insolent swine was leering at her. He might not, by his dress, be one of King Charles's courtiers, but he certainly shared their morals. It did not help that Sir Thomas's smile remained pasted to his face as he informed her that she was to pack her bag immediately, and be ready to leave as soon as Tom Trenchard called on her.

"Which will not be until after your last performance tonight. And then you will do as Tom bids you—so far as this mission is concerned, that is."

Catherine ignored the possible *double entendre* in Sir Thomas's last statement. Instead, looking steadily at him, she made one last statement of her own.

"I may depend upon thee, Sir Thomas, that should I succeed, then my brother's safety is assured."

"My word upon it, mistress. And I have never broke it yet."

"Bent it a little, perhaps," added Tom Trenchard, disobligingly, viciously dotting Sir Thomas's i's for him, as appeared to be his habit.

Catherine, after giving him one scathing look, ignored him. She thought again that he was quite the most ill-favoured man she had ever seen, with his high forehead, strong nose, grim mouth and determined jaw. Only the piercing blue of his eyes redeemed him.

She addressed Sir Thomas. "I may leave, now? After the commotion your tipstaffs made, my neighbours doubtless think that I, like my brother, am lodged in the Tower. I should be happy to disoblige them."

"Indeed, mistress. I shall give orders that your brother be treated tenderly during his stay in the Tower, my word on it."

And that, thought Catherine, is as much, if not more, than I might have hoped. She gave Sir Thomas a giant curtsy as he waved her away. "Tell one of the footmen who guard the door to see thee home again, mistress," being his final words to her.

She had gone. Tom Trenchard rose to his feet, and drawled familiarly at Sir Thomas, "Exactly as I prophesied after I toyed with her at the play. The doxy has a ready wit and a brave spirit. I hope to enjoy both."

He laughed again when the wall hanging behind Sir Thomas shivered as Black Wig, otherwise Hal

Bennet, m'lord Arlington, emerged from his hiding place where he had overheard every word of Catherine's interrogation.

"The wench will do, will she not?" said m'lord. "She may have been the fish at the end of your line, Thomas, but you had to play her carefully lest she landed back in the river again. I observe that you did not directly inform her that she is to use her female arts on Grahame to persuade him to turn coat yet once more—he being a noted womaniser. That may be done by Master Trenchard in Flanders or Holland—wheresoever you may find him!"

He swung on Tom Trenchard, otherwise Sir Stair Cameron, who was now pouring himself a goblet of wine from a jug on a side-table. "She knew thee not, Stair, I trust?"

"What, in this Alsatian get-up?" mocked Stair, referring to the London district where the City's criminals congregated. "I doubt me whether she could have recognised the King himself if he were dressed in these woundy hand-me-downs."

"Well suited for your errand in the Netherlands, Stair. None there would take you for the King's friend, rather the King's prisoner."

"Or the friend of m'lord Arlington who turned the Seigneur de Buat away from the Grand Pensionary and towards the Peace party—which cost Buat his head," riposted Stair.

Arlington's reply to his friend was a dry one. "His fault, Stair. He was careless, and handed the Pensionary a letter from me, not meant for the Pensionary's eyes. Do you take care, man. No careless heroics—nor careful ones, either."

Stair Cameron bowed low, sweeping the floor with his plumed hat that had been sitting by his feet. "An old soldier heeds thee, m'lord. My only worry is the lady. She may, once she knows what her part in this is, take against Grahame and refuse to enchant him. Furthermore, playing the heroine at the Duke of York's Theatre is no great matter, and coolness shown on the boards might not mean coolness on life's stage when one's head might be loose on one's shoulders. We shall see."

Arlington dropped his jocular mode and flung an arm around his friend's shoulders. "If aught goes amiss, Stair, and the heavens begin to fall on thee, then abandon all, and come home. Abandon Grahame to the Netherlanders if you have cause to suspect his honesty. Let the wolves have the wolf—we owe him nothing."

"And the lady?"

Arlington looked at Sir Thomas Gower, who shrugged his shoulders. "Deal with her as common sense suggests. She is there not only to seduce Grahame, but to help you with your supposed insufficient Dutch and to give an air of truth to your claim to be a one-time solder turned merchant. You will both claim to have Republican leanings and in consequence are happy to spend some time in God's own Republic—which is the way in which the Netherlanders speak of Holland."

Stair toasted Arlington with an upraised goblet. "Well said, friend, and I swear to you that I shall try to persuade the Hollanders that I am God's own soldier—however unlikely that is in truth."

Arlington ended the session with a clap of laughter. "The age of miracles is back on earth, Stair, if thou and God may be mentioned in the same breath. Forget that—and come home safely with Grahame and the lady in thy pocket. Great shall be thy reward—on earth, if not in heaven."

Stair Cameron bowed low again. "Oh, I beg leave to doubt that, Hal. From what I know of our revered King Charles and his empty Treasury, I shall have to wait for heaven. What I do I do for you, and our friendship. Let that be enough."

Sir Thomas Gower, who had poured a drink for himself and Arlington, had the final word. "Long live friendship, then. A toast to that, and to the King's Majesty."

Chapter Two

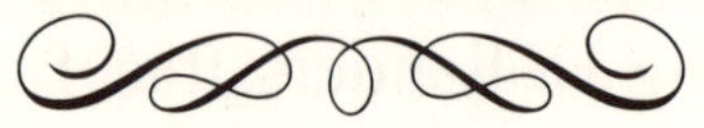

Catherine Wood, posing as Mistress Tom Trenchard, hung over the packet boat's side, vomiting her heart up. A spring crossing from London to Ostend was frequently unpleasant, and this one was no exception.

Nothing seemed to have gone right since the afternoon on which Tom Trenchard had called at her door to escort her to the docks. His appearance was as fly-by-night as it had been forty-eight hours before in Sir Thomas Gower's office. Behind him stood an equally ill-dressed manservant who had been pulling a little wagon on which Tom's two battered trunks rested.

The day was cold and a light drizzle had begun to fall. Tom was sporting a much darned cloak about his shoulders: it suitably matched his shabby lace. He leaned a familiar shoulder on the door post, grinning down at her from his great height.

“Well, mistress, do you intend to keep me standing in the rain forever? A true wife would invite her husband in.”

“I am not your true wife, sir,” Catherine riposted coldly, “but natheless you may come in.” As Tom removed his hat in order to enter, she added, “Do you intend your man to remain outside growing wet whilst his master enjoys the fireside indoors? He may sit with my serving maid in the kitchen.”

Tom was nothing put out. “Ah, a kind wife, I see, who considers the welfare of her husband’s servants, as well as her husband. Do as the mistress bids, Geordie.”

Geordie doffed a much-creased hat whose broad brim drooped to his shoulders. “And the trunks, Mistress Trenchard, may they come in, too?” He was so ill-shaven that it was difficult to tell whether he was as poorly favoured as his master.

Catherine nodded assent and followed Tom in. He was already seated before the hearth, and was pulling off his beautiful boots.

“You have made yourself at home, I see.” Catherine could not help being acid. He was here on sufferance, solely because she was being blackmailed into doing something which she had no wish to do, in order to save her silly brother’s life, and Tom was already behaving like the master of the house.

He must learn—and learn soon—that he could

take no liberties with her. Alas, his next words simply went to prove that he had every intention of doing so. "Look you, Mistress Wood, or rather, Mistress Trenchard, from this moment on you are my wife, and what is a wife's is her husband's for him to do as he pleases with. If you are to pass as my wife without attracting comment, then I suggest that you remember that. A tankard of ale would not come amiss, *wife.*"

Oh, it was plain that the next few weeks—pray God that they were not months—were going to be difficult ones, if the start of this misbegotten venture was a sample of her future! Unwillingly, Catherine bobbed a mocking curtsy at him in a broad parody of a stage serving maid before bustling into the kitchen to do as she was bid. She could hear him laughing as she stage-exited right, as it were.

Once in the kitchen, she found that Geordie had made himself at home also, and was not only drinking her good ale, but was eating a large slice from a fresh-made loaf, liberally spread with new-churned butter. At least *he* showed a little gratitude, pulling a greasy forelock and offering her a bobbing bow.

The whole effect was spoiled a little by his bulging cheeks and eyes as he stuffed more bread into his mouth. Plainly Master Tom Trenchard did not feed his servant well.

Tom accepted the ale she handed him as his due—

waving her to a seat by her own fireside as though the house were already his. From what pigsty had he graduated to arrive at King Charles's court? If he were from the court, that was. His rank and standing seemed dubious to say the least.

By his clothes he was virtually penniless, some sort of hireling, called in to serve the nation's spy-master—for that was surely Sir Thomas Gower's office. Yet Sir Thomas had treated him almost as an equal, and he had not hesitated to mock at Sir Thomas. Sir Thomas had said that they would pose as merchants. He seemed an unlikely merchant.

So, was he a gentleman down on his luck? And what matter if he were not? These days gentlemen were as nastily rapacious where women were concerned as their supposed inferiors, and at Whitehall the courtiers, led by such debauchees as m'lord Rochester, were the nastiest of all. No woman was safe with them. It would be as well to remember that.

"You are very quiet, wife? What ails you? A silent woman is a *lusus naturae*—almost against nature."

"I mislike sentences which assume that all women are the same woman. Men would not care to be told that because some men are dissolute rakes, then all must be so."

"Oh, wittily spoken—good enough for Master Wagstaffe, I vow. Tell me, my dear wife, does reciting the well-found words of learned playwrights result in your own lines in real life becoming as witty as theirs?"

Catherine widened her eyes. "La, sir, your intelligence quite overthrows me! Let me try to enlighten you. Am I, then, to suppose that Sir Thomas Gower and Lord Arlington's wisdom must transfer itself to you when you frequent their company?

"I see little sign of that; on the contrary, you maintain your usual coarse mode of speech. From this I deduce that my wit is therefore my own, and not the consequence of mixing with the geniuses who frequent the Duke's Theatre, be they actors or scribblers."

Tom was laughing as she finished, and before she could stop him he had put a large arm around her waist and hefted her on to his knee. "Shrew!" he hissed affably into her ear. "It is a good thing that you are not my true wife or you might earn a lesson in civility. As it is, let this serve."

He tipped her backwards and began to kiss her without so much as a by your leave, just like the rapacious gentlemen whose conduct she had just been silently lamenting. First he saluted each cheek, and then her mouth became his target.

The devil of it was that she would have expected him to be fierce and brutal in such forced loving, but no such thing. His mouth was as soft and gentle as a man's could be, stroking and teasing, rather than assaulting her, so that her treacherous body began to respond to him!

Fortunately, just when Catherine's senses were beginning to betray her, he loosed her a little to free his right hand, and her common sense immediately reasserted itself. Wrestling away from him, she broke free—to slide from his lap to the ground, and found herself facing his man Geordie, who wandered in still chewing as though he had not eaten for a week.

"I gave you no leave to do that, sir," she told him severely.

"Oho, that were quick work, master," Geordie announced, spewing crumbs around him, "not that one expects slow work when an actress is your doxy."

Catherine picked herself up from the floor and slapped the face, not of her unwanted would-be lover, but of his servant.

"Fie and for shame," she cried, "after I have warmed and fed you. I gave him no leave to kiss me, nor you to call me doxy."

"Bonaroba, rather," suggested Tom from behind her, using Alsatian slang to describe a whore.

Enraged, Catherine swung round and boxed his ears, too. "We might as well start as we mean to go on," she announced. "I will not allow liberties *to* my person at your hands, nor liberties *about* my person from his tongue. You, sir, are a hedge captain, and your servant is naught but a cullion who needs to acquire a wash as well as manners."

Tom was openly laughing at her defiance. "Well, I at least am clean," he told her smugly. And, yes, that at least was true as she had discovered when trapped on his knee. His clothes might be shabby but his body smelled of yellow soap and lemon mixed.

"Oh, you are impossible, both of you," she raged. "Like master, like man. How am I to endure this ill-begotten enterprise in such unwanted company?"

"By accepting that, for the duration of it, we are man and wife, and Geordie is our only servant." Tom's tone was suddenly grave.

"I may not take my woman with me, then?"

"Indeed, not. The fewer who know anything of us, the better."

"But Geordie—" and Catherine's voice rose dangerously "—is to be relied on?"

"Very much so. We have been to the wars together, and he has twice saved my life."

To her look of disbelief at the mere idea of such a scarecrow saving anything, Geordie offered a brief nod. "True enough, mistress. Only fair to say that he saved mine more times than that."

"I trust him," said Tom belligerently, "and so must you. Your life may depend on it."

"Oh, in this ridiculous brouhaha everyone's life depends on someone else," declaimed Catherine bitterly. "Mine on you, yours on me, and both of us on Geordie, and poor Rob's life depends on all three of us. It's better than a play. No, worse than a play, for no play would be so improbable."

"You're the actress, so you should know," was Tom's response to that. "In real life, my dear, everyone *does* depend on everyone else. 'Tis but the condition of fallen man."

Fear, impotence and anger, all finely mixed together, drove Catherine on. Her tongue turned nasty.

"Oh, we have turned preacher now, have we? Not surprising since we are to pass as canting Republicans. Canst thou whine a psalm through thy nose, preacher Tom? Or is that a trick to learn on the way to Antwerp? Pray learn it quickly so that you may leave a poor girl's virtue untouched as a good preacher should."

To her own surprise Catherine found herself half-laughing as she finished, and Tom's powerful face was also glowing with mirth. Geordie was watching them both with his rat-trap mouth turned down.

"Loose tongue," he muttered, "may loosen heads on shoulders, master. Because you have allowed your tongue to wag in the past and paid no forfeit for it, doth not mean that you may escape punishment for ever."

"There," exclaimed Catherine triumphantly, "even your servant can teach you common sense."

"Oh, is that what he is muttering at us? Come,

mistress, we must have a council of war, but only when you have sent your serving maid to market to buy our supper for us."

This shocked Catherine a little. "You intend to stay here tonight?"

"Aye, mistress. The packet doth not sail until early tomorrow. We must be up at dawn and away."

What can't be cured, must be endured, would obviously have to be her motto, was Catherine's last despairing thought as she turned away from him. But he had not finished with her yet.

"Your baggage is packed, mistress?" he asked her commandingly. "You have an assortment of clothing both plain and fancy and are ready to leave?"

She had the satisfaction of assuring him that she was more than ready—at least so far as her luggage was concerned.

"And there is yet another thing, mistress. No good follower of the late Lord Protector would be saddled with a wife called Cleone—a heathen name, indeed. Your true name is Catherine, and so you shall be known. Or would you prefer Kate?"

More to annoy him for the orders he was throwing at her than for any other reason, Cleone replied tartly, "Catherine will do. As old Will Shakespeare said, 'A rose by any other name would smell as sweet,' so what shall it profit that I am called Cleone or Catherine: they both begin with a C."

Tom bowed as gracefully as any court cavalier. "Catherine it shall be. And I am Tom, always uttered with due humility as befits a good wife."

He gave her his white smile again and, for the first time, Catherine saw that it quite transformed his face. Not only were his teeth good, but the relaxing of his harsh features showed her the boy he must once have been.

Nay, Catherine, she told herself sternly, you are not to soften towards a hired bully who plainly sees you as his prey. To do so is to deliver yourself into his hands.

Surprisingly he made no demur when, later, after they had supped, she showed him into Rob's bedroom. She had thought that he might take advantage of her, try to pretend that she was his wife and must do a wife's duty. Instead, he had flung down the small pack he had carried upstairs, given her another of his slightly mocking bows and told her to try to get a good night's sleep.

"For, madam wife, we have several hard days ahead of us, and I would wish that you arrive before Grahame as fresh as a daisy in spring—or the violets that your eyes resemble."

"Fair words butter no parsnips with me, Master Trenchard," Catherine told him tartly.

Only for him to say, blue eyes mirthful, "Tom, dear wife, always Tom. Most wives would be happy to receive such a compliment from a husband to whom they have been married for the last five years."

"Ah, but as a Puritan and a preacher such fair words would lie ill upon thy tongue."

"Oh, a man may be a Puritan and a preacher, but he is still allowed to love his wife, lest the world end. Go forth and multiply, the Lord hath said, and how shall we do that if there be not love?"

"And the Devil can quote Scripture to achieve his own ends," Catherine replied smartly. "Goodnight, dear husband, and sleep well."

"I would sleep better if I did not sleep alone," Tom informed the door soulfully as it closed behind her—and chuckled as she banged it.

And now, after boarding the packet without further incident, or much talk, and enduring a morning that began fair, but ended in storm and a high wind, Catherine found herself in the throes of seasickness. More than ever she wished that Rob had had the wisdom not to put his treasonous thoughts on paper.

A hand on her shoulder as she straightened up had her whirling around. It was Tom's. He was not being seasick, no, indeed, not he. Far from it—he looked disgustingly healthy, rosy even. Behind him lurked Geordie, looking green; a violent lurch of the ship brought him to the rail to join her in her offerings to the sea.

"Below with the pair of you," ordered Tom, laughter in his voice. "You will be better below decks."

"Not I, master," and, "Not I," echoed Catherine, but Tom was having none of it.

"Do as I bid you," he ordered Geordie, and as Catherine reached a temporary halt in her heavings he swept her up, to set her down only when they reached the companionway into the hold.

Below decks was truly nasty, as Catherine had expected, smelling of tar and worse things, but the boat's heavings did seem less distressing. Tom, having laid her down on what he called a bunk, brought over to her a large tin basin. Sitting beside her, he said, still vilely cheerful, "Use that if you feel sick again."

"I am over the worst, I think," Catherine told him, hoping that she was, but a moment later a huge wave sent the boat sliding sideways, which had her stomach heaving again. With a tenderness that surprised her, Tom held her head steady in order to help her, and when her paroxysms at last ended, he laid her gently down and pulled a dirty sheet over her.

How shaming to behave in such an abandoned manner before him! Not that he seemed to mind. On the contrary, having removed the basin, he came back again with it empty, carrying a damp cloth with which he gently wiped her sweating face.

This seemed to help, and he must have thought so,

too, for he said in a kinder voice than he had ever used to her before, "This time, I think, the worst *is* over. Do you feel able to sit up yet?"

Speech seemed beyond Catherine, so she nodded, and struggled into a sitting position. From nowhere Tom produced a pillow with which he propped up her aching head.

"Geordie!" he bellowed at that gentlemen, who had been engaged in heaving his heart up into a bucket, but now seemed a little recovered. "Bring me my pack, if you can walk, that is."

Geordie appeared to take the "if' as an insult. "Course I can walk. I ain't been ill."

This patent lie amused Catherine, and she gave a weak laugh. Tom looked at her with approval as the staggering Geordie handed him his pack. He opened it, and produced a small pewter plate, two limes and a knife.

Catherine watched him, fascinated, as he cut the first lime in half, handing one half to her, and the other to Geordie.

Geordie began to suck his, and Catherine, after a nod from Tom, followed suit, her mouth puckering as the acid liquid reached her tongue.

"Good," Tom told them both, "that should make you feel better!" He cut the second lime in half, and began to suck it vigorously also. "And now, some schnapps." His useful pack gave up a small tin cup, and first Catherine, then Geordie and finally himself, offered what he called, "a libation to the Gods of the sea, only down our throats and not over the side!"

Like the lime, the strong liquor seemed to settle, rather than distress, Catherine's stomach. She began to feel, as she told Tom, the drink talking a little, "more like herself".

He put a friendly arm around her which she felt too weak to reject—and then he gave her his final present, a disgusting object which he called a ship's biscuit.

"Eat that, and you will be quite recovered."

Her head spinning from the combined causes of an empty stomach brought about by seasickness, followed by a large draught of the strongest liquor she had ever drunk, Catherine managed to force it down. Her poor white face bore testimony to her revulsion as she did so.

Her reward was "Good girl!" and a tightening of Tom's arm. Her gratitude to him was expressed by her leaning against his strong warm body for further comfort. This resulted in a soft kiss on her cheek before Tom laid her down again, covering her with the sheet that had slipped its moorings during his ministrations.

"Try to sleep," he told her. "I am going on deck to stretch my legs a little." He beckoned at his man. "You, too, Geordie."

"Growing soft, are we, master?" growled Geordie at Tom as they reached the deck. The storm had lifted and the sea had grown calm again whilst they were below decks. "The schnapps did its work right well and the doxy would not have objected to a little—well, you know what!"

Tom's expression was an enigmatic one. "Oh, Geordie, Geordie—" he sighed "—you would never make a good chess player. At the moment I need her trust more than anything else in the world. Later—when it is gained—might be a different thing, a very different thing!"

Oh, blessed sleep "that knits up the ravell'd sleave of care", as old Will Shakespeare had it, thought Catherine drowsily as she awoke to feel refreshed. She was not alone. Tom Trenchard was seated on a bench, watching her, a tankard in his hand.

He lifted it to toast her. "You are with us again, dear wife, after sleeping the day away. Your colour has returned, I see." He drank briefly from the tankard, his brilliant blue eyes watching her over its rim before he handed it to her.

"Drink wife. We shall be in Ostend shortly, and there we may find shelter."

"Oh, blessed dry land," sighed Catherine, taking a long draught of ale. "I shall never wish to go to sea again."

"You were unlucky," Tom told her, "to find yourself in such a storm on your first voyage."

"And was it luck that you were not overset like poor Geordie and me?"

"Oh, I am never seasick," grinned Tom. "I have good sea legs. It is but one of my many talents," he added boastfully.

Catherine laughed and, easing herself out of the bunk, handed the tankard back to him. It was odd not to be sparring with him. She decided to prick the bubble of his conceit a little.

"Why, dear husband, I vow that you would well match the play wherein I late acted. *The Braggart* by name—*or Lackwit in Love.* Which title best befits you, do you think?"

Tom met her teasing look and answered her in kind. "Why, Master Will Wagstaffe may write a play taking me as hero, calling it *St George, or, England's Saviour*—and, if you do but behave yourself, you shall be the heroine. A new Belinda, no less."

Something in his tone alerted her. "You saw me play Belinda, then? At the Duke's Theatre?"

"Indeed, mistress, I had that honour. And a fine boy you made. I ne'er saw a better pair of legs—not even on a female rope dancer—and that is a splendid compliment, is it not?"

The look in Tom's eyes set Catherine blushing. He was stripping her of her clothing in his mind, no doubt of it. She swung away from him lest she destroy the new camaraderie that had sprung up between them since he had succoured her in the storm.

After all, they were to live together for some time, although how long or short that might be Catherine did not know, and t'were better that they did not wrangle all the time.

By good fortune, to save them both, Geordie came down the companionway, his long face glummer than ever.

"Bad news, master, I fear."

"And when did you ever bring me good?" Tom exclaimed. "'Tis your favourite occupation! Spit it out, man. We had best all be glum together."

"Nothing less than that we may not dock at Ostend. There are rumours that the plague may be back, and the packet's master has decided that we must risk all and go on to a harbour near Antwerp."

"And that is bad news?" Tom taunted him, brows raised.

"Aye, for those of us who do not like the sea."

"Antwerp or Ostend, it is no great matter. I have enough schnapps left to make both you and my dear wife drunk and insensible for the rest of the sea trip should the storms begin again. Tell me, wife, will that do?"

For answer Catherine made him a grand stage curtsy, saying, "I know my duty, husband, to you and to our gracious King, and if I must be rendered unconscious to perform it, I shall be so with a good grace."

Tom rewarded her with a smacking kiss on the lips as she straightened up. "You hear that, Geordie? I shall expect no less from you."

"Oh, aye, master. But don't expect any pretty speeches from me."

"Certes, no. The next one will be the first! Back to your bunk, wife, to rest. So far, so good."

He was being so amazingly hearty that he made Catherine feel quite faint—and he was apparently having the same effect on Geordie, who sat grumblingly down on the dirty floor, complaining, "It's as well that some on us are happy."

Tom came over to sit on Catherine's bunk. "And that shall be our epitaph, or, as you stage folk say, our epilogue. Will Wagstaffe himself could not write a better, nor his predecessor, Stratford Will. Rest now, wife."

So she did, her mouth still treacherously tingling from his last kiss. Oh, he knew all the tricks of seduction did Master Tom Trenchard, and she must never forget that.

Chapter Three

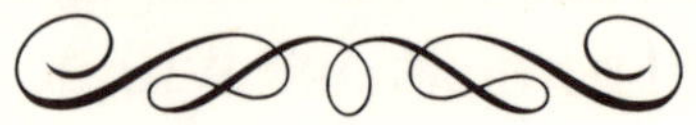

Oh, the devil was in it that Hal Arlington had decided that William Grahame could best be snared by the wiles of a pretty woman so that, instead of carrying out this mission on his own, Stair was saddled with an actress who carped at his every word. And *her* every word was devoted to denying him her bed, which would have been the only thing that made having to drag Catherine around the Low Countries worthwhile!

The pox was on it that he had ever volunteered to try to turn Grahame at all! One last such junket, the very last, he had told Arlington and Sir Thomas, having at first refused to oblige them.

"I am seven years away from being a mercenary soldier for anyone to hire. If anyone deserves a quiet life, it is I. I have served my King both before his Restoration and after—as you well know."

"The Dutch War goes badly—as you equally well know, Stair, and yours are the special talents we need."

In a sense that had pained him, for were not those talents the ones that he had needed to survive in the penury which exile from England had forced upon him during the late usurper Cromwell's rule? Cunning, lying, cheating and killing, yes, killing, for that was the soldier's trade. Leading men in hopeless causes that he had won against all the odds, by using those same talents.

He thought that he had done with it, that he was now free to live a civilised life in peace. Not simply enjoying its ease, but also the pretty women to whom he need make no commitment, as well as music, the playhouse, books and the blessed quiet of his country estates, both in England and Scotland, when he was no longer at Court. Estates most fortunately restored to him when Charles II had come into his own again.

God knew, he no longer needed the money in order to survive. If he did this thing, he would do it for nothing, which, of course, Gower and Arlington also knew and was partly why they had asked him to be their agent in the Netherlands. As usual, the King's Treasury was empty, and not needing to pay him would be a bonus.

So, he had agreed. Only to discover that they had also decided that he needed a woman to pose as his wife, and a pretty woman at that, skilled in seductive arts, for Grahame had a reputation for being weak where women were concerned.

"As a bird is caught by lime, so will he be caught by a pair of fine eyes," Sir Thomas had said. "And we know the very doxy who will turn the trick for us."

In consequence, he had found himself in his own proper person at the Duke's Theatre, in company with Hal Arlington, trying to test the nerve of the young actress whom Sir Thomas knew that he could blackmail through her indiscreet and foolish brother.

And nerve she had, no doubt of it, by the way in which she had refused to let his unsettling jests with oranges, posies and gloves disturb her. She had also displayed a pretty wit, which she was now constantly exercising at his expense—except when she was seasick, that was.

Sir Stair Cameron, to be known in the Netherlands only as Tom Trenchard—Trenchard being his mother's name, and Tom his own second Christian name—was leaning disconsolate over the packet's side as it neared land, musing on his fate.

He lifted his face to feel the rain on it. Blessed, cleansing rain. By God, when this is over, he vowed, I shall refuse to engage in such tricks ever again, but now I must go below and help my disobliging doxy to ready herself to be on dry land again.

Tom did not reflect—for he never allowed the possibility of failure to trouble him—that having to take a young, untried woman with him might put his mission in hazard, even cause it to fail. He had made such a point to Gower and Bennet but they had dismissed it. And so, perforce, had he to do the same.

All the same, the idea was there, very like a worm that secretly eats away at the foundations of a seemingly secure house until at last it falls.

He shrugged his broad shoulders. No more mewling and puking over what was past and could not be changed, he told himself, no looking backwards, either. Forwards, ever forwards, was the motto his father had adopted on being made a baronet, and he would try to live up to it, as had always been his habit.

The day was growing late, and it was likely that they would not dock until the morning. Once on shore they would travel to Antwerp where they might, please God, find Grahame and finish the business almost before it was begun.

Time to go below to wake his supposed wife from her schnapps-induced sleep.

"Aye, that will do very well, mistress, very well, indeed," announced Tom Trenchard approvingly. Catherine had dressed herself in a neat gown of the deepest rose. Its neckline was low and boat-shaped, but was modestly hidden by a high-necked jacket of padded pale mauve satin, trimmed with narrow bands of white fur, which reached the knee and was fastened with tiny bows of fine gold braid.

Round her slender neck was a small pearl necklace, and her hair, instead of being arranged in the wild confusion of curls popular at King Charles's court, was modestly strained back into a large knot, leaving a fringe to soften her high forehead.

This had the effect of enhancing rather than diminishing the delicate purity of her face and profile.

For his part, Tom had also changed out of his rough and serviceable clothing. Although he was not pretending to be a bluff and conventional Dutch burgher, he looked less of a wild mercenary captain and more of a man who was able to conduct himself properly out of an army camp as well as in it.

He was wearing jacket and breeches of well-worn, but not threadbare, black velvet, trimmed with silver. His shirt was white, not a dirty cream, and he sported a white linen collar edged with lace that, if not rich, was at least respectable. His boots, as usual, were splendid. He had also shaved himself carefully so he looked less like the wild man of the woods, which Catherine had privately nicknamed him.

His hair was, for the first time since she had met him, carefully brushed and fell in deep red-gold waves to just below his ears. He carried a large steeple-crowned black hat with a pewter buckle holding its thin silver band.

The whole effect was impressive. No, he was not handsome, far from it, but he had a presence. The

French had a saying, Catherine knew, that a woman of striking, but not beautiful looks, was *jolie laide,* which meant an ugly woman who was pretty or attractive in an unusual way. It could, she grudgingly admitted, be applied to Tom, who was better than handsome.

It did not mean that she liked him the more, simply that his brute strength attracted her more than the languor of the pretty gentlemen of King Charles's court did. She had held them off when they had tried to tumble her into bed, and so she would hold off Tom. She would be no man's whore, as she had told Sir Thomas Gower.

"Deep in thought?" offered Tom, who seemed to be a bit of a mind reader. "What interests you so much...wife...that you have just left me in spirit, if not in body?"

She would not be flustered. "Nothing, except that this morning, for the first time, I feel dry land firm beneath my feet again."

Forty-eight hours ago they had docked at a wharf on the coast well outside Antwerp itself, which by the Peace of Westphalia was closed to shipping. Antwerp was not Dutch territory, being situated in Flanders, territory still under the heel of the Austrian Empire, and it was always known as the Austrian Netherlands. Being so near to Holland, it would be a useful place to work from—if one were careful.

Once safely on land again, Catherine had found the ground heaving beneath her feet as though she were still on the packet. It had needed Tom's strong arms to steady her.

Today, however was a different matter. The inn at which they were staying was clean after a fashion that Catherine had never seen before. Its black-and-white tiled floors were spotless. A serving maid swept and washed them several times a day. The linen on her bed was not only white, but smelled sweet, as did the bed hangings. It was a far cry from the inns in which she had slept on the occasions when the players took to the roads in England.

The furniture in the inn was spare, but had been polished until it shone, as did the copper, pewter and silver dishes that adorned the table and sideboards. In the main inn parlour there was a mirror on one wall, and on the other hung a tapestry showing Jupiter turning himself into a swan in order to seduce Helen of Troy's mother, Leda.

Few private houses in London boasted such trappings as this inn in Antwerp. Tom had told her that everywhere in the Low Countries might such wealth and such cleanliness be found—"We are pigs, by comparison, living in stys," he had ended.

And now they were to visit the man whom Tom hoped would be their go-between with Grahame, one Amos Shooter, who might know where he was to be found. Early that morning, Tom had visited the address of the house that Sir Thomas Gower had given him as that of Grahame's lodgings, but had been told that no one named William Grahame had ever lived there!

"Not true, of course," Tom had said to her and Geordie, who was also tricked out like a maypole—his expression. "But this business is a woundy chancy game."

Game! He called it a game! Catherine was beginning to think of it as a nightmare.

"Now for my second man. One I think that I might—just—trust."

"Thought you trusted no one, master," sniffed Geordie.

Tom ignored him. "We must look well-found," he had ordered her. "Not as though we are beggars come to cadge money from a rich friend. Do not overdo matters, though. That would be equally suspicious. Do you not have a small linen cap that you might wear, mistress? Bare heads are for unmarried women."

Catherine shook her head. "A pity, that," he sighed. "Well, a good husband would be sure to buy his modest wife one, so we shall go to market tomorrow. Too late to go today!"

So, here they were, knocking at the stout oak door of a respectable red-brick mansion in Antwerp, not far from the market place, which was lined with medieval guild houses. It was opened by a fat, red-cheeked serving maid who bustled them through into a large room at the rear of the house, which opened on to a courtyard lined with flowers in terracotta tubs.

"Amos has done well, I see," Tom whispered in Catherine's ear as they followed the maid, for the house was even cleaner and better appointed than their inn. "I had heard that he had married wealth, but had not realised how much wealth. Ah, Amos, my old friend, we meet again," he said as Amos, a man as large as Tom, came to meet them.

Amos's welcome was warmer than Tom's. He threw his arms around him and embraced him lustily. His wife, a pretty woman, plump and rosy, greeted Catherine much more sedately.

Embraces over, Amos held Tom at arm's length, saying, "Old friend, you are larger than ever, and the world has treated you well enough, I see. And this is your wife? I thought you vowed that you'd never marry, Tom. Not after the beautiful Clarinda deceived you so!"

"Aye, Amos, but 'tis not only a woman's prerogative to change one's mind. This is my wife, Catherine, and yes, I thrive—a little. But not like you," and he gave Amos a poke in his fair round belly. "You carried not that when we were comrades in arms together, nor were you so finely housed and clothed!"

"Oh, but that was long ago. I am quite reformed these days. I am a respectable merchant now—and it is all Isabelle's doing." He threw his arms around his blushing wife and gave her a loving kiss.

So, the beautiful Clarinda—whoever she might be—deceived him, did she? thought Catherine. She must have been a brave lass to manage that! But she ignored this interesting news for the time being, concentrating instead on talking of polite nothings in French to Isabelle.

Polite nothings, indeed, seemed to be the order of the day. Amos bade Isabelle see that food and wine were served to their unexpected guests, and then began a loud discussion of long-gone battles and skirmishes with Tom, as well as memories of comrades long dead.

Tom had volunteered to her earlier that the greatest virtue a successful agent needed was patience. It was, perhaps, just as well that Catherine had learned it in a hard school, for at first Tom talked of everything but anything connected with their mission. It was very pleasant, though, to sit and laze in this well-appointed room, drinking wine and eating what in Scotland were called bannocks, well buttered.

Was Tom lazing as he laughed and talked and drank the good red wine? Or was he picking up hints and notions from his idle gossip with his friend? Catherine could not be sure. Names were flying between him and Amos. Tom had told her earlier, before they had left the inn, that Amos had no true convictions and had always signed up with the side that paid him the most. "Republican or Royalist, Turk or Christian—all were the same to him."

"And you?" she had asked him. "Were you like Amos?"

"Oh," he had told her, giving her the white smile that transformed his face, "you shall tell me your opinion of that when this venture is successfully over."

He was as slippery as an eel—which in this kind of an enterprise was almost certainly an advantage. Seeing him now, one booted leg extended, wine glass in hand, one might have thought that the only care he had in the world was to gossip with an old friend, chance met.

"And William Grahame," Tom said at last. "What of him? I had heard that he had set up his household in Antwerp these days."

Was it her imagination or did something in Amos Shooter's bland, amiable face change? Did it harden a little so that something of the severe mercenary soldier that he had once been peeped through his genial merchant's mask? If so, the expression was so fleeting that it was gone almost before Catherine had seen it. He was laughing again.

"William Grahame, Tom? I had not thought that you knew him. Not your sort of fellow."

"True. I know him not. But I was told that he might be a useful man to make a friend of."

"No doubt, no doubt. He lodges but a mile away from here. He wanders, I am told, from town to town. About his business. Whatever that might be."

Did Amos Shooter truly not know aught of Grahame but his possible resting place? Both Tom and Catherine were asking themselves the same question, and getting the same answer. He did, but for whatever reason he was not admitting that he did.

Tom took a deep draught of wine—and changed the subject. The rest of the afternoon passed without incident. Mistress Shooter showed Catherine around the courtyard, and then took her through a little gate into a garden where herbs and vegetables grew, and, in summer, fruit on a sheltered wall.

Before they returned indoors, she said in her fractured English that she had learned from Amos, "Your husband should not trust this man Grahame overmuch. I tell you for your own good."

"Why?" asked Catherine, trying to look innocent, and succeeding. After all, she did not need to be a great actress for it to appear that she knew nothing—for that was true.

Isabelle Shooter shook her head at her. "I cannot tell you. I should not have said what I did. But you seem to be a good girl, even if your husband is perhaps not quite the jolly man he pretends to be."

Like Amos, then, thought Catherine cynically. But I would never have called Tom jolly. But, of course, he had been a jolly man this afternoon.

She said no more—for to know when to be silent is as great a gift, if not greater, than the ability to talk well, her Dutch mother had once said—which had the result that, when they returned to the big living room, Isabelle was holding her affectionately by the hand. She said to Tom as they left, "You have a pretty little wife, sir. Take care of her, I beg you."

"Now what brought that on?" Tom asked her once they were on their way back to the inn, Geordie walking behind them. He had spent a happy few hours in the servants' quarters, and was rather the worse for drinking a great quantity of the local light and gassy beer, although he was still able to walk.

"What?" Catherine asked, although she knew perfectly well what he meant.

"Amos's pretty wife holding you so lovingly by the hand?"

"She thought that I was an innocent, and needed protection. She told me that you were not to trust William Grahame overmuch."

"Did she, indeed? Believe me, I have no intention of trusting him at all—or Amos, either. And…?"

"There is no and… She said nothing more. Other than that you seemed a jolly man, but she did not think that you were. That you were pretending to be."

Tom stopped walking, with the result that the overset Geordie, his head drooping, walked into him and earned himself a few curses from Tom, before he answered her.

"Did she so? A wise lady, then. Which begs the question, that being so, if she were wise, why did she wed Amos?"

Catherine shrugged her shoulders. "Why does one marry anyone? For a hundred reasons—or none at all. And did the jolly Amos tell you where William Grahame might be found?"

"That he did. But he did not warn me, as his wife warned you. I fear that he may think me as devious as he is and that therefore I do not need warning. That bluff manner of his is not the true man."

"So I thought. But you and I are not the true man or the true woman either. So we are all quits—except, perhaps, for Isabelle."

Tom gave a great shout of laughter, which had the heads of the few passers-by turning to look at them, and Geordie absent-mindedly walking into him again.

"I can see I must watch my words, wife. You would make Will Wagstaffe a good secretary—the kind who embroiders his master's words. There are many such around Whitehall. Why not in the playhouse?" He turned to throw a second set of oaths at Geordie for treading on his heels.

"Why not, indeed? And do not curse poor

Geordie, for I swear that you probably drank more than he did."

"Ah, but I hold it so much better. Remind me to teach you the trick of it."

"I thank you, husband, but no. No man would wish a toping wife."

"Well said, and now we are home again. We must begin our campaign by deciding on what to say and do when we at last meet the elusive Master Grahame. Battles are won by those whose planning is good, and lost by those who do not plan at all. Remember that."

"As a useful hint to employ in the kitchen? My soldiers must be carrots and cabbages, all arranged properly in rows."

Bantering thus, they reached their rooms, where Tom called for more drink, and some food to stay them for the morrow.

Well, thought Catherine later that night as he staggered to the bed that he had made no attempt to share with her, sharing the unfortunate Geordie's instead, one thing was sure. Whatever Tom Trenchard might, or might not be, life with him was certainly never dull.

Nor did it so prove the next day. This time Catherine was told to dress more modestly, in an old grey gown, with a large shawl. On the way to the address that Amos had given them as that of William Grahame's, Tom brought her a white linen matron's cap, elegant with its small wings, and its lace frill that framed her face prettily even if it hid the dark glory of her hair.

Tom was soberly dressed too, in a brown leather jacket, coarse canvas breeches, his frayed cream shirt, and, of course, his beautiful boots. They were always constant! As was his black, steeple-crowned hat with its battered feather.

Geordie, their ghost, followed them. Since arriving in the Low Countries, he was wearing something that passed as a livery: a shabby blue jacket and breeches, grey woollen stockings and heavy, pewter-buckled shoes. He carried a large staff with a silver knob on the top. His sallow face was glummer than ever. One wondered why he served Tom at all since he seemed to take so little pleasure in the doing.

Tom had talked seriously to Catherine before they left. "Hal Arlington told me that Grahame has a weakness for pretty women. Now you are a pretty woman, but a married one, so if you are to attract him—and distract him—you must do so modestly. Killing looks from swiftly downcast eyes. A glance of admiration should he say something witty. Later, when you know him better, then you may go further."

Catherine threw him a furious look. For the last

few days she had been spending her time worrying over Tom seducing her, and all the time she had been brought along to try to seduce Grahame!

"And, pray, how far is that 'further' to be? Are you here to play pimp to my strumpet? For if so, I tell you plainly that you may be in love with your role, but I am certainly not about to play the part which you and your two masters have assigned to me."

"No need for that," Tom told her swiftly. "You are to tease him only. Draw him on. Nothing more."

Distaste showed on Catherine's face and rang in her voice. "And that is almost worse than going the whole way! To lure a poor devil on with hopes that you are never going to satisfy is more indecent than being an honest whore."

"Your choice," grinned Tom. "If you prefer being the honest whore…"

"Oh—" Catherine stamped her foot "—if I were not between a rock and a hard place so that Rob's life depends on my complicity, I should take ship for England straightaway."

"Well said, wife. I like a woman who knows the way of the world—so few do."

"Oh…" Catherine let out a long breath. He was impossible, but there was no point in telling him so. So she didn't.

After that, when he bought her the cap, she was minded not to thank him, but the expression on his hard face was so winning when he gave it to her, that she did so—even if a little ungraciously.

Grahame's house turned out to be a small one-storied wooden building on the outskirts of the city, surrounded by vegetable gardens with a dirt road running through them. A boy was poling along a small flat boat loaded with cabbages on the small canal that ran parallel with the road.

"Not lodgings, I think," Tom said thoughtfully as they left the road and walked up the path to the house through a neglected garden. "Something rented." He looked around him. "It's deathly quiet."

He shivered. "Too quiet. I would have thought a man of Grahame's persuasion would prefer to be lost in a crowded city than isolated here. Safer so."

It was the first time, but not the last, that Catherine was to hear him say something which had an immediate bearing on what was about to happen—and of which he could not have known.

For, as they reached the door but before they could knock on it they heard, coming from inside, the noise of a violent commotion, and male voices shouting.

"What the devil!" exclaimed Tom—and pushed at the door, which was not locked and opened immediately. He strode in, Geordie behind him, pushing Catherine on one side, and telling her not to follow them but to wait outside.

An order that she immediately disobeyed.

Chapter Four

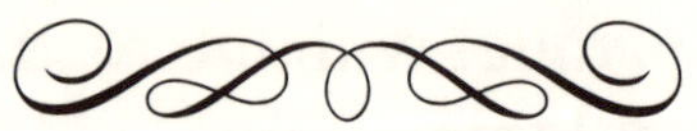

Catherine found herself in a large room in which two, no three, men were struggling together. Tom was standing to one side, doubtless trying to decide which of them was the one he had come to meet—and must try to rescue.

It suddenly became plain that one of the men was losing an unequal fight with the two others and therefore was almost certainly William Grahame. Tom seized Geordie's staff and brought its metal tip hard down on the head of the man who now had Grahame by the throat.

He fell to the ground, unconscious. Tom then tossed his staff back to Geordie, and drew from inside his coat a long dagger. On seeing Tom coming at him with the dagger, Geordie behind him, the fellow of the unconscious man loosened his hold on Grahame and threw him bodily at Tom with such force that Tom lost his balance and collapsed across a settle, Grahame on top of him.

Having done so, the would-be assassin ran through the open door at the far end of the room, Geordie in pursuit, for Tom was busy disengaging himself from Grahame who was gasping his thanks at him.

"For," he said feelingly, "had you, whoever you are, not arrived in such a timely fashion, I was dead meat. I give you my thanks."

"My pleasure," said Tom. "And you, sir, must be William Grahame, whom I have come to speak with. Who is this—" and he prodded the man on the floor who was now stirring and groaning "—that with his fellow he sought so desperately to kill you?"

"Why, as to that, I know not," replied Grahame, who was visibly distressed by what had just passed. There were bruises on his face and throat and he had some difficulty in speaking. "Only that the two of them broke in through the door there and set about me." He pointed at the one through which his assailant and Geordie had disappeared.

For some reason Catherine—who had been standing back staring at the action, which was far more exciting and dangerous than that in any play in which she had acted—did not believe him. She wondered whether Tom also thought that Grahame might not be telling the truth.

Tom had sheathed his dagger again inside his

coat, was hauling the groaning man to his feet and throwing him down on the settle, since he appeared to have difficulty in standing.

"Come, *mijnheer,*" Tom began in broken Dutch, for he was of the opinion that these might be assassins sent by the Grand Pensionary, John de Witt, to dispose of a double agent whom he might now consider dangerous, "who sent you here to kill Master Grahame—and why?"

The man shook his head and seemed not to understand what Tom was saying. Grahame began to interrogate him, but Tom stopped him, saying, "Do not distress yourself, sir. My wife speaks good Dutch. Mine is poor and he may not understand what I was asking him. Wife?"

Catherine stepped forward, just as Geordie reappeared, looking glummer than ever.

"My apologies, Master, but I lost him. There is a small wood beyond the gardens where the path forks and I must have taken the wrong track..."

"No matter." Tom was brief. "Our friend here will soon tell us all. Begin, wife."

Catherine questioned their captive in Dutch and then in French, being proficient in both. He understood not them, nor English either—or so his shaking head and uncomprehending face appeared to say.

Tom lost patience. He surveyed the man silently for some minutes. He was anonymous in both face and dress, being like a score such as one might see in the street. At last he leaned forward to pull the man upright.

"Wife," he said, not turning his head towards Catherine, "do you go into the garden and not return until I call for you. I would fain question this piece of scum more severely and I would not have you present. Go!" he ordered her fiercely as she hesitated.

Nothing for it but to leave with Geordie, for Tom bade him to go with her and, "to look after the mistress with a little more care than you chased yon assassin!"

Catherine never quite knew what followed next for her back was towards Tom, Grahame and the would-be assassin when, just as she reached the door, she heard a shot behind her.

Shocked, she swung round to see Tom facing the assassin who was sinking to the floor, blood gushing from his mouth. Behind him stood Grahame, his face grim, a pistol in his hand.

"Now, why the devil did you do that?" enquired Tom of Grahame.

"To save you, of course," returned Grahame hardily. "See, he had drawn a dagger on you, it is on the floor near his hand. I had a pistol in my belt that I was not able to use against my assailants, their attack being so sudden, and I used it to save you, as you had saved me."

Tom's expression was deadly, thought Catherine,

shivering a little, and he did not seem at all grateful to Master Grahame for saving his life.

"No," he said, his voice so cold and severe that Catherine scarcely knew it, "I was in no danger from this poor fool, despite his dagger. And now that you have slain him so incontinently, we can know no more of who paid him to slay *you.*"

Grahame's expression was a sad one, but his voice was patient. "Forgive me. I had no time to think. I saw you being attacked, and acted accordingly."

Tom stood silent before giving a short laugh. "No, you must forgive me. You thought I was in danger and you acted promptly. For that I must thank you. You were not to know that I have been for many years a mercenary soldier who would not easily have fallen victim to such an amateur creature as this. After all, he and his accomplice were making heavy weather of killing a solitary man, unable to use his weaponry."

Well, Catherine thought, a trifle indignant on Grahame's behalf, at last Tom had thanked Grahame, even if his thanks were belated.

Grahame inclined his head. "We are quits, I think," he said, smiling. "And now you must tell me who you are, and why you have sought me out here. And, most of all, who told you where to find me. I had thought this place unknown to all my enemies, and most of my friends.

"Then, in a few short minutes, there arrive both enemies and friends, for I take you, your wife and your servant to be my friends. Indeed, if you arrived as strangers, your actions have made you my friends."

He smiled at them, before announcing, "Wine," and going over to a *buffet*—the Low Countries word for a sideboard—where stood a decanter and several goblets of fine glass, a little at odds with the rough style of the house and the furnishings of the rooms in it. "We must drink a toast to our survival." He had needed to step over the assassin's corpse to get there. Catherine felt quite faint at the casual way in which all three men were treating his death.

She was not surprised when Tom shook his head, saying, "Wine later. First we must decide what to do with him," and he pointed at the body. "If I am wrong in supposing that you do not wish to inform the authorities of what has passed this day, forgive me. If I am right, however, the evidence needs to be disposed of."

Grahame continued to pour wine as though discussing murderous attacks and the hiding of dead bodies was an ordinary, everyday matter.

"There are enough canals about here, to hide a dozen such as he. Depend upon it, no one will seek to know what happened here today. The odds are on it that his companion will not return to confess his failure. These were but poor hirelings sent to dispose of me. It was their bad luck that you arrived."

And ours that we did, thought Catherine to whom a glass of wine seemed a most desirable thing. I have had a real baptism of fire today. If I had ever imagined that this enterprise was not a risky one, this episode has proved exactly how risky it is! I feel quite faint, but will not confess it.

She looked away from the dead man, and saw Tom gazing at her enquiringly. She gave him a small wry smile to try to tell him that, whilst she was shocked, she was not about to disgrace herself—or him—by doing anything so stupid as faint.

Pleased—and relieved—by her stoicism, Tom handed her his glass. "Drink up," he bade her. "It will make you feel better."

She made no demur, but drank down the good Rhenish wine, and listened to Tom and Grahame discussing what to do with the corpse.

"Your man may help me to carry this poor fool to the shed in the garden. He may lie until darkness falls when the canal shall be his resting place—for the time being, that is," said Grahame, his manner almost cheerful.

Geordie pulled a long face, but did as he was told. Tom said nothing, but he was thinking a great deal. No stranger to violence himself, he found that Grahame's equanimity in the face of violent death—and a violent death which he had needlessly inflicted—was telling him something of the man quite other from what Gower and Arlington had believed of him in London.

This was no puling scholar who simply paid for the information which he painstakingly—almost safely—gathered and used to sell to either the Dutch or the English government, according to whichever would pay him the most at the time. He had killed before, and would doubtless kill again.

No, Grahame was a very dangerous man and not to be trusted. And who, exactly, was trying to kill him? And why? These questions ran through Tom's head, as he took the empty wine glass from Catherine and refilled it for himself. Other thoughts were troubling him.

Were Gower and Arlington playing a double game with him and Catherine? Had they employed the assassins who had tried to kill Grahame—and so nearly succeeded? And had he and Catherine been sent as a blind so that they might disclaim responsibility if Grahame were found murdered? Their argument being that they would scarcely waste time sending emissaries to deal with a man they intended to kill.

Or was the Grand Pensionary responsible? Was it not possible that he, like Gower and Arlington, might have tired of Grahame's devious games, and decided to do away with him?

Worse still, were he and Catherine being manoeuvred by Gower and Arlington into a situation where they might be accused of killing Grahame? The possibilities were endless; instead of cursing poor Catherine's presence, as he had been doing, might he not be better employed asking himself why he had been so foolish as to agree to this dubious venture at all!

"So, sir," Grahame said, handing Tom his glass of Rhenish and seating him in a large chair opposite to him, Geordie having been left in the garden to keep watch at the back of the house. "Pray tell me who you are, and why I am honoured by your presence," and he lifted his glass to Tom, almost fawning on him.

Oh, the greasy swine! Tom had difficulty in not laughing out loud at such a seductive attempt to charm. There was something odd about Grahame, but exactly what the oddness consisted of Tom did not yet know.

"My name is Thomas, Tom, Trenchard. I am a member of that family, noted as a supporter of the late Lord Protector. Colonel Ned Trenchard, now a soldier for the Hapsburgs and the Empire, is a distant cousin. I met him once in Nurnberg, when I was still a mere lad."

Now that, at least was true, for Tom mixed truth with lies to achieve a greater truth—as all such conspirators do, and if pushed could describe Ned Trenchard accurately, aye, and others who were opposed to King Charles as well.

"Indeed, indeed, Master Tom Trenchard. And what does this cousin of Ned Trenchard come to me for? On whose behalf? Not on his cousin's, I dare swear."

"No, indeed. On the contrary, for although my inclination lies towards the late Cromwell's cause, I do not wish to see my country brought low by a foreign power, even to bring down King Charles. That were to leave us helpless before any European state which might wish to conquer us. And knowing my mind on this, I am sent by my masters in London to offer you what they believe you most dearly wish…"

Tom paused, and waited for Grahame to answer.

"And that wish is? Tell me, Master Trenchard, since you have just claimed to know my mind, what my mind is."

Oh, a devil! A most cunning devil! He and Tom were a good pair, were they not? This was Catherine's immediate reaction to this conversation between two men, neither of whom could be trusted to tell the truth. She waited for Tom's answer.

It was his turn to raise his glass to Grahame before speaking. "Why, Master Grahame, I believe that you have a great mind to return to the land of your birth, but that you do not wish to meet the headsman's axe shortly after arriving there!

"That being so, I am to inform you that a pardon awaits you if you give my masters, through me, not only what you know of the dispositions of the Dutch Army and Navy, but also what you have learned of the arrangements of the French forces. You see, I am being frank with you," Tom ended, trying to look as sincere as a man being insincere could.

"Oh, I do like a frank man," exclaimed Grahame, "frankness not being much of a commodity on any exchange these days! You will, I know, be well aware that I may not be equally frank back. For it is my head that will roll if I accept this offer at face value. Pray forgive me for speaking the language of commerce, but we are in the Low Countries where commerce reigns, and commerce is what we are engaged in, is it not? Yes, I must have time to think."

"I am authorised to give you time," Tom told him, "but not a great deal of it." Which last, at least, was truthful.

He had not expected, nor had Gower or Arlington, that Grahame would fall on his neck, and agree to come home immediately—hence their insistence that Catherine accompany him to act as bait.

Grahame's next words were unexpected. "Your wife speaks Dutch well, and French also, not always accomplishments which English women possess. How so?"

Truth would serve again, Tom thought, and

Catherine should tell it. "My wife must answer you, Master Grahame, if she be so willing."

So this was to be her baptism into the devious business of spying. She must not falter—nor did she, saying eagerly, "Indeed, husband. My father was married to a Dutch lady of good birth who spoke both Dutch and French well, and insisted that I learned to speak both languages well. And Latin, too, for she thought that girls as well as boys should have the education that the Dutch gave them, which the English do not."

She ended by rising and dropping Grahame a neat curtsy.

"Convenient," was all that Grahame had to say to that. Tom did not inform him that Catherine was an actress—for that was no business of his, and he was pleased that her answer had been short and sweet with nothing volunteered that had not been asked for. She was now sitting down again, head bent, looking both submissive and wifely.

A strange warm feeling swept over Tom. It was not a feeling he had ever experienced before. He had no time to analyse this new sensation further, for he had more pressing matters on which to ponder.

He had probably gone as far as he could in this first meeting. He had laid Gower and Arlington's proposition before Grahame, and whether, if he returned to the English fold, they would hold to their promises to him, he did not know. It was not his business, but it was Grahame's. And if Grahame were as wily as Tom thought he was, it was likely that he would take a deal of time before making up his mind.

So far as Tom was concerned, there were other questions that needed an answer. Item: Why was Grahame living alone in the country without servants or helpers? Item: What was his connection with Amos Shooter, that Shooter should know the whereabouts of a double agent who was obviously in hiding?

All this whilst watching Grahame watch him as they drank their wine. Silences, Tom thought, often told one as much as words. Grahame ended this one by pouring Tom more wine, saying as he did so, "And who, may I ask—for perhaps I may not—told you where to find me?"

Again the truth was best. "Oh, you may ask, no secret there. None but my old friend and late companion in arms, Amos Shooter, now a fat burgher with a rich and pretty wife."

"He does not need to run back to England, then," was Grahame's dry comment. He looked across to where Catherine sat, silent and demure. "And *your* pretty wife. Why have you brought her along?"

Tom had a quick answer for him. "She has no family with whom she might stay, and I did not care to leave her alone. A woman alone is a target for the unscrupulous. My mission is surely not a dangerous one for me, and I would be happier with her by my side."

He came out with this in the dieaway tone of a man still in love with his wife, but who was well aware that others found her attractive.

"I would speak with you further, Master Trenchard, upon your position. Know that I am heartily sick of being an exile, and I have thought long on the matter. I am not yet completely at the point where I accept that the King's cause is the just and proper one, but my mind inclines that way."

Grahame was looking away from Tom as he said this, as though he were half-ashamed to say it. Tom took the bait offered. "I shall be most ready to entertain you at the inn where we are lodged, and where we may arrange to speak privately. Unless you prefer to meet me here."

Grahame flapped a wary hand. "No, no. Not here, nor at the inn, neither. Safer that you hire a coach and that you pick me up on the main highway at the point where the road leading to my house turns off. Thus we may speak in peace with none to overhear us."

"Except the coachman," Tom could not help saying.

"We shall speak in English. In any case, I shall not stay long here, but must find a safer place now that my enemies have tracked me down. Bring the coach to the spot of which I have spoken at noon tomorrow, and we will take matters further."

That appeared to be that. Grahame would say nothing further, but spoke largely and vaguely of having met the Grand Pensionary, and of one Benjamin Tite, who he said, pretended to be a merchant inclined to the English, but who was selling details about the British Fleet to the Dutch. Tom had never heard of Benjamin Tite, but did not tell Grahame so.

It was time to go. Time to leave Grahame to wonder how much Tom Trenchard and his masters knew of his double-dealing, and whether Tom Trenchard's pretty wife was a player in this new game that London had inaugurated. Tom swallowed his wine, and put down his glass, silently admiring its costly beauty, which was a little at odds with the shabby dwelling where Grahame had gone to ground.

To hide from whom? Why, everybody, of course, Tom thought, watching Grahame's deference to Catherine as she rose to put on her shawl. Geordie was summoned from the garden, and they made ready for the long walk back to the centre of Antwerp.

"At least," Tom said to Catherine, as they tramped steadily back to what was to be regarded as home, "we shall have the doubtful pleasure of riding in a coach tomorrow, for which I am sure Master Grahame expects us to pay."

Catherine had something to ask him. Something

which had been troubling her as she had listened to him and Grahame tip-toe around one another.

"Sir—" she began, only to be interrupted.

Tom stopped, looked down at her, took her chin familiarly in his hand, tipped her face up towards his, and said, "Tom, husband, or Master Trenchard, if you please, Mistress Trenchard. To call me 'sir' sounds as though you are my servant, not my wife."

To her astonishment, the touch of his big hand was doing strange things to Catherine. Oh, men had touched her in the past, and some, trying to overcome her resistance to their blandishments, more familiarly than this. She had always slapped their hand away, but no one's touch had affected her so strongly as Tom's did, here, in an Antwerp street.

She wanted to put her hand over his, so that the tingling pleasure that had invaded her whole body would not stop. Looking up at him, she saw, for the first time, his face clear and plain. Since their first meeting she had always avoided looking straight at him—something she was sure that he must have noticed, although he had never spoken of it.

But now she registered every detail of him. She saw the red-gold stubble on his chin, which had grown since his close shave early that morning. She saw the laughter lines around his eyes, and his eyes' amazing blue, clear and shining. Their whites, too were clear, with the faintest pale blue tinge, not bloodshot through debauchery, like many of those of the hangers-on around Charles II's court.

She saw also the power of his face, which seemed to cancel out its harshness and give him a strange handsomeness of his own. That transformation was something that she had seen before, but never so plainly as now.

It seemed to depend on the strong jut of his nose, the strength of his jaw and chin, and on his mouth, long and slightly curling so that his errant sense of humour—which she was so strongly resisting since it made her vulnerable to him—was plainly visible.

For a moment it gave him the appearance of a man of power, and she must never forget that he was not that, but was simply a penniless adventurer using her for his own ends—and she had no idea what they were.

"Master Trenchard, then—" she said at last, but before she could go on he interrupted her again.

"I had supposed that I might be Tom. I had even dared to suppose that *dear* Tom might be offered me, but, alas, the Gods are not kind, I see."

He released her chin as he spoke—and his spell was broken. He was ordinary Tom Trenchard again, not someone who appeared to be infinitely more powerful.

But the memory of how she had felt and what she had seen remained with Catherine even after their walk was over and they were back at the inn. Meantime, she finished her sentence.

"Now that I have met Master Grahame, I see why you are right to mistrust him, and Amos Shooter also. For if Shooter is an honest man, the simple merchant he pretends to be, how does he come to know of Grahame's secret hiding place?"

She hesitated, picking her words carefully before going on, "There is another thing. Why did Grahame kill the man who was attacking you? Were you really in danger? You seemed to think that you were not. And if you were not, why should Grahame needlessly kill a man who could give him useful information on the enemy who had hired him? Surely it was in Grahame's interest *not* to kill him?"

"Well argued, wife. I can see that you are going to be a useful aide-de-camp, for that was the most suspicious thing that Grahame did during our time with him. The only reasonable inference is that he did not want me to know who his enemy was. And for the life of me I cannot think why Grahame should think that important enough to kill him. If you can think of a reason, pray tell me."

He was testing her, Catherine was sure, for she was also sure that Tom had already thought of a reason—perhaps more than one.

"I suppose that it might reveal that he was not only spying on us for the Dutch, and on the Dutch for us, but that he might also be involved with the Spanish or the French."

If Geordie had been travelling behind them as he had done on the way, Tom's sudden stop would have had Geordie almost tripping him up again. As it was, Geordie was walking ahead of them on the way back, his staff importantly raised as though she and Tom were substantial citizens instead of a pair of fly-by-nights, so Tom went unscathed.

It was she who was scathed, for Tom bent down and gave her a smacking kiss on the lips, bellowing "Well done, wife," when he lifted his head again. "My thoughts entirely, but I had not reckoned that you were such a fly customer as to read Grahame so quickly. I suppose all those confounded plays you have acted in, with double-dealing going on around the stage, have alerted you to the ways of the world."

Tom's kiss had an even more powerful effect on Catherine than his hand on her chin. She felt quite faint. And where had all that come from? He had kissed her lightly when they had first met in London without it having had such an overpowering effect on her. What had changed?

It must have been the kind way he had treated her when she had been seasick. Yes, that was it, no doubt of it. She became aware that Tom was saying urgently, "Wife! Wife! Where have you gone?" and was passing a hand before her face. "Is aught wrong?"

Now why the devil was she suddenly dumbstruck and moon wandering in the middle of the day? "No, there's nothing wrong," she said, a trifle crossly. "I was possibly overcome by the compliment you paid me. Most unlike you!"

"That's better," he told her approvingly. "I would think that there was something wrong with *you* if you did not try to bite me. Now, since you have worked out why Grahame killed that poor wretch, perhaps you might like to try to tell me why Grahame was being so cautious with us. After all, we are only here because it was he who sent word to London, and yet he is behaving as though we took the initiative and are pursuing him."

"But we are pursuing him, are we not?" This seemed so plain to Catherine that she thought that it was scarce worth saying. "After all, he has the whip hand, has he not? It is he who has information to sell, and he who can dictate his terms to us. The reverse is not true. It is no loss to him if we retire empty-handed."

Better and better, thought Tom as they turned into the road where their inn was situated. I have brought along a clever doxy—one who echoes my thoughts entirely. If I had feared, as I did, that I would have to spend my time explaining matters to her, I was wrong.

He looked down at her as she trotted by his side. The only trouble is that it would be dangerous if I allowed myself to feel anything for her—for my principal spur of action must be my mission—and not my companion on it.

All the same, he could not dismiss the supposed Mistress Catherine Trenchard from his thoughts—nor did he particularly wish to. Would she be as bold and adventurous in bed?

Time might tell.

Chapter Five

"How now, wife? What thought you of your first day in action?"

Catherine and Tom had eaten their supper in the upstairs parlour from which their bedroom led. Geordie had shared it with them, but had then been allowed to retire to the taproom downstairs—on condition that he did not get drunk.

Tom—a tankard of ale in his hand—was lounging before a fire in the great hearth for it was a cold day for early May. His unbooted legs were stretched out before him, he had wrenched off the linen cravat that had encircled his neck, and loosened the strings of his shirt. He appeared to be as unbuttoned and easy as a man might be. Violent death and the conspiracy in which they were both involved seemed far away.

His question caught Catherine both unawares and uneasy. It was the first time that she had found herself alone with him. Until now Geordie had been their constant companion, and she was a little worried as to what his dismissal might mean.

"I was somewhat surprised," she said slowly, "at what an ordinary man William Grahame appeared to be. Had I met him in the street, I would not have thought that he was a violent man engaged in villainous doings. For sure, a man such as Grahame must be a villain."

"Dear wife and dear actress," mocked Tom. "You have grown too used to the stage where a man announces himself to be a villain from the moment in which his script says enter. He sidles, he leers, he speaks with exaggeration. Now, were Grahame to behave like that as he goes about his treacherous business he would be immediately identified for what he is. Your true villain hides his colours, he does not flaunt them. He is anonymous, overlooked, lost in the crowd."

"And does that mean that you are not a villain, Tom Trenchard? For you are not lost in the crowd, and no one would overlook you!"

"True, dear wife. But then, I am a villain of a different kind from Grahame. No one expects subtlety from me. I am openness itself. I am your true, simple-minded and honest villain." He was laughing as he finished speaking.

Your true, simple-minded honest villain! Well, at least he knew that he was. But was that a blind? To pretend that you were something of a fool might be the trick of a clever man. And, for sure, Tom Trenchard was not simple-minded, even though he might claim to be.

"Yes, wife," he continued, "you have been deceived by such as Will Wagstaffe, your newest playwright. And tell me, since he, too, is a deceiver, have you any notion of who he might be, and what his true name is?"

Catherine dropped her eyes and looked at her hands, neatly folded in the blue wool of her modest gown. She was silent for so long that Tom twitted her on it.

"Come, is the matter so secret that you may not answer me?"

"Why speak you thus of Master Wagstaffe? Why suppose him to be, as you say, a deceiver?"

"If your true honest villain has one thing, it is a nose. And my nose tells me that Wagstaffe is a false name. Come, mistress, tell me, have you not heard of Will Shakespeare, the very original Wagstaffe himself!"

Catherine began to laugh, as much at the comic face Tom was pulling as at what he was saying. "Of course I have. But it still might be an honest name? Why suppose otherwise?"

"I think, mistress, that someone is playing a joke, laughing at us behind his hand. For the jests in *The Braggart, or, Lackwit in Love* are those of a man who likes to laugh at what others do not know. So, have you met him, this Wagstaffe? Or know of those who have met him?"

Catherine wondered why he was being so persistent over a matter of such little import. Here they were, dealing in life and death—for if William Grahame was fit to be a target for illwishers, so were they—and all that Tom Trenchard was worrying about was the true name of a hack playwright!

She told him so.

It troubled him not at all. For he laughed again, and said, "Now, I wonder why you will not answer a simple question with a simple answer. Have you met him, mistress? Yeah, or nay?"

"Nay, then, I have met no such he," Catherine replied, her eyes down, busy looking at her restless hands that she could not command to stay still.

"And you have met those who have met him? Yea or nay?"

"Yea. Or rather, I know that Betterton hath met him. But Betterton doth not talk much, and he has said nothing of Wagstaffe. Only that he values his privacy."

"Bravo, mistress, the truth at last. And why I had to wrench it from you, like pulling teeth, defeats me."

"I respect a man who wishes his privacy to be respected. But you, I take it, as an honest villain, respect nothing."

Tom rose and bowed low to her, pulling off an imaginary hat and sweeping it along the ground. Catherine began to laugh; she could not help it. He was parodying a player pretending to be a gallant. When he straightened up, it was to see her laughing face.

Instead of staying upright, he dropped to his knees before her. "What would Master Wagstaffe have his honest villain say now?" he whispered before taking her face in his hands. "Come, mistress, this comedy has gone on long enough. Let's to bed, and pleasure the night away."

His hands were at her bosom, and his mouth met hers, to stifle any protest, she supposed. Or was it that he thought that no protest would be forthcoming? In any case Catherine found it difficult to pull her own mouth away, for it was a treacherous thing, which wanted to be kissed by him whether she willed it or no.

Oh, but this must stop—for who knew where it might end? Perhaps in the bed of which he had spoken! So she pushed him and his invading hands and mouth away, saying, "Fie on you, sir. I thought that I had made it plain back in London that we were only to pretend to be man and wife, and would not carry the pretence into bed."

"And fie on you, mistress, for assuming a virtue though you have it not, as the first Will once wrote. All the world knows that the virtue of actresses is but a cracked thing, a pot long broken."

"Not so with this actress," cried Catherine, jumping

to her feet and making her way to the door. "Try to touch me so again and I'll return to London by the next boat, and leave our mission unaccomplished."

Tom was no whit daunted. Like the true and honest villain he claimed to be, he stood back to laugh at her, no whit deterred.

"What, mistress, would you run away and condemn your brother to the hangman? Go to, thou wouldst not do that!" He was speaking the language of the playhouse in the playactor's high stage voice, mocking her and it. But he was not attempting to try her virtue again.

Instead, "You are a pearl among women if you have remained unspotted, and since I have never met such a pearl, nor do I believe in one, why then, it is Tom Trenchard who is unlucky enough to be unable to please you. No matter, mistress, propinquity they say is a great thing, and I am a patient man. You may go to your bed alone—tonight."

"As I do always," Catherine came out with proudly. It had been hard work keeping her virginity in the cruel world of the theatre. It was true that most actresses sold themselves in order to live, their pay being poor, but she had another string to her bow of which she was determined that Master Tom Trenchard should know nothing.

It was true that in some strange way he was attracting her more and more—but was not that simple lust speaking? Lust of which all the sages and poets had written again and again. True love might exist, but it was a rare commodity, hard to find—though it beckoned often—and certainly she would not find it in the arms of a scheming mercenary captain who scarcely ever spoke the truth—if he knew what the truth was, which was doubtful.

But if she were honest something in him called to her and for the life of her Catherine did not know what that something was. Perhaps she feared to look for an answer because she was afraid of what it might be, and of what it might tell her about herself!

She had often dreamed of a lover, someone whom she could admire and trust, and the kind creature whom she had always conjured up bore no resemblance at all to Tom Trenchard. Quite the contrary. Tom symbolised everything that she detested about the gallants who infested London and the court since Charles II's Restoration.

Loose, untrustworthy, selfish and ready to sacrifice anyone else to gain a moment's pleasure. Lackwits all, so far as she was concerned, fit only to be tricked as they went their merry way. Their master at King Charles's court, m'lord the Earl of Rochester, even called his followers The Merry Gang—and they pursued virtuous and unvirtuous women alike.

Well, Tom Trenchard would not gain any such

pleasure with Mistress Catherine Wood, known also as Cleone Dubois, and now Catherine Trenchard. It was enough to make a poor girl dizzy to have such a multitude of names—only one of which was truly hers—and that being the only one she never used!

Which, I suppose, makes me as big a liar as he is. But I am only one through necessity! And even as she thought this a little voice in her head said, But what if it is necessity which drives him on, too? What then?

Catherine took this somewhat unwelcome thought to bed with her. She had no notion of what thoughts Master Tom Trenchard took to bed with him—if any.

It was raining in the morning. The sky was grey, and as they ate breakfast Tom said cheerfully, "It is as well that our meeting today is to be by coach. We need not venture into the open. The coachman will drive his carriage into the inn yard, to save us from walking to it in the rain. Or so the innkeeper says. He thinks that we are off on a pleasure jaunt."

Could the innkeeper really believe that we are rich enough to spend our time doing any such thing? thought Catherine. Perhaps he could. Tom was looking a little magnificent this morning; he was in his black velvet again. As he had bidden her the night before, she matched him in one of her best gowns, violet with silver trimmings. Geordie, to his disgust she later found, was to be left behind, unbeautified.

"You may guard our rooms," Tom told him privately. "Not that there is anything either incriminating or valuable in them, but it would be useful to know whether anyone thought that there might be."

He received a sullen nod of the head, but Tom knew that despite his surly manner Geordie was as faithful a friend and servant as a man could have. Someone who was prepared to guard his master's secrets and carry out his orders, complainingly, it was true, but always obediently.

And so he told Catherine as their coach rolled towards their assignation with Grahame. Not that he had secrets, but that Geordie was a good and faithful servant—"nay friend," he added quickly. "And you may trust him too. You may not be my true wife, but Geordie will treat you as though you were."

Some time later Catherine was to have occasion to remember these words and act upon them—to her own consequent advantage. But on that grey morning she received them lightly, and thought little of them. Geordie was Geordie, Tom Trenchard's surly servant, and that was that.

The coach reached the meeting place where the road to William Grahame's home diverged, but he was not there. Tom ordered the coachman to stop a moment. To admire the view, he said. Which, seeing that there was no view worth speaking of, must have sounded a little odd. Doubtless the coachman was used to the vagaries of the notoriously mad English, for he said nothing.

Tom and Catherine alighted, "To stretch our legs," Tom said. The rain had stopped so they walked a little way down the road, loudly admiring the unadmirable canal. They had gone about two hundred yards when they saw Grahame running towards them.

He was carrying a small pack, and his face was white and strained. Fortunately they were out of sight of the coach and its driver, the road having taken a sharp turn to the left.

"Thank God you're here," he gasped at them. "Someone sent another assassin after me—I should have gone with you yester afternoon. Fortunately I was ready for him, I sat up all night, and he came just before dawn. I was delayed by having to dispose of him. You have a coach with you?"

"Beyond the bend," Tom said, waving his arm in that direction.

Catherine found that she had an unseemly desire to laugh—and worse, to laugh without restraint. For she had a sudden grim vision of the small canal growing full with all the bodies that Grahame was throwing in it, and for some odd reason this seemed droll. Tom later told her that shock, combined with the macabre, frequently had such an effect. Hysteria, the old Greeks called it, he said, and it seemed a strange thing for him to know.

Grahame refused to slacken his pace and she could only keep up with the two men by running—something her heavily skirted gown made difficult.

"At last," said Grahame breathlessly, when they were in the coach again. "Drive me back to Antwerp if you would. In the crowded city we shall not be conspicuous—as we are here."

"I would have thought," said Tom Trenchard, that true, simple-minded, honest rogue, "that Antwerp would have been a safer bolt-hole than the one where we met you yesterday."

"I had reason to believe that I was safer there, for I thought that none knew of the house—but I was wrong. Some traitor has informed on me, and now I must try to hide myself again."

He said nothing more for a time, but sat there mumchance, although the meeting had supposedly been arranged for him to have a private word with them.

As they reached the outskirts of the City Tom asked him gently, "Have you had any further thoughts, Master Grahame, on those matters which we spoke of yesterday?"

"Indeed and indeed. There is, in fact, little for us to discuss. I have decided that I shall say no more until I have the King's pardon in my hand, here in the Low Countries. I am not minded to risk my life by passing on information to you without any such guarantee. I have no wish to find myself facing the gallows, or the headsman's axe, the moment I reach England."

This came out in a surly, grumbling voice, as though he had been taking lessons from Geordie. It was plain to both Tom and Catherine that two attempts at his life had rendered Grahame not only fearful, but non-amenable.

"I can think of nothing further," Grahame complained, "until I find a safe haven in Antwerp itself. You will bid the coachman drive me to the main square. From there I have a safe house to go to—the address of which I shall reveal to no one—and from thence I will send you a message when I am ready to speak to you again."

"No more than that?" asked Tom.

"Not until you have sent word to England by the next boat, asking for a letter containing a written promise of a pardon. Only after that letter arrives shall we talk again. I do not expect the pardon itself to arrive immediately, you understand, I know that such matters take time."

"And how do I contact you?" asked Tom. Things had not gone as well as he had hoped, but in such enterprises as these, they rarely did.

Grahame smiled. "Can you not guess, man? Speak to Amos Shooter. He will act as our go-between. You may trust him."

"Trust Amos Shooter!" exclaimed Tom when

they had set Grahame down in the main square, and had paid and dismissed their coach. "After meeting him again, I had as lief trust the devil. But as he is all we have, then trust him we must. But not much."

He, too, fell silent until they were safely back in their parlour at the inn where Geordie had a cold meal waiting for them.

"Prepare to work, wife," Tom said through a mouthful of good Dutch ham. "I want you to write a letter to London in the code we were given before we set out, informing them of Grahame's demands. I know you write a better hand than I do."

He had discovered this on the previous day when they had been practising the use of the code. Catherine's script was clear and clerkly, Tom's was ornate, flowing and hard to read.

"You shall be my secretary," he told her. "I shall devise strategy. Between us we must bring this awkward dog to heel."

Enciphering the letter, not the actual writing of it, took some time. Tom had told her what to say, and after that left her to it, going downstairs to join Geordie in the taproom.

Painstaking as always, Catherine reread the letter before adding her codename at its end. It was Oenone, the name of the nymph with whom

Paris of Troy had fallen in love on Mount Ida before the three goddesses had made him choose between them.

He had given Venus the golden apple as the loveliest of the three, and she had rewarded him with the most beautiful woman on earth, Helen, the wife of the Greek King Menelaus. Paris had carried her off and as a result the Trojan War had been fought, Paris had been killed, and Troy had fallen.

Some jester back in London had chosen their names, for Tom had been given that of Menelaus, the deserted husband. Well, thought Catherine, they could scarcely have called him Paris, for Paris had been as beautiful as a god, which Tom Trenchard was not.

She thought that it would be some time before he returned so when she had finished the letter, she went over to her small trunk and fetched from it several sheets of paper and began to write on them.

She laughed to herself a little at Tom's surprise if he were to read what she was so busily putting down on paper.

For Catherine had not lied when she had told Tom that she had not met the man, Will Wagstaffe, who had recently taken the London stage by storm and whose next play, *The Braggart, or, Lackwit Married,* had been commissioned by Betterton and was eagerly awaited. None but Betterton knew that Will Wagstaffe was no man, but the young actress who had played the heroine Belinda in *The Braggart, or, Lackwit in Love.*

When Catherine had handed the manuscript of her first play, *Love's Last Jest,* to Betterton, she had told him that she had been given it by a friend who wished him to read it, for she feared that if Betterton knew that she, a mere woman, had written a play, he would not have taken it seriously.

He had been fulsome in his praise of it, but had told her that at least two scenes needed to be rewritten to suit the talents of the actors whom he thought might play in them. "I shall have to meet Mr Wagstaffe to discuss the matter with him," he had ended. "I take it that Wagstaffe is not his real name."

"No, indeed," Catherine had said uneasily. She hardly knew how to tell him the truth, but needs must, she could not falter now.

"Wagstaffe is not a man," she blurted out at him. "Oh, Mr Betterton, pray forgive me, but 'tis I who wrote *Love's Last Jest,* and none other."

At first he had not believed her. But she had finally convinced him, and as she had originally thought, he was unhappy about the fact that a woman had written it. "Will the public come to see it?" he asked her. "We cannot afford a failure."

It was Catherine who had solved the problem for him. Much though she wanted to be acknowledged as the play's author, she knew that there was little chance of Betterton, or Tom Killigrew, the manager of the Duke's Theatre, putting the play on if they knew that she had written it.

"Need you," she suggested, "advertise it as by a woman at all? Wagstaffe was the name I gave myself, and Wagstaffe it may stay. You can tell Killigrew that that is not the author's real name, but that he is a recluse who wishes to have nothing to do with its staging, and desires no public acknowledgement as the play's author. You and I can work together to make any necessary alterations when it first goes into rehearsal."

"A splendid notion," said Betterton approvingly, "for your play is too good to lose. You, having been on the boards yourself, obviously know what will come well over the footlights. Will Wagstaffe shall take the credit, whilst you take the money."

And so it was. And it was strange that no one but Tom Trenchard had thought the name odd, although Catherine had, as he surmised, christened herself so in jest to get Betterton to read the play—and was then compelled to go on with the jest once it had been successful.

"The trouble is," Betterton had told her frankly, "that this play is so down to earth about the relationships between men and women, that it would ruin your reputation if it came to be known that you had written it. And you cannot want that. No, no, you must be Mrs Wilhelmina Wagstaffe only to me!"

The very last thing which Catherine wanted was that prying Tom Trenchard should discover who Will Wagstaffe really was. For he would be sure to think, as Betterton had suggested, that only a whore could have written it.

It was a pity that Wagstaffe's name had intrigued him so much. He had obviously seen the jest contained in the name, and not for the first time Catherine was surprised, not only by the depth of his knowledge, but also by his intuitive grasp. It was interesting, to say the least, how much that he did or said was at odds with his description of himself as a simple-minded rogue.

Given all this, it was really unsafe for her to be writing it in Antwerp at all, but the devil of it was that all the exciting things which had happened to her were spurring her on to write. New scenes, new jokes and new denouements were pouring into her brain so rapidly that she could scarce write quickly enough.

Sighing—for she thought that she heard Tom's footsteps on the stairs—Catherine stuffed her papers into the writing case inside her trunk and sat down demurely at the table. When Tom arrived, Geordie following, she was reading the letter which she had apparently just completed to make sure that it was correct.

"So, Mistress, you have finished this woundy business for me?"

"Aye, as a good wife should," Catherine told him sweetly—and caught Geordie's approving nod. Here was a woman who knew her place!

Tom read it over swiftly, scarcely mouthing the words aloud as he read—a trick that also betrayed to Catherine that she could not trust a word he said of himself. Few men but scholars could read anything without reading it aloud.

"Very fine," he told her. "Plain and simple. That may go as it stands. I shall ride this very night to the nearest harbour where an English packet leaves for home, for time is something that we have little of.

"Geordie shall stay with you as protection. You may let slip to our landlady that I am off on a business mission. As a good Lowlander, that will please her and prove that we are people of substance."

For no reason at all, for surely there was no danger here, Catherine was afraid for him. "How long will you be gone?"

Tom read her aright. "Never fear, sweeting. I shall be safe enough. I am not Grahame, who has never been to the wars." He was buckling on his rapier as he spoke, and picking up the horse pistol that Geordie had loaded for him.

"I have supped well, which is the first rule for a soldier on campaign. If by some mischance I do not return within two days, then you and Geordie must continue our mission without me, and pray that I may at last return here better late than never. I have left Geordie enough money to keep you both from starving. Follow Grahame, do not lose him, and use Amos Shooter—which may prove a little hard without me. You see, I trust you, sweeting. Here is my farewell to you."

Before Catherine could stop him he was enveloping her in a bear hug, and was well and truly kissing her goodbye.

"Miss me a little, sweetheart," he told her, "and do you look after her for me, Geordie," and with these final words he was gone.

The room was strangely empty without him. And quiet, too. In the short time that they had been together, Catherine had grown accustomed to him; to his mockery as well as his rare tenderness and—confess it, Catherine!—to the feeling of safety that his mere presence gave her.

Geordie said, breaking the unaccustomed silence, "Do not fret, mistress. He will be back. It would be a rare man who could kill my master. He's a match for any three of 'em."

His earthy comfort set Catherine laughing, a tearful laugh. "Oh, Geordie, I wish that you could have gone with him. I would have felt happier so."

He shook his head, "Not on, mistress. My master

would never have left you alone, not him. Oh, he trusts you, as he trusts me, but he would not leave a lone woman here among the wolves who would have murdered Grahame… No, no," and he shook his head again until Catherine thought that it would fall off his shoulders.

And so to bed, alone as usual. But it was strange not to think of him there, in the next room, with Geordie, and whether she trusted him, or no, Catherine was beginning to find that her world without Tom Trenchard in it was a quieter, but also a lonelier, sadder place.

Chapter Six

"Mistress Trenchard, is it not?"

To while away the second morning of Tom's absence, Catherine had gone shopping in Antwerp's vast market place, larger and busier than any she had visited before. Even though Antwerp might no longer be the richest port in Europe and one of its wealthiest cities, it was still a bustling and thriving place.

Not only was it famous as a centre where diamonds were cut, bought and sold, but it did a brisk trade with other European countries. Catherine had just been admiring some fine Brussels lace—far too expensive for her to buy—when Isabelle Shooter, a footman in attendance, came up to her.

"Indeed I am," Catherine replied. "We have the pleasure of meeting again."

Mrs Shooter—or should it be Madame? Catherine was not quite sure—looked around her. "Your husband is not with you, I see."

Some explanation seemed to be called for. Catherine offered it. “No, he is away on business, and I expect his return this evening. Meantime, his man, Geordie, guards me as you see.”

Isabelle Shooter quite saw. Geordie was staring glumly at her, his usual expression, but not one that she expected to find on a servant’s face. Her own man stood by, his face coldly impassive—as a good servant’s should be.

I really ought to know Geordie’s surname, Catherine thought, not that Isabelle Shooter needs to be aware of it, but I should.

Isabelle was speaking again. “My husband was saying only this morning that he would like you and Captain Trenchard to sup with us one evening. He would like to reminisce about old times when they were very young men together. I was on my way to the inn where you lodge when, by good fortune, I caught sight of you.

“Amos suggested that tomorrow evening would be a good time—he has a friend whom he would like Captain Trenchard to meet. You could send word by your man in the morning as to whether that would be convenient or no.”

Captain Trenchard, was he? What next? There seemed to be no doubt that Tom had been a soldier—as he had claimed. But what else had he been? Catherine was sure that he had been something else. This spying business appeared to be catching, for now she was practising it on him—and hoping that he would not practise it on her.

"Certainly, madame. I am sure that Tom, my husband, would be as pleased as I am to sup with you."

"Excellent, Mrs Trenchard, then that is settled," and she gave Catherine her kind smile. "Now I understand that this is your first visit to Antwerp and, if you so wish, it would give me great pleasure to show you some of its fairest sights. We are near to our cathedral, Notre Dame, which is not only the largest church in Flanders, but has the tallest spire. Even better, inside it are paintings by Peter Paul Rubens, which no one who visits Antwerp should miss seeing."

"That would give me great pleasure," said Catherine truthfully. "It is most kind of you to offer."

"Not all, my dear," and chatting agreeably, Isabelle Shooter was as good as her word. Catherine spent a happy hour forgetting about spies and plotting, and whether Tom was safe or not.

It was as they were walking away from the cathedral that Isabelle Shooter said something that set Catherine thinking.

"Amos has given me some letters to post to his family in England, and I must not enjoy myself with you so much that I forget to call at the office and see them on their way."

"There is a regular service to England, then, despite the war?" Catherine asked as casually as she could.

"Indeed, and since trade is our country's life blood a good postal service is essential. If you are to be here for some time, you may wish to use it to correspond with your family in England. I will show you where to go."

Whilst Catherine was busy thanking Isabelle for her continuing kindnesses, she was also busy remembering that Tom had told her and Geordie that in order to send their letter to England he would need to leave Antwerp to find a packet boat which would deliver it! Either he was ignorant that an efficient postal service existed, or he had been lying to her, and was engaged in some secret activity whilst almost certainly leaving his letter at the post office before he did so.

Given what she knew of him, Catherine was sure that he had been lying. The moment she and Isabelle had parted among exclamations of mutual friendship and gratitude, she turned on Geordie.

"Exactly what has your master been doing for the last two days, Geordie?" she asked him, her voice dangerous.

Geordie showed her his most defeated countenance. "Sending your letter on its way," he mumbled. "What else?"

"What else, indeed! You heard what Mrs Shooter

said. That there is a good postal service between Antwerp and England. And since our letter was enciphered, there is no reason why we should not use it."

Geordie shrugged his shoulders. "He *said* that he was taking the letter to post elsewhere—that's all I know." He spoiled this a little by remarking ungraciously, "He don't tell me everything. That he don't. Only to look after you."

Catherine gave up. For the time being, at least. When Tom arrived back in Antwerp, *if* he arrived back, that was, she would ask him what games he was playing with them.

Her opportunity to do so came sooner than she had expected. On her return to the inn she found Tom seated in their small parlour, pulling off his boots.

"Oh, you're back," she said coldly, well aware that she sounded ungracious, and unwelcoming.

"And a very good day to you too, wife," Tom returned cheerfully. He was always cheerful, damn him, thought Catherine crossly. "And did you have a hard time of it, husband? Shall I send for a tankard of ale for you, my dear husband?" he added, tossing his second boot into the corner where Geordie retrieved it and began to polish it lovingly.

"Did you have a hard time of it, my dear husband?" Catherine echoed sardonically. "Travelling miles to deliver a letter which you could have safely posted in Antwerp? Or so Isabelle

Shooter tells me. Where exactly were you? And what were you doing that you needed to lie to me?"

Tom was too busy tying the broad ribbons of his shoes to answer her immediately. At last he said, "Suppose I tell you that I did travel some distance to post the letter, would you believe me?"

"No!" Catherine's expression was mutinous.

"Then I shan't. And you are right not to believe me. It's a curst business that Isabelle Shooter chose to put a finger in the pie and enlighten you."

"She didn't do it deliberately. It only came out in passing."

"And now you are hectoring me *in passing,* I suppose."

Tom rose and walked over to where Catherine was standing, head high. Behind her Geordie was watching them both, a half-smile on his usually hangdog face.

"Suppose something had happened to you while you were away? How were Geordie and I to help you if we had no notion of where you were? Unless you had told Geordie what you were up to, that is."

"Nowt said to me, mistress," grumbled Geordie, admiring his handiwork on Tom's boots. "As I told you earlier."

"True enough," said Tom. "And know this, wife and servant. I had good reason to go on a dangerous errand without telling you. Mainly because what neither of you don't know you can't blab about—either in light conversation, or in answer to the questions of a torturer to save yourself further pain. Let that be enough—for that is all I shall tell you."

There was suddenly nothing light or cheerful about him. The unleashed power that Catherine had once or twice scented in him was fully in evidence. There was no gainsaying or arguing with him in this mood, that was plain.

"Yes, wife." He was very near to her now, his voice light and mocking again. "Nothing to say? Strange that, you are usually full of words."

Why should tears prick behind her eyes? Why should Geordie look so downcast?

"Yes, I *do* have something to say. By chance I met Isabelle Shooter in the square. She told me that she was bringing us an invitation to sup with them tomorrow evening. She said that Amos was inviting an old friend of yours so that you might speak of days gone by. I accepted on your behalf. Was I right to do so?"

He bent down to give her a gentle kiss on her nose, the kind of careless caress with which a man rewards an obedient wife.

"Very right. I wonder of whom Amos speaks? I shall discover tomorrow night perhaps. Did she say aught else?"

"Nothing of import. She showed me the cathedral

and Rubens's paintings. Afterwards we drank tea at a stall not far away—and that is all."

"Quite enough," he told her, kissing her lightly again. "Geordie," he said over his shoulder to his servant, "if you clean my boots much more, you will wear them away.

"If you are hanging about because you harbour fears that I may beat the mistress for scorning me, then dismiss them. She is a clever lady, and sees far too much—which in this Godforsaken venture is an advantage, not a disadvantage. Be off with you, and arrange for our supper to be sent up before the hour is out."

So Geordie had appointed himself his supposed wife's protector—even from her supposed husband. This amused Tom Trenchard not a little. But it saddened him also. The devil of it was that he had had to deceive them both—but with the best of intentions.

Like Geordie, he shrugged his shoulders. Surely he was running mad to care what his supposed wife, the actress and doxy, Cleone Dubois, and his servant, Geordie Charlton, thought about his actions—which were no business of theirs, since he, and he alone, was the master agent whom Gower had sent to do the business of the State.

Both Tom and Catherine dressed themselves in the very finest garment that they had brought with them to Antwerp in order to visit Amos and Isabelle Shorter on the following evening.

There was a kind of armed truce between them. Tom had spent the day God knows where. He had gone out shortly after breakfast—without Geordie—and he did not return until the late afternoon—a little the worse for wear. He had plainly been drinking, but was by no means drunk.

Before he had left the inn that morning, Tom had ordered Geordie to keep watch over Catherine whilst he was gone. "Since you have appointed yourself my wife's knight, then knight you must be," he had said. "She is not to go anywhere without you, and you are to guard her at all times, even in the inn."

Geordie had made no reply so Tom added sternly, "You hear me, man?"

"Aye, master. I hear you. Your voice ain't a soft un."

So his supposed wife was making his usually taciturn servant mutinous, was she? No matter.

Tom was going to meet a man whose name he had been given by yet another agent during his two days' absence. It was that of one Giles Newman, who was a former crony, and now an enemy, of Colonel Bampfylde, the leader of a small army of Puritans in exile in the Netherlands who were busy plotting to start a revolution in England. Newman knew of Grahame's involvement through his informant, a deserter from Bampfylde's army.

It was probably a fruitless errand, and whilst Grahame might yet fall victim to Catherine's charms, his informant had also told him that Newman was a dour man, a woman-hater, since his wife had deserted him to become the mistress of a member of Charles II's court.

He was to be found most days at a tavern called The Princess of Cleves where he had a room. Whether he was disaffected enough to give away both the secrets of the Dutch Navy and of Grahame, his informant did not know, "But no harm in trying, eh?"

The Princess of Cleves proved to be a small tavern in a dirty back alley, and was a notable exception to the general cleanliness of the taverns in Antwerp. It was more like one in St Giles back in London where the bully boys of Alsatia hung out, was Tom's verdict on it.

He looked pretty shabby himself, having left behind his good boots and his fine clothes. He had rammed a dirty-grey-felt steeple hat over a ratty-looking black wig which concealed his betraying red-gold hair. No one looked askance at him when he walked into the smoke-filled parlour, where games of chess and draughts were in full swing, since he looked like every seedy adventurer who was already there.

He asked the pot-bellied landlord whether Giles Newman was in his room—no one in the parlour seemed to answer to the description he had been given.

"Aye. Upstairs, first door on the right," drawled the landlord round his clay pipe.

Upstairs was reached by a crude, open-stepped wooden stairway that led to a long landing from which several doors opened. Tom rapped on Newman's, but no one answered. He rapped again. Still nothing—and he could hear no signs of life coming from inside.

The landlord might be mistaken, but Tom thought not. He pushed at the door—which opened. He found himself in a dark room, pitifully furnished, which stank vilely of tobacco. There was a small table in the centre of it on which a clay pipe rested, gently smoking. One wall contained a bunk bed, its curtains shut.

There was no sign of Giles Newman other than a pair of battered boots standing against the door and a shabby black cloak hanging above them. Tom hesitated a moment before pulling out the long dagger that he always carried with him, concealed by his dirty buff jacket.

Holding it at the ready, he walked over to the bed and flung its curtains back to find there, lying on his back, a man, horribly dead. He had been strangled, a useful method for a murderer who wanted to make sure that his victim could not cry for help. By all seeming the man was Newman, and his murderer was not long gone, for his body was still warm.

And now Tom was in a quandary. To go downstairs to tell the landlord what he had found was to invite both suspicion and investigation—neither of which a secret agent of the British crown wished to incur. To disappear through the dirty window on the opposite wall—which was wide open—and not to reappear in the tap room below was also to invite suspicion when Newman's body was found.

On balance, the second option seemed safer. But before he left he might as well take the opportunity to search Newman's room in case it contained anything that would give him some clue as to who had murdered him, or to his recent activities.

Tom looked carefully around him. A pack, half-full, had been thrown down on a chair beside the bed. A small book, and a pair of worn gloves, had spilled from it on to the floor.

He picked up the book and leafed through it. It was a collection of prayers and homilies. Newman's name had been written on the fly-leaf in a cramped hand. Whether or no he had used it to pray was doubtful. What he *had* used it for, however, was quite plain.

Certain letters had been ringed and others had been written below them. This told him that Newman had been corresponding with someone—who?—and this was the code that they had been using. The other man, or men, would possess a copy of the same book, similarly marked.

It was the work of a moment to slip it into the pocket of his buff jacket. Who knew how useful it might be in the future? From such small discoveries might a great secret be unravelled. Otherwise, though, the room was empty of anything but the sad and soiled bric-a-brac of Newman's lonely and wasted life.

He was considering what to do next when he heard the sound of footsteps outside. Someone was mounting the stairs and walking along the landing! It would not do to be found alone with a man brutally murdered. There was nowhere secret to hide, so Tom flattened himself against the wall by the door so that if anyone opened it he could leap upon them, and stun them before they knew that he was there.

He heard a man cursing loudly, and a door banging…followed by silence. Whoever had come upstairs had done so in order to go to their own room, not to find out what Tom Trenchard—or Giles Newman—was up to. He let his breath out in a great whoosh, and considered what to do next. Common sense told him to get as far away as possible from The Princess of Cleves as soon as he could.

He looked out of the window, which he judged to be just large enough for him to escape by. It was doubtless the means by which the murderer had entered to do his fell work.

Below it was a lean-to shed, whose roof was not

more than ten feet above the ground. No one appeared to be about—other than a goat tethered in the corner of a small yard-cum-garden of a kind often found in the Low Countries. Beyond the garden was a narrow unpaved lane that ran behind the tavern and the adjoining houses.

Tom thought for a moment. It would be to his advantage if it were some time before Newman's body was found. Well, he could easily arrange that.

He walked over to the bed, threw Newman's body over his shoulder, and carried it to the open window. After that, as gently as he could, he manoeuvred Newman through it and allowed him to slide slowly down the sloping lean-to roof before he fell to the ground. With a bit of luck the ignorant yokels in the inn might assume he had fallen out of the window and killed himself in a drunken stupor.

All this Tom accomplished with a minimum of noise before he wriggled with some difficulty through the open window. From thence he slid down the roof, before jumping to the ground—just avoiding Newman's body.

He recovered himself, and walked away as coolly as he could, meeting no one either in the narrow lane at the back of the inn, or in the larger one to which it led.

When Newman's body was ultimately found, the landlord would be bound to remember the man who had asked for him—and who had never reappeared. Tom knew that there had been nothing distinctive about him, and fortunately the landlord had seemed half-asleep and quite indifferent to what was going on about him, as had been most of his customers.

He could only hope that the luck that had been with him so far in Antwerp would hold. In any case, it was likely that the death of such a man as Newman, down to his last groat, would not be considered worth an enquiry by the authorities. Good riddance to bad rubbish was probably their motto where such as he were concerned!

To allay any suspicions as to his own activities he carried on walking until he reached a more respectable tavern, The White Horse, where he called attention to himself by appearing to drink more than he actually did. Most of his ale went to water one of the large pot plants that adorned the inn. He also started a noisy quarrel, which he picked with a man against whom he played chess.

He had played to lose—but loudly complained when he did so. His presence there was sure to be remembered. Quietened down at last by the landlord and his recent opponent, he finally staggered out, reeling round the corner, only walking steadily when he was out of sight of the inn before returning to Geordie, Catherine, and something resembling normality before preparing to visit Amos.

Chapter Seven

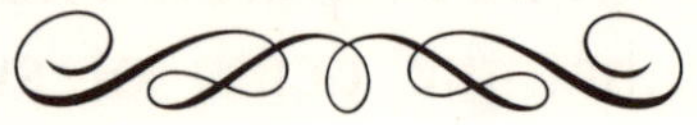

"This is better than a slice of bread and hard cheese before a campfire on a cold night, eh, Tom?"

Amos Shooter raised a glassful of his best red wine high in order to toast Tom, Catherine, and the guest to whom he had wished to introduce Tom—who had turned out to be William Grahame. This evening Grahame was no longer the shabby man whom Catherine had first met. He was splendid in dark blue velvet and a collar of Brussels lace. His signet ring was a showy one: altogether he looked as rich a merchant as Amos himself.

The Shooters' dining room was truly a haven of comfort and wealth. The *buffet,* loaded with silver plate, was of richly carved oak, as was the massive dining table and its matching chairs. A tapestry, showing the *Judgment of Paris,* hung on one wall. Opposite to it was a painting of a young woman in a blue gown playing the virginals. When Catherine had admired it, Isabelle Shooter had told her that it was by a little-known Dutch painter, Jan Vermeer.

A convex mirror, framed elaborately in gold, and supported by two gilt cherubs, adorned the third wall and reflected the company, turning them into caricatures of themselves. Catherine had never seen its like before.

On the fourth wall brocade hangings of the deepest blue, embroidered with silver fleurs-de-lis, hid a large lattice window. The dining room's black-and-white tiled floor stretched from it into the corridor outside. A Persian rug had been thrown down before the empty hearth beneath the mirror. Everything in the room and the house spoke of wealth and taste.

Isabelle had inherited the house from her father, but most of the furnishings had been acquired since her marriage to Amos. Earlier, flown a little with wine, he had twitted Tom about his apparent lack of success in life, and Tom had shrugged his shoulders sadly.

"We are not all winners like you, Amos," he had said, lying in his teeth. "But I have survived exile and am now reasonably content with my modest station. And after all, I have my greatest treasure with me, my dear wife Catherine."

"And Geordie, your faithful servant," Catherine could not help saying. "Do not forget Geordie!"

"Nay, I'd never do that—as Amos knows. Through poverty and modest affluence Geordie has always been faithful to me. Remember Geordie liberating a fowl for us, Amos, when we were besieging that town the Turks took in Macedonia—I forget its name."

"And a damned skinny thing it was, too—saving your presence, ladies," Amos had bellowed. "But better than starving, eh, Tom?"

It was then that he had reminisced about their difficult life together on campaign, and Tom had answered him in kind. Grahame smiled benignly at them as they spoke of battle, hardship, and death.

Neither he nor Tom were drinking heavily, leaving that to Amos, who quietened down a little when a great dish of oysters, new bread and butter, and sundry sliced lemons, accompanied by a small ewer of a spicy sauce, had been brought in, as well as a flagon of white wine and several large cheeses. The business of eating became more important than the business of talking.

Catherine had never seen such food nor such magnificence on a table before. In the middle of the snowy white damask cloth stood a centrepiece of gilded silver, consisting of two cherubs holding up a great dish on which reclined a pair of lovers in classical dress. "Venus and Adonis," Isabelle told Catherine. "It is a neat conceit, is it not?"

Neat, indeed! If we sold it it would keep Tom and

me for years, was Catherine's inward thought—and then she blushed at herself. Tom and me! Whatever was she doing? She was going on as though they were really married, and not pretending to be so in order to find out what Amos Shooter and William Grahame were up to.

She was also troubled by Tom's behaviour—again as though she were his wife. Something was wrong with him, and had been wrong ever since he had returned to the inn smelling of drink and tobacco. He was oddly distrait, as though he were thinking of something else whilst he laughed and talked so easily over the supper table. With a sense of shock, Catherine realised that she only knew this because she had come to understand him so well.

I am turning into a female Geordie, was her amused response to this discovery. She caught Tom's eye on her, and gave him a dazzling smile. This seemed, for once, to overset him, for he looked away before squeezing lemon juice on to his oyster and swallowing it.

The oyster despatched, he spoke directly to Amos and Grahame. He thought that for once being straightforward might pay more than being devious. "Did either of you ever meet Giles Newman? He was one of those who joined Bampfylde's small army. A little bird told me that they had a falling out.

I seem to remember that he was with us when we fought the Turks."

This was true. Tom had spent some time since finding Newman's body trying to puzzle out where he had met him before. It was only when he had idly mentioned Macedonia to Amos that he had remembered the man who had served with them there so briefly.

"That canting Puritan," snorted Amos through a mouthful of bread and cheese before Grahame could speak. He had long since demolished his share of the oysters. "Glad to see the back of him. Odd fellow. He had a little prayer book he used to read from. Always asked God to give us victory before we engaged in even the mildest skirmish.

"I could never imagine why he wasn't back in England, sharing in his kind's victory. Haven't thought of him for years. Certainly haven't seen him since then."

He cut himself another large chunk of cheese before asking Grahame, "Did you ever meet him? Once seen, never forgotten," and he gave a noisy laugh.

"Heard of him," offered Grahame, accepting more wine from the manservant who was unobtrusively waiting at table. "Never met him—or if I ever did I don't recall him. Many like him, you know."

Tom, who was watching Grahame and Shooter, too, in case either of them betrayed that they knew more about his affairs than they ought, wondered cynically whether one of the two men sitting opposite to him was Newman's murderer—or had hired his murderer. He also wondered how Amos had come to know Grahame.

Why he had been invited to meet Grahame was a simpler question to answer. Grahame almost certainly wished to speak to him and Catherine privately on neutral ground.

And so it proved, for once the topic of Giles Newman was over and then the meal, Amos helped his wife out of her chair, announcing jovially, "I believe that Master Grahame and our two other guests have business to do together, and would be happy to engage in it in the privacy of our home. That being so, we shall leave them to talk for a little before we serve coffee in the parlour overlooking the garden."

"A tactful man, our host," Grahame remarked once they were alone.

"Not always," Tom replied drily. "But he has supplied a convenient opportunity for you to speak further with me on the matter we raised with you the other day."

"True," said Grahame, "for it would be wiser for you not to be seen visiting me, nor me visiting you. There are curious eyes everywhere—as I'm sure you know."

Tom had no time for further havering. "So?" he asked, raising his brows.

"So, *I* am curious. Have you yet written to your masters back in London, concerning the pardon of which we spoke?"

Tom looked meaningfully at Catherine, giving her, as the actors said, her cue, which she promptly accepted.

"Certainly, Master Grahame. On the very evening of the day on which we met you, I enciphered a letter to London containing your demands, and my husband saw that it was posted immediately."

"Good, very good. I see that you have a useful wife, Captain Trenchard."

"Master Trenchard or Tom, I am no longer a captain in any army," Tom returned. "We shall speak with you when we receive a reply from London. And yes, my wife is useful—and loving! She is particularly adept at translating coded messages."

This last, suitably cryptic, remark, Catherine assumed, was meant for her, not Grahame. She rewarded both men with her sweetest—and falsest—actress's smile.

Grahame responded to it. "I will only say this to you, that the information I have relates to the plans of the Dutch Navy, and is of the greatest importance."

Tom nodded thoughtfully on hearing this. Catherine, watching him, was suddenly seeing a different man. She was beginning to wonder how many sides there were to Tom Trenchard.

"Moreover," Grahame added—Catherine thought that he was enjoying dangling bait before them—"I have other, most pertinent information regarding other great matters of state. But these must await my pardon."

Catherine took a hand in the game. Smiling her sweet smile again, she asked softly, "And there is nothing that will make you reconsider that decision, Master Grahame? For would not London look more favourably on you were you to send them such vital information without demanding an immediate return for so doing?"

Grahame rose and came over to where she sat to take her hand and kiss it. "Oh, you are a clever lady, are you not, Mistress Trenchard!" He paused before adding significantly, "I can think of some inducements that might persuade me..."

To his astonishment, Tom, who fully understood what Grahame was asking of Catherine, was filled with as much jealous rage as would have been appropriate were she actually his wife! A most inapt response, since beforehand he, Gower and Arlington had all agreed that to tempt Grahame with Catherine would be the ploy he would use in case he proved intransigent.

What had changed was that then he did not know her, and now he did. For the first time in his adventurous life he had come to respect a woman, not merely for her looks and the charm of her sex, but for the intelligence and courage which she also possessed, and was constantly displaying. It took him all his strength of will not to say something cutting both the Grahame—and to his supposed wife.

For Catherine, playing the game that she and Tom had previously agreed on, was still allowing him to hold her hand and was saying softly, “Oh, Master Grahame, something may be arranged, you may be sure of that.”

Tom spoke at last in a cold voice. “I beg you to do as my wife asks, and reconsider.”

Grahame bowed. “I note what you say, sir. And now we must adjourn in order to drink the Shooters’ excellent coffee, a new and rare experience. They live well—as tonight’s entertainment has proved.”

It was plain that he intended to say no more. Nothing further of any great import was said by any of the company. Isabelle Shooter produced a guitar and sang to them, Catherine joining in at her bidding. The men listened and applauded. It was not, indeed, until they were walking home, Geordie behind them—he had been entertained in the kitchen—that anything serious was said at all, and that by Tom.

“Did you have to hold that scaly traitor’s hand so lovingly?” he almost snarled at Catherine.

He was jealous! He must be. By the light of the

moon Catherine looked up at him and his hard face was thunderous. He looked like a very Jove about to cast down a lightning bolt to destroy his enemies!

"Why, husband," she replied gaily and naughtily, for it was her turn to twit him, and she did not intend to miss the chance he had offered her, "I was but doing the bidding of you and those who sent me here. Charm William Grahame, you all said, if it be necessary. And since it seemed necessary, this poor girl did your bidding. And, having done so, I have earned from you, not praise, but blame. You leave me all at sea."

She spread her hands out, and assumed an expression of charming bewilderment, looking both innocent and bewitching.

Yes, bewitching, thought Tom Trenchard savagely. But he must never forget that she was an actress, used to deceit. For was not all acting a deceit? The actor assumed courage, pity, despair, and innocence. And it was all a sham. How the devil was he to know, when dealing with such a Circe, whether she was innocent or not?

He told her so. Oh, thought Catherine gleefully. It is I who have him on the end of a string now, and not him me. Can it be that he is beginning to feel—oh, so inconveniently—a little of what I am beginning to feel for him?

For if he were jealous, what did that tell her about his feelings for her? A man could not be jealous of a woman whom he regarded as a mere tool, a sprat to catch a mackerel, as the saying had it. A mackerel called William Grahame!

Well, Master Tom Trenchard need not trouble himself overmuch, for the so-called Mistress Catherine Trenchard had not the slightest intention of getting into bed with William Grahame—or with any other man.

Keeping Tom Trenchard out of it, though, was quite another matter, Catherine was to find. His foul mood continued all the way back to their inn and was still there when they reached the parlour. He cast his hat down on one chair after sending Geordie away, before flinging himself into another and looking steadily at her.

"You seemed to take great pleasure in beginning to seduce Grahame—wife!"

"I was neither taking pleasure in seducing him, nor am I your wife," Catherine said evenly, removing her cap. An action that resulted in her hair falling about her shoulders. A glorious sight that did nothing to improve Tom's temper. He could only think how much Grahame would enjoy seeing it.

What Catherine was enjoying was that for once she was possessing power over Tom. At the same time the knowledge of his jealousy was doing strange things to her. Besides the desire to bait him a little, another stronger desire was growing.

She wanted to comfort him, to take his hand and stroke it, saying, "Nay, dearest heart, it was not his hand I wished to hold, but yours. Not he whom I wished to kiss, but you. Kiss me, Tom! Be comforted"—for her whole body yearned to comfort him.

Maudlin! She was growing maudlin, just like the girl in the play that she was writing who was equally besotted with a man whom Catherine had not yet decided was worthy of her.

But what had worth to do with love—or lust? For this must be lust, must it not? These internal quiverings at the mere sight of him, this desire to touch and hold him—to be touched and held by him—could only be lust. Was this splendid savage truly the one, the only one, whom Catherine Wood could love?

Tom rose and strode towards her. "What now, sweeting? Shall we practise together what you have offered Grahame? It would not do for your arts to be a little backward through lack of use."

His voice was gentle, not angry, and the arms he slipped around her were gentle, too. And his kiss...Catherine drowned in it—again. Until she remembered the insult that he had offered her before the kiss. Her arts, indeed! They were of quite a different order from those of which he had accused her. He might rather have referred to *his* arts, for he was never the same with her twice together.

Now he was being gentle where before he had been

rough: as gentle as he had been when he had been succouring her on the packet. Which was the true man? The one who had almost assaulted her the other evening—or the one who had been kindness itself when she had been seasick—and was being kind now?

"No, don't fear me, sweeting," he told her softly, his hand rising to stroke the lips which he had just kissed. "I shall not hurt you—quite the contrary. Let us make the sweetest music of all together. I know that you are drawn to me, your bright eyes and your soft mouth tell me so—so why refuse me? Let us love the night away."

Oh, the devil was in him, for he knew so well how to tempt a poor girl! This poor girl was almost ready to fall before him. How could she say to him, "If I were not virgin I would gladly lie with you. But I am and wish to remain so. I have sworn my vows both to God and to Diana, and I will not break them." What did the other Will say? "To thine own self be true, thou canst not then be false to any man."

"No," she told him, and was proud of how steady her voice was. "I will not lie with you. I am no whore, no matter that you think all actresses must be fallen women. I will tempt Grahame for you, but I shall not lie with him—how ever often you may ask me to do so."

His arms were around her again, and he was lifting her up. "Your pretty refusals only tempt me the more," he whispered to her. He was holding her as though she were a child and he kissed her as one might kiss a child as he carried her towards their bedroom. "If you wish me to woo you slowly and patiently so that you may regard your surrender as no surrender, then I will do as you wish."

Catherine had been so surprised by the speed with which he had scooped her up that at first she made no resistance, but as he kicked the bedroom door open, she began to struggle. "Let me down, you big bully. I vow you are worse than any Mohawk."

As she might have expected, this reference to the gangs of bully boys who roamed London's streets by night did not daunt him. He simply laughed at her. "If you think that, then you don't know Mohawks very well. Any self-respecting Mohawk would have pleasured you twice on the floor by now."

"And any self-respecting man would not take me against my will at all," she raged at him, beating on his broad chest with her fists.

"Hush, woman, and enjoy yourself," Tom said, throwing her on to the bed before bending over her and beginning to kiss her again, butterfly kisses, his hands behind his back, as though to emphasise that what he was doing was not against her will however much she cried out and protested.

Oh, she was nearly lost, for he knew the truth of her, damn him. Knew that, whatever she said, she desired him as much as he desired her. She also discovered another truth—an unwelcome one. In the past it had always been easy for her to keep her virginity for she had never truly been tempted before. No man's attraction for her had ever been powerful enough to breach her defences.

Whether or not she would have surrendered to him on the spot, without so much as an attempt to resist him, Catherine was never to know. "No," she whispered, half-heartedly. "No," trying to pull his hands away as Tom clambered on the bed to lie beside her and began to untie the laces of her bodice.

Even as he did so there was a noise of a door opening in the room outside, and of Geordie's voice, "Master?" he was calling plaintively, "Master?"

Tom's oath was ground out between his teeth as he rolled away from Catherine, and consigned Geordie to the lowest pit of Hell. Only the urgency in his servant's voice had the power to move him at all. Catherine, dazed, prostrate on the bed, could only regard Geordie as her unlikely saviour. She sat up slowly as Tom walked through the door to confront Geordie, who was looking even more hangdog than usual.

"Now what the devil is all this about, man?" he

demanded. "And your explanation had better be a good one or I shall strangle you with your own guts."

This last came out in a half-comic, half-threatening growl that had Geordie cringing away from him.

"Be very sure, master, that I would not interrupt you at your…work, but that the reason is urgent. There is a sort of constable downstairs demanding to speak to you immediately, and threatening us all with arrest if you don't agree to see him at once."

"A constable? At this hour? What kind of constable?"

"A captain, a sort of soldier," Geordie whined. "How the devil should I know what these foreigners call themselves? I only know that he had a pair of dirty great pikemen with him, and I was like to be scared out of my wits."

"Difficult that," said Tom unkindly, "since you don't appear to possess any. Do you go downstairs, and tell him to come up at once."

"Too late, master," Geordie announced miserably, "for he is already here."

Pushing by him as he spoke came an important-looking fellow, wearing a steel bonnet and a steel cuirass over some sort of uniform. Two pikemen followed him. He was carrying a paper in his hand.

He looked from Tom to Catherine, who had advanced to stand beside him, before bellowing importantly, "If you are Thomas Trenchard, then my master, the chief magistrate, would have words with you on a matter of some urgency. You and your wife will accompany me to the Town Hall immediately."

Chapter Eight

Yawning behind his hand, the chief magistrate, one of the local representatives of the Austrian Empire, rose from his seat at a long table to greet them.

"Exceeding gracious of you to accede to my request so late into the night, Master Trenchard—and your good wife, too."

He spoke as though they had had any choice in the matter, thought Catherine sardonically, storing up all she saw and heard for future use in a play when she got back to London. If she ever did get back to London, that was!

The Town Hall was a splendid place, decorated with old arms and armour, recovered from Antwerp's long-ago sack. The tapestries on the wall were new and portrayed various episodes from the Bible: Abraham and Isaac, Joseph being sold into Egypt and the Judgement of Solomon—all in the richest of colours.

Despite his effusive greeting the magistrate, a still handsome and impressive man in his late fifties, made no attempt to offer them a chair but kept them standing whilst he sat and talked idly to them, asking how long they had been in Antwerp, from whence had they come, had they journeyed outside the city walls, and what was their business?

"I was a soldier, sir," replied Tom smoothly, telling the tale which he, Gower and Arlington had agreed on back in London. "My father left me a small competence and I have set up as a merchant in London, hoping to make a living out of importing luxuries from the Austrian Netherlands and Holland."

The magistrate steepled his hands together and remarked, as smooth as Tom, "Ah, that accounts for your visits to Amos Shooter, does it not?"

So they had been watched—as Tom was certain they would be. Had they trailed him on his visit to Giles Newman? Doubtless he had not long to wait to find out. He inclined his head and nodded, "Indeed. But I cannot believe that you have hailed me here in order to speak on matters of business."

This was, Catherine thought amusedly, the polite way of saying, "Hurry up and tell us exactly why we are here. We waste time otherwise." The magistrate was by no means put out.

"These are dangerous times," he said. "The French are at our borders, the English fight the

Dutch. Naturally when foreigners arrive in our city we like to keep an eye on them and on their activities—and when a foreigner is found dead in our city we like to know how he came by his end—and why."

He paused. "I should be grateful for your help, sir."

This was cat-and-mouse tactics with a vengeance. It was difficult to know whether they were being threatened or not. Catherine, who not long ago had been fighting for her honour, now began to wonder whether she was fighting for her life. Tom seemed not a whit put out. He was as large and cheerful as ever.

"Whatever small thing we can do," he offered, smiling, "my wife and I will do it. Though I can guarantee that if a man was murdered, she for one did not do it. She faints at the sight of blood—and all violence distresses her."

Do I? Well, there's a thing about myself that I never knew—but a highly convenient one. I must remember to swoon if I am anywhere near a Flemish official when blood is about! With one clever stroke Tom has exempted me from all suspicion if the man was stabbed or cut down.

Catherine pulled out her kerchief and wiped her face with it as though the very idea of anything untoward distressed her.

"Interesting," said the magistrate with a frown. "I commiserate with you, Mistress Trenchard."

Why interesting? Was Tom's unspoken response. He had deliberately spoken of the murderer as being stabbed because he knew that Newman had been strangled. He hoped that, if it were Newman whom they were being questioned about, the magistrate would be likely to think him innocent of any knowledge of Newman's death if he got the mode of his dying wrong.

Catherine dropped a curtsy, and gave the magistrate a sweet smile, meant to disarm him. The magistrate smiled back before saying, "I wish to show Master Trenchard something, and now that he has told me of your aversion to violent death, I will spare you the sight."

He turned to Tom. "Come, sir. You will not object to doing me a small favour, I am sure. Your good wife will not be harmed during our absence. Blaise," he shouted to the footman who stood unobtrusively before a small door between the tapestries, "fetch Mistress Trenchard a glass of water. She looks a little faint. You, sir. This way."

The captain and the two pikemen behind them, a man carrying a branched candlestick before them, the magistrate walked Tom out of the main doorway, down a long panelled corridor to some stone steps that led down into the bowels of the building. He chatted agreeably all the way along the stone-floored passage that led to a heavy oak door.

He stood back to allow the captain to throw the door open. Before them was a large windowless room, lit only by a crude brass candelabra that stood by a long table which was covered by a grimy sheet. The magistrate led Tom to the table, threw back the sheet to reveal a very dead body, and said, looking sternly at him, "Do you know this man, Master Trenchard?"

Tom knew the man. It was Giles Newman. He decided to be exactly as truthful as he dared to be. "Yes. I knew him slightly. I last saw him in Macedonia when we were fighting the Turks. He left long before the campaign was over—sent on a mission to Vienna, it was said. Since then, nothing."

"Look well on him, Master Trenchard," said the magistrate, still holding the sheet back. "You came to speak with him, did you not? That is why you are in Antwerp, is it not?"

Tom said, and this at least was the truth. "No, sir. I had no notion that Newman was resident in Antwerp, and my visit was, as I have said, solely concerned with trade." Which was what he had told Amos when they had talked privately together in the absence of the women.

"You may ask Amos Shooter, if you need confirmation of what I have told you," he added.

"Oh, I will, Master Trenchard, be assured of that."

"I don't understand," said Tom slowly, "why you

should connect me with Newman, a man I have not seen for many years."

The magistrate threw the sheet back over the body and pulled a grimy piece of yellowed paper from his pocket. "This was discovered on Newman's body. Nothing of any value, and little in the way of private possessions was found in his room. This is the only thing which connects him with anyone else."

Tom took the paper and read what was on it. Written there was the name Tom Trenchard—and nothing more. He shrugged his shoulders and handed the paper back to the magistrate. "I have no notion at all as to why he should have my name in his possession. Or of how he came to his death."

"Oh, no, you know exactly how he came to his death," smiled the magistrate, watching him keenly. "You must have plainly seen when I showed you his body that he had been strangled. Did you strangle him, Master Trenchard?" and he looked pointedly at Tom's large hands.

Tom spread those same hands, and shrugged his shoulders again. "No, indeed, I did not. My visit to Antwerp, as I have already told you, is a peaceful one. I can shed no light on this poor fellow's murder."

The magistrate had said nothing of where Newman had been found, nor of a stranger visiting the inn where he had lodged. Best, Tom thought, to say as little as possible himself, and let his interrogator lead the conversation. Were he in such a position in England, he would have used his superior rank and his considerable powers of mockery to unsettle the man before him. Here, however, in a foreign country, such a course of action would not be wise.

He could, however, ask a question that an innocent man might expect to put to someone who was questioning him so keenly.

"May I ask where his body was found?"

"Perhaps, Master Trenchard, you could tell me?"

Tom shook his head and smiled. "I was not lying when I said that I had not seen Giles Newman for many years. I regret that I cannot help you further."

"Or will not."

Tom shook his head again. "Cannot. You may question my wife on the matter—so long as you do not distress her."

"Oh, I will, Master Trenchard, I will, but not yet. You are sure that you have not spoken to Giles Newman today? At the inn where he lodged they said that a stranger called to see him, went to his room and did not return. Disappeared, in fact. Were you that stranger, Master Trenchard?"

Tom decided that bewilderment was the best defence. "Indeed not, sir. As I said, I have not seen Newman since Macedonia." He decided that his best defence was to be bold, to behave as though he had nothing to hide. "You have a description of this stranger?"

"Only that he was a large man, shabbily dressed. You are a large man, Master Trenchard, are you not?"

Tom looked down at his fine clothes. "There are many large men in Antwerp, sir, and many are shabbily dressed. Now I may be large but I am not shabby—as you see."

The magistrate smiled. "I see that you are dressed finely now, Master Trenchard—but were you this afternoon? Let us leave that for the present. I should now like to question your wife."

Well, it was a piece of luck, Tom thought, that the landlord of The Princess of Cleves had been half asleep and had been unable to give any details of the chance-come stranger that the magistrate could use.

What did worry him a little was the thought of an unprepared Catherine being quizzed by such a persistent and cunning inquisitor. But there was no help for it. He dared not protest. To do so would be suspicious. He followed the magistrate and his cohorts back to the courtroom.

The attendant who had brought Catherine a goblet of water, also handed her to a chair, for which she thanked him gratefully. The day had been a long one and she was tired. Had the magistrate deliberately ordered them to be brought before him at such a late hour in the hope that if they were tired they might be unintentionally indiscreet or careless when questioned?

If he had, then it behoved her to be careful. For she knew of two dead men, not one, and both had been killed by William Grahame and thrown into the nearby canal. The best thing for her to do was to pose as a weak woman, easily overset. Which, she conceded glumly, was at the moment no pose at all. She had seldom felt weaker. On the other hand, this was more grist for the playwright's mill, and no mistake.

She wondered where Geordie had been taken and what he might be saying. For he had been led away from them by two burly lackeys as soon as they had arrived. At least he now had something real to complain about. And what were they doing to Tom—and where was he?

Catherine had rarely felt such relief from worry as she did when he walked back through the door by which he had left. His expression told her nothing, for it was as coolly cheerful as it always was.

"Good. Excellent," intoned the magistrate. "You have seen Mistress Trenchard to a chair, Blaise. Just as well, for I have some questions to ask her, and I would wish her to be comfortable when I do so. Your husband has asked me to treat you gently, my dear, and so I will. Answer me freely and truthfully and all shall be well."

"Yes, sir. I have nothing to hide." Except that I am growing to be as big a liar as Tom. She folded her hands in her lap and tried to keep them from trembling. She looked away from Tom so that the magistrate should not suspect that he was coaching her in any way.

Afterwards, she was to think how useful her stage training had been in this difficult new life into which Rob's folly had precipitated her. She tried to pretend that she was on the stage, and that it was Master Betterton who was confronting her, a false smile on his lips. She was sure that the magistrate's smile was false.

"What brings you to Antwerp, Mistress Trenchard?"

That was an easy question to answer. "I am accompanying my husband to help him in his business venture. We are not rich and so I act as his secretary and clerk."

"Useful as well as beautiful, I see. And this dead man, Giles Newman, whom your husband once knew. Did you ever meet him?"

Catherine lifted her hands and clasped them before her. "No, indeed. We have met few in Antwerp so far. We supped this evening with Amos Shooter."

"Yes, we know that, Mistress Trenchard. And this man Newman, do you know how he died?"

How useful to be able to tell the truth, to say earnestly, "I have no notion, but I suppose that he was stabbed—from what was implied earlier."

"Would it surprise you to know that he was strangled, and his body thrown into a back alley from his bedroom window at the inn where he lodged?"

Catherine's reply was genuine and heartfelt—her actress's skills were not needed. "Oh, the poor man! Who could have done such a thing?"

"Who indeed? Your husband, perhaps?"

Catherine widened her eyes to their fullest extent. "Oh, no, for I would have known. He tells me everything, you see."

The magistrate shook his head. Every word the woman before him uttered rang true. He had one eye on her husband and his expression never changed. It was one of husbandly pride.

What the magistrate could not know was that Tom was watching a consummate actress at work. His admiration of Catherine's quivering lips, her faltering voice, her expression of wide-eyed innocence, grew with each sentence she uttered. Nothing she said gave away the truth, that she, like him, was an agent of the British Crown.

He could see that, despite himself, the magistrate was gradually falling under her spell.

"Suppose I told you that Newman was trying to contact an agent of your government and was looking to sell information to him about the Dutch fleet. We know that your government has agents in the Low Countries. What we don't know is whether you and your husband are spies, or for whom you spy, and whether your husband killed Newman rather than pay him for his services—or because your masters ordered him to."

Catherine put her hands before her mouth, and then took them away to murmur faintly, "Oh, no. You cannot believe that of my husband and me. We are but simple merchants. Besides, why should you trouble whether or not such terrible things go on? You are neither English nor Dutch."

"That is so, but murder is murder, Mistress Trenchard, and we do not wish our neighbours and allies, the Dutch, to believe that we are aiding their enemies. Moreover, I think it possible that you may not be aware of all your husband's activities since you reached Antwerp. We know that on your first day here you walked into the country. May I ask why?"

A simple question again, requiring a simple answer. "To see the countryside, of course—so different from our own."

"You were not making a rendezvous with a possible informer, then?"

Catherine put on an expression of extreme and innocent puzzlement. "Why, no. As my husband told you, we are here on business. There would be no one in the countryside with whom we might do business."

Oh, you clever girl, thought Tom gleefully. Those quick wits, which I last saw demonstrated on the stage of the Duke's Theatre, are working now—to our advantage. He wondered what the magistrate was making of her.

It was difficult to tell. He changed tack a little, saying, his voice still mild, "And this man, Giles Newman. Your husband has never spoken of him? You seemed to say that you had never met, or heard of him."

Tom waited anxiously for Catherine's answer. If she lied and said that she had never heard his name, and if the magistrate's informant was Amos Shooter—for there was an informant, Tom was sure—then all her seeming innocence would go for nothing. For Shooter would be sure to have reported that Tom had spoken of Newman before his wife and the other guests at the supper party.

Catherine's brow was furrowed. She said slowly, "I am not certain," and then, as though recalling something slight and scarcely heard, she murmured, "Oh, yes. I remember now. He asked Amos Shooter at supper this evening if he had known Master Newman. It seemed that they were soldiers together, against the heathen. It was said in passing when they were gossiping of old times and old friends."

She smiled at the magistrate as though she were relieved at being able to help him.

As a piece of acting it was masterly. Tom wanted to applaud. Catherine's answers were seamless—leaving little opportunity for further questioning. At each move on the magistrate's part, she had countered by using her pawn to attack his Queen.

"And that is all?" he asked.

Catherine nodded. "Yes. I am sorry that I cannot be more helpful, sir."

Tom closed his eyes. This was either a master stroke—or a gross mistake. On balance it was probably the former—offering the image of a woman cocooned in naïve innocence. The magistrate gave a great sigh—and turned his attention to Tom again.

"One last question. Where were you this afternoon, Master Trenchard? With your wife—looking for bargains? Or were you looking for Master Newman?"

"Neither, sir. I wished entertainment and I visited an inn which seemed to provide it. It was not far from where we lodge. The White Horse it was called."

He was being straightforward and bluff where Catherine had been straightforward and delicate. Both responses were designed to give an appearance of absolute truth.

"You could prove that, Master Trenchard?"

For the first time Tom hung back, as if he disliked having to answer.

"Alas, yes. I fear the landlord will remember me. I drank overmuch and made a fool of myself with one of the other drinkers over a game of chess. He had to call us to order." He paused, and offered the company a shamefaced smile. "I was not proud of my behaviour and consequently did not tell my wife of it, though I think she knew that I was a trifle unhappy—but could not guess the reason. Was not that so, wife?" he appealed to her.

So he had noticed that she was aware that something was wrong. How little he missed of what was happening about him! She would have to be careful in future not to betray her innermost feelings to him. For the moment it was enough for her to smile and blush prettily—and confirm what Tom had said.

It was over. The magistrate steepled his hands again and regarded them thoughtfully: the pretty, helpless-looking woman and the strong-faced man with the air of the soldier still about him. He had seen many such. Why did he not believe them? The evidence he had before him was flimsy and he could not detain them on it. They would both bear watching, that was for sure.

He rose to his feet again, and called the captain over to speak to him privately, his eyes on the woman, not the man, to see whether she did anything to betray fear or uneasiness.

She did not. She was smoothing her gown down and playing with the linen bands at her wrists as though she had not a care in the world. Presently she glanced at her husband and smiled at him. Not once had she shown any signs of the distress of which her husband had spoken. She was either a consummate actress—or a total innocent—and he had no notion which.

The captain departed. The magistrate sat down again, saying nothing, his hands performing their favourite trick. Tom looked from him to Catherine and back again. He was almost ready to speak when the captain reappeared, Geordie in tow. He abandoned him before the table and spoke briefly and rapidly to the magistrate in an undertone.

The magistrate waved a hand at Tom. "A word with you, Master Trenchard. We have spoken to your servant here, and he has confirmed what you have told us."

"The truth," Geordie wailed at them all. "I told 'em the truth, master. What the devil else could I do, even if I'd been tortured with hot pincers?"

The glance which the magistrate threw at him was one of a man compelled to look at some creature far beneath his notice.

"Be quiet, fellow. No one has harmed you. You, your master and mistress, are free to leave. But I warn you all that you will be watched. Should I have reason to believe that you are other than you claim to be, you will be brought before me again—and dealt with. Antwerp is not a city which takes kindly to the presence of spies and assassins. That is all."

"Not all, too much—" growled Geordie rudely.

To be silenced by Tom, who said sharply, "Behave yourself, Geordie. None of us has been badly treated. We must respect the right of the governors of this city to see that its peace is kept."

The bow he gave to the magistrate before he turned to offer his arm to Catherine saying, "Come, wife, let's to bed," was a low one. It was imperative that they did not rage and storm loudly about their innocence.

He was both pleased and relieved that Catherine had chosen to act with bewildered simplicity—which must have made a much more favourable impression than behaving like a wounded virago. What was it that the Bard had said? "The lady doth protest too much, methinks."

Nevertheless, her hand on his arm was trembling, and he knew what an effort it must have been for her to remain cool and steady beneath the cannonade of questions directed at her.

It would have been difficult if she had been prepared for such an ordeal, but for her to go straight from their jousting in the bedroom to a court of inquisition must have imposed a strain on her under which many women might have buckled. Even her training as an actress had scarcely prepared her for this night's ordeal.

"That's my brave girl," he told her once they were safely away and walking back to the inn, Geordie behind them keeping up a constant litany of complaint. He, too, had played his part manfully—but he had done so before and would do so again.

But this night had been Catherine's baptism of fire, and she had acquitted herself brilliantly.

Catherine found sleep long in coming. She replayed the scene with the magistrate over and over again, trying to remember whether she had said anything incriminating, anything that the magistrate might remember and so call her back to question her again.

Tom made her drink a glass of wine and eat some bread and cheese before she retired to bed. He had put an arm around her, hugged her, kissed her on the cheek, and said only, "Thank you." There had been nothing overtly salacious about the hug or the kiss. They had merely been part of his thanks.

His last words had been, "We must talk in the morning when we are rested. Not now."

The worst thing was the feeling that they had been watched—and were being watched. If, up to now, Catherine had felt that she was simply playing a game, had not taken their mission seriously, what had passed at the Town Hall had proved exactly how serious it was. She was deep in a conspiracy that might prove fatal to all three of them if anything went wrong.

Worse, she now had three dead men to worry about, not two. If murder could be accounted straightforward, then the deaths of those who had been thrown in the canal could be described as such. Grahame had killed them because they were trying to kill him. But who was Newman? And why had he been killed? Tom had been out all that day—not simply during the afternoon. Had he killed him? And if so, why? Could she imagine him capable of strangling a man?

This was the thought which she struggled with. For, in truth, he *had* been disturbed when he had returned that evening. Was it possible that what had disturbed him was that he had killed Newman?

Everything went round and round in her tired brain exactly like a caged squirrel bounding round and round in its wheel. To imagine Tom as a solider was one thing: as a cold-blooded murderer was quite another.

She was still tired when morning, and breakfast, came. Tom seemed as disgustingly hearty and cheerful as ever, Geordie as glum. But then, they were used to this double life; she was not. Tom had ordered coffee and made her drink two cups of it. She was not sure that she liked it. It was too dear a luxury for her and Rob to buy.

Tom told her that it was an acquired taste. "It

stiffens the sinews, drives away fear and the more you drink of it, wife, the more you will like it. I have drunk a great deal of it in London's coffee houses."

"Where decent women may not go," Catherine grumbled, as disconsolate as Geordie for once. "And coffee is a luxury that I cannot afford."

"Then you must drink as much of it as possible while we are in the Low Countries, and when it has made you bright and lively again we must speak of what passed last night and decide on our future plans."

Yes, disgustingly cheerful was the only way to describe him, but he was right. Either the good food or the two cups of coffee did the trick, because she felt much livelier when breakfast was over and she was sitting before the hearth, opposite to Tom, each of them in a big leather-padded chair.

To her amusement, he began by imitating the magistrate, steepling his hands together and leaning his elbows on his knees. He adopted the same dry voice, too, to ask her, "What do you consider the most important things we learned from the questioning to which we were subjected last night? At least two possibilities must be considered: neither of them pleasant. Can you guess what they are? You may take your time in answering me."

Catherine's laughter was as much for his clever

mimicry as its difference from his usual forthright and robust manner. She checked herself and tried to answer him seriously. To do so meant that she needed to think carefully. It might be useful to imagine that it was part of the plot in a play that she was writing.

"Well, wife?" said Tom after several long moments of silence. Catherine thought with some annoyance that the happy smile pasted on his face was a superior one. Well, if it was there because he was expecting her to say something foolish, she would remove it.

"So far as I can see," she said slowly, "we must assume that the authorities in Antwerp know why we are here—even though they may not be able to prove it. Which means that either they were waiting for us when we arrived in Antwerp, which raises the possibility that we were betrayed before we left England, and before we even began our mission—or…" and she paused.

"Good, very good, wife." Tom's superior smile had disappeared. Yes, she was clever, this doxy Gower had foisted on him, and he would do well to listen to her. He always named her doxy to himself because he was refusing to admit that she was beginning to touch his heart, his mind and his senses. "Go on. I am agog to learn what comes after 'or'."

"Or we were betrayed soon after we arrived by someone whom we met—or who was watching not us, but Amos Shooter or William Grahame. I do not know which of these suppositions I like the least. All of them are unsettling."

Tom nodded his approval. "Exactly my thinking. And consider this. If Newman's body was found only late this afternoon how was it that they were able to find us so quickly? There may be no either/or, dear wife and Geordie, for we may be part of a double betrayal."

He considered the time had arrived for him to be truthful. Not perfectly truthful, of course, for he had his necessary secrets.

"I must confess to you both my own secret doings. My journey the other day was to meet an informant whose name I was given before we left London. He, in turn, gave me Giles Newman's name, and his lodging, and I visited him this afternoon."

He stopped in order to watch Catherine carefully. After all, for all he knew, she might be a traitor sent to keep watch over him—and ensure that he failed. It was not likely, but a wise man guarded his back at all times.

So far in his adventurous life, Tom had been good at guarding his back.

Catherine said and did nothing suspicious. Her glorious eyes were fixed on his, her lips were parted:

she was all attention. Tom continued, “When I reached The Princess of Cleves, I found him dead in his room. Strangled. It was I who pitched him out of the window to delay discovery of his death. I also came away with this, the only thing of interest in his room,” and he produced the prayer book, which he handed to Catherine.

She leafed through it in some puzzlement until she came to the passage with the ringed letters. She looked up at Tom.

“A code?” was all she said.

He nodded agreement. “Yes, proving that he was an agent, but for whom or what, we have no knowledge. We have too many fingers in the pie to know which hand they came from.

“Consider, all those with whom we have been associating could be working for any one or more of the following: the English, the Dutch, the French or the Austrians. To say nothing of the Spanish or the Cromwellian sympathisers and their so-called Republican Army. Pick any one or more of your choice.”

What interested Catherine almost as much as this was that Tom had not only kept his involvement with Newman from Geordie and herself, but had confronted the magistrate with an aspect nearly as innocent as her own, giving nothing away. Her busy mind ran through more possibilities. She decided to provoke him, for now she could not trust him at all, and she wished to discover whether provocation might not spill some more truth from him.

"There is one person, or possibility, you did not mention," she said coolly, smiling at him.

He was genuinely puzzled. "I thought that I had covered everything. What have I missed?"

"Why, who but you, Tom Trenchard, adventurer, who might possibly be an agent for no one but himself!"

Before Tom, struck dumb by this sudden accusation, so cheerfully made, could answer, Geordie let out a cackle of laughter.

"Oh, aye, she has you there, master. A hit, a hit. A pity females cannot fence. She has given you the true *coup de Jarnac* without knowing what it is." And he bent double, laughing and cackling like a mad hen, as Tom rudely told him.

"Damn you, Geordie, you of all people know full well that I am no traitor."

"Aye but does she? And you play your cards damnably close to your chest, master, and no mistake."

Seething inside at the impudence of his two dependants, Tom came out with, "And that is why I so often win. What are you grinning at, wife?" he roared at Catherine, who was laughing at the commotion that her pointed remark had provoked.

"Everything. Nothing. Will someone please tell

me what a *coup de Jarnac* is?" Her face as she asked this was a picture of innocent, inquiring mischief.

For a moment Tom looked as though he were about to explode like the frog in the fable, Catherine thought irreverently. And then he began to laugh, his head flung back, before he bent down to scoop her up and dance her around the room before depositing her back in her chair.

"A trick. The *coup de Jarnac* is a trick in fencing when one man attacks the other, not in the expected manner, straightforwardly, but severs his hamstring, injuring him so that he cannot walk, or fight."

"I see," cried Catherine breathlessly. And she did, for had she not done the equivalent of that to Tom in questioning him so sharply, so suddenly? Geordie had put his finger on the heart of the matter.

Geordie was watching them benevolently, head on one side. "Have no fear, mistress," he told her kindly. "You may trust the master. Oh, not as to detail, but as to the Grand Plan."

"Well, thank you, Geordie, for nothing," riposted Tom, giving his servant a hearty clap on the back that nearly had him on the floor. "And now we must go carefully. For we are suspected—and rightly. Only the lack of evidence prevented us from ending the night in the dungeons. Our only safety is in behaving as innocently as possible until the letter comes with Grahame's pardon.

"After that, who knows? We must act as the occasion demands, and that we do not yet know. And in the meantime, we trust no one, for we have no means of knowing who are friends, and who are enemies."

Chapter Nine

"Make way! Make way!"

Swords uplifted, horses foam-flecked with hard riding, a party of horsemen galloped madly across Antwerp's main square towards the Town Hall, its citizenry running to escape being mown down.

"What is it? What is it?" was a cry raised by many. One of the riders, lagging behind the others because his horse was falling lame, called out to them, "The French are coming! The French are coming!"

This threw the people in the square into a worse terror than before. A woman near Tom and Catherine—who were walking to the post office to see whether any message had come from London—fell on her knees and began to pray. The dreadful sack of Antwerp by the Spanish nearly a hundred years earlier was a folk memory that remained strong in the consciousness of its citizenry.

She was not the only one who felt the need to call

on God to save them. Many others began to run in the direction of their homes, ready to abandon them as refugees if the French marched on the town. Catherine clutched at Tom's arm for support. "Can this be true?"

"I fear so. It would be a master stroke for the French if, while the Dutch are concentrating their forces and their treasure on fighting the English, they could conquer Flanders. For then Holland lies before them, another possible conquest—and a richer prize than Flanders even."

He said this coldly, like a scholar considering a mathematical problem. Catherine shivered. "What shall we do if they reach Antwerp?"

Tom put a large reassuring hand over hers. "That I will tell you when we have collected our post—if there is any. But one thing, I'm sure, is certain. I don't think that the French can be very near to us yet, for if they were, we should have heard the sound of their cannon by now. But you are right to be afraid. At present, the French are the best soldiers in Europe and their leader, Turenne, is Europe's greatest general.

"On the other hand, it is also possible that, threatened by the French, the Dutch may be driven to offer us peace at Breda. They cannot wish to fight us both. But that is for the future. The present is murky."

Catherine's shivers arose from the fact that this

adventure of theirs was growing more and more dangerous. The notion of flying before an invading army was not an attractive one. But Tom was right. They must collect their post and then decide what to do. She had awoken this morning feeling happy for the first time since the magistrate had questioned them. There had been no further word from him, nor from Grahame.

She and Tom had spent nearly a week visiting various shops and booths where beautiful glass, lace, silverware, leather goods and pottery were sold. Tom had ordered various items and paid for them from what seemed a bottomless purse. They were to be delivered to London Docks by packet boat. Catherine wondered what Tom would do with them all when they returned to London.

If God did allow them to return to London. This was a litany Catherine constantly repeated, not daring to be too hopeful lest she tempted Fate to punish them for having an overweening faith in their own ability to survive.

Tom had also stopped trying to get her into his bed. In one way this was a relief, but oddly enough, Catherine found herself regretting his cheerful advances, and the merry glint in his eyes that told her when they were coming. He had been much more serious in his manner to her and to Geordie since their arrest. After his first lengthy discussion with her about their mission when they had been allowed to return to the inn, he had refused to refer to it at all.

"We have claimed that we are merchants here on business. Let us behave at all times as though that is true. Walls have ears. Geordie, do you be careful in what you say. Particularly when you have been drinking. But I do give you permission to gossip about my success as a merchant whenever you please."

"Oh, aye, master, trust me. I never say nothing, and that's the truth. I don't ask questions, neither. Not even to know where you went yesterday when you left me and the mistress alone."

He dodged the light blow Tom aimed at him. "You know perfectly well, man, that if I tell you and the mistress little of some of my doings, it is in order to protect you both." He didn't add, and myself, in case either of you should care to betray me. No, he didn't really believe that either Catherine or Geordie were traitors, but as his old nurse used to say, What you don't talk about, others can't know.

What Catherine also did not know was that she had suddenly become a temptation so great that Tom dared not so much as touch her lest he fall upon her and brook no refusal. And that she did not deserve.

Since his last mistress, a pretty little widow, had deserted him to marry a City merchant, he had been continent—a state to which he was not used. Always before when he had lost his mistress he had made it his business to console himself immediately with another. He had vowed never to take a wife, having been a sad witness of his father and mother's unhappy marriage.

Unfortunately, having reached the age of thirty-five as a bachelor, he had suddenly grown tired of the free life that he and his fellows about Charles's court were following.

Not only the fear of disease, but boredom and a feeling of weariness at the prospect of chasing yet another woman who would fill his bed for a time—and then depart—were overwhelming him. When he had first watched Catherine on the stage, and afterwards when she had joined him in his mission, he had seen her simply as yet another woman with whom he might amuse himself.

What was it that he wanted of her—and from her? He and his friends, The Merry Gang, were contemptuous of women, viewing them as either light-minded toys or mere milk cows one married solely to produce heirs—and to neglect. But he could not persuade himself that Catherine fitted into either of these categories.

She was witty, spirited, amusing, clever and brave. He could talk to her as though she were a man, and she would respond to him in the same way. He had been surprised by the depth of her replies to him when he had discussed the problems of their mission with her. And even when confronted for the first time with sudden and violent death, she had not fainted, had a fit of the vapours, or needed to be comforted and consoled.

She had more than held her own with the magistrate when it would not have been unnatural for her to be overwhelmed by his ruthless inquisition. For all these reasons he could not dismiss her as he had been in the habit of dismissing most women. That she held him off also intrigued him, for he was used to conquest and had been spoiled by his successes.

He could not, dare not, believe that he was falling in love with her. For love was an illusion believed in by fools. A beckoning dream which could never come true. And he was not a fool. Lust was all. But was it enough?

Undoubtedly he was a fool for allowing himself to be distracted by such unnecessary and untimely considerations when he was on a mission rendered more difficult by her presence.

Reaching the post office after threading their way through the growing crowd—for after the first flight from the square of many of the citizenry, others had flocked to it to discover what further news, if any, was to be heard—ended Tom's musings.

And there *was* a letter waiting for them, which

he handed to Catherine to carry, saying loudly, "This must be from my clerk in London, telling me the latest news of my enterprise. Do you guard it well, wife."

Back at the inn, Catherine settled down to the laborious business of deciphering what was apparently an innocuous letter, documenting the day-to-day occurrences of Tom's supposed shop near the Strand. What she found in it was dismaying, and so she told him when she finally handed it over to him to read.

Tom flung the paper down in disgust. "Reasonable enough, in all honesty," he said sadly, "but it does not move us a whit further forward. I cannot believe that Grahame will accept this."

He read aloud from the letter. "At this moment, matters being as they are, it would not be wise to forward the actual pardon for Grahame, but you may assure him most heartily that a pardon awaits him once he returns to our shores, having given us those assurances about the Dutch which he has promised and we expect."

He looked across at Catherine, who sat opposite to him, her quill pen in her hand, her face as disappointed as his own. "I fear that he will give us nothing when he reads this. I understand why my masters have acted so—but will he? The peace discussions at Breda, and the possible knowledge that the French intended to invade have caused their caution—but has left us with no carrot to offer the donkey and persuade him to oblige us."

Catherine laughed, and said demurely. "I don't think that Master Grahame would be happy to learn that we see him as a donkey."

"I don't give a damn for Grahame's happiness," growled Tom, "only for any information that he may care to give us. Now we must go to Amos Shooter straight away and ask him to tell us where Grahame may be found—or, if he will not do that, then arrange for us to meet Grahame at his home."

This was no easier to accomplish than Tom had expected. Shooter was not at home, but at his warehouse on the banks of the Scheldt. He was not pleased to see Tom and Catherine arrive.

"What now?" he asked, his manner surly. "The French may be here at any time; they are well over the border and are besieging Lille. They will soon be on their way to Ghent and Brussels. This is no time for me to be seen with those under suspicion of being agents of the English government."

So Amos knew that they had been arrested. And the question was, how? But this was no time to consider that.

"We need to see Grahame at once, and the sooner we see him the sooner we leave Antwerp and you are free of us," said Tom shortly. "Can you arrange a meeting for us?"

"Not at my house, no." Amos was no longer the friendly host who had eaten, drunk and laughed with them. "I can tell you where he lodges and you may find him yourself. He is at The Oriflamme, a hostelry by the river, not far from the Town Hall. It is not difficult to find. And now you have learned that, I bid you good day."

"Something—or someone—had frightened him, that is plain," Catherine said to Tom as they walked away, unnecessarily, she knew, for he surely was aware of that without her telling him! But he was obviously pleased that she had grasped that, as well as the need to go to The Oriflamme without delay. For if there was any danger of the French taking the city—and rich Antwerp must be one of their main targets—it would be well if they had left before the French arrived.

It was true that The Oriflamme was not difficult to find. What was difficult, though, was that when they reached it, Grahame was not there. He had left his rooms the day before and had gone, the landlord thought, to Amsterdam, though he could not be sure.

"He must have learned of the French invasion," Tom told Catherine, "and decided that discretion was the better part of valour."

"What do we do now?" Catherine asked him, although she already knew the answer.

"We make for Amsterdam, of course, and try to

find him there. A useful turn, perhaps, for at one stroke by leaving Antwerp, we avoid the French and the possibility of further trouble with the magistracy. We must go to the inn and pack immediately."

If Catherine had been surprised by the cleanliness and order of life in Flanders, she was even more struck by what she found in Holland.

"It's as though the whole country is scrubbed clean every morning," she told Tom as they sat eating bread and cheese and drinking strong ale for breakfast in a tavern near Utrecht on their way to Amsterdam. "I thought that I was clean, but these people, and their clothes, look as though they were new-minted every morning. Look at this floor."

Mirth on his face, Tom obeyed her. "Yes, wife, what is it that you wish me to admire?"

He was mocking her, but Catherine was too full of what she was seeing to take any notice of that.

"Look," she told him gravely, pointing at the spotless black and white tiles, "imagine what this floor would look like in a London tavern. The filth of weeks of neglect, spilt ale, dogs' droppings, straw—and worse. But here..."

Even as she spoke, a burly peasant sitting in the corner of the room accidentally knocked over his pot of ale. Almost before it reached the floor a little serving maid appeared, her cap, collar, cuffs and apron snowy white, a mop and bucket in her hand, and began to restore the floor to its pristine condition.

"There!" she exclaimed triumphantly as the girl ended her task. "They can't leave the place dirty or untidy for a moment."

"Yes," agreed Tom equably, looking around him, apparently admiring the remarkable cleanliness of the Dutch. What he was actually admiring was not Dutch hygiene but the sharp wits and knowing eye of his supposed wife. She was becoming a true helpmeet to him because she had all the best instinct of an agent: an intense curiosity about the life around her.

Catherine could have told him that her success as a playwright was based on her observation of life and her fellows, for one cannot write convincingly without being acutely aware of the passing show that makes up the world. It was that talent that Betterton had seen in the play she had given him, and that, he was sure, would make her future plays worth staging. It was a talent he had found surprising in so young a woman—or in a woman at all.

Tom had watched her watching Geordie, and—like a true actress—even imitating his walk and gestures, but never when he was by. For she also had a delicacy about her that made her unwilling to hurt people and animals unnecessarily.

On their ride north, Geordie and a packhorse

trailing behind them, she had always refused to eat the food and drink that they had carried with them from the inn where they had stayed the night before, until he had caught them up. She also insisted that he supped with them in the evening, instead of being consigned to the yard or the kitchens to eat his meal.

Now she was offering Geordie the ale she could not finish, which he took from her gratefully.

"You are spoiling him," Tom told her lazily.

"No, indeed. A happy servant is a good servant. One of my father's maxims."

"So you say," Tom drawled back at her, still lazy.

Geordie looked from one to the other of them. They might not be married, or even share a bed—yet—but they were beginning to behave like a happily married couple, freely laughing and talking together. Even when they argued they remained cheerfully friendly—except when the master was trying to get her into bed, that was.

He spoke, and what he said surprised him as much as his hearers. "I wish you were my true mistress, for a kinder lady never breathed. Remember that, master." He put the empty pot of ale down and strolled off into the yard. "To find the necessaries," he grumbled, for here, in Holland, one did not use the nearest wall as a privy. Stinking back alleys were few.

"Great God," exclaimed Tom, amused. "I thought

Geordie despised all women since his wife ran off to live with the Turks."

"He has been with you as long as that?"

"All my life," said Tom, before finishing off his own ale, and following in Geordie's wake. "I suppose," he added, a little surprised at the thought, "that he is my oldest friend, one on whom I can always depend, despite his never-ending wailings. Geordie enjoys being miserable."

It was apparently a day for revelations, for sitting alone, finishing her bread and cheese, Catherine had seen a side to Tom that was new to her. It struck her that, unlike many men with their servants, he was never actually unkind to Geordie. She had never seen him beat, or even strike him in anger.

Oh, he might rail at him, but that was all, and she had never seen Geordie cringe away from him as many servants did with their masters. He took Tom's sarcasms for granted, and rode over them. As she was beginning to.

"How do we find Master Grahame?" she asked Tom later in the day, when they sat by the roadside eating the inevitable bread and cheese and drinking water from a skin refilled that morning.

"We ask." Tom was being uncharacteristically brief. He looked about him. Holland was flat and there was little shelter or comfort to be found near the road—which was itself nothing more than a dirt track. Once or twice a wagon or a farm cart jolted by. Nearer to the towns through which they passed the roads improved and coaches, large clumsy things, rolled along them.

"But surely that will draw attention to us—and we cannot want that."

"Not at first. I have kept careful watch and we are not being followed. One thing the French have done for us is to give the authorities in Flanders more to worry about than possible English spies. It may take some little time, I trust, for the Dutch to become suspicious of us. Unless we have been betrayed."

"And we go on pretending to be merchants?"

"Indeed, and it is not only pretence. The goods we have bought in Flanders and shall buy in Holland will be shipped to London to be sold there. I might as well gain some profit from this adventure."

Well, that certainly answered her question as to what was to become of the beautiful things that she and Tom had bought. On one of their last buying excursions in Antwerp, they had bought bolts of exquisitely patterned cloth that Tom had held up against her to see whether or not it matched her eyes.

"Is that what you do now that you are no longer a soldier?" she had ventured.

Tom had smiled one of his secret smiles. "Not

exactly, but the wise man takes advantage of any situation in which he finds himself. Do you do the same."

The only advantage Catherine could think of arising out of her present adventure was that it was providing a great deal of material to help her to write future plays. But she could not tell him that.

Amsterdam, she found when they at least reached it, was not as large as Antwerp, but was much more compact, being built round a series of canals, often parallel with the cobbled tracks along which they rode in search of a suitable tavern.

The narrow streets and the bridges across the canals were full of people who took little interest in them. Strangers, she knew, were easily identifiable in small towns, but not in large ones. This would help them in their wish to be anonymous.

"Here, we'll stop here," exclaimed Tom, pointing to an inn whose sign board showed the portrait of Piet Hein, the Dutch admiral who had captured the rich Spanish silver fleet thirty years earlier.

It was set at the corner of a lane that opened off a long road on which stood some of the most splendid houses Catherine had ever seen. That they were narrow, terraced and many-storied, added to their rich splendour rather than took away from it. She was later to discover that they had been riding down one of the richest streets in Amsterdam, the

Herengracht, where many of Holland's great merchant princes lived.

Tom turned into the inn yard, Catherine and Geordie following him. They had not hired any servants to accompany them, partly because Dutch roads were safe, and partly because the less anyone knew of them, the better.

Their rooms were even cleaner and, although smaller, were more impressive than the ones they had occupied in Antwerp. The window looked out on a view of the bridge, the canal, the Herengracht and the distant road leading to it.

"A soldier," Tom announced, looking out of it, "would say that this was a splendid vantage point, since no enemy could advance on us without being seen."

"Unless they came by the back way," Catherine announced naughtily.

She was less amused on exploring their quarters to discover that the great four-poster bed in their room dominated it forbiddingly. Geordie was housed in a minute ante-room off theirs, which boasted a narrow bunk bed in a niche in the wall. There was no way in which Tom could sleep in either room other than by lying on the floor: they would have to share the great bed!

"Did you arrange this deliberately?" she demanded of Tom who, sprawled in a large armchair, was watching her, smiling at her agitation and knowing what was causing it.

"No, *wife,*" he said, laying emphasis on the word wife. "This is, alas, the only room left."

"I told you," she said frostily, "that I did not intend to pose as your wife other than in public. In private is quite a different matter. May we not move to another inn?"

"Amsterdam, dear wife, is not Antwerp, and the inn-keeper assures me that we are fortunate to find a good room at all. We could, of course, try our luck in the seamen's alehouses on the waterfront, but I fear that you would like their attentions even less than mine.

"But do not trouble yourself; the bed, as you see, is large, and we may put the bolster down the middle to preserve your honour, for I have no intention of sleeping on the floor."

"It's not my honour I'm worried about," Catherine told him bluntly, "but yours."

"Very wise of you. As Geordie will inform you, my honour is a fickle thing—it comes and it goes, but do not fear, I have never forced a woman yet, and I do not intend to begin now."

Oh, damn his smiling impudence! And why did she find such an unhandsome man so attractive? Why should a craggy face, a grim mouth and a shock of red-gold hair undo a poor girl so?

Later, alone, for Tom went drinking with Geordie, reeling from tavern to tavern to try to find news of Grahame without drawing too much attention to themselves, she found herself remembering him and his taking ways all too often. Pray God they took not her! These days when she was composing impudent speeches for her dashing rake, Lovewell, he grew more like Tom every time she wrote of him!

"Do not think that your last declaration makes me feel any happier," she told him.

"Oh, wife, if you wish to feel happier, then let us remove the bolster, and we can fly to heaven together."

Best to say nothing to that, for whatever she said, he would be sure to cap it with a witticism that would be difficult to refute. A plain and straightforward villain he might call himself, but he was as slippery as an eel and possessed a tongue as sharp as Satan's.

Catherine was still thinking of him later that night after she had finished writing another scene of *The Braggart, or, Lackwit Married,* and was carefully putting her manuscript back into her pack. It had grown dark outside and the noise of the revellers leaving the inn to stagger home had died away.

She lit the candle beside the bed and decided that it was time for her to retire. Tom had been adamant that they share the bed, and she had reluctantly given way. She put the long bolster down the length of it and stared at it hopefully. She knew that when men married young children who were not old enough to become their true wives, they shared the bed for a night with a bolster between them to signify that the ceremony had been performed.

But I am not married, and if I am truthful I fear myself as much as I fear him. Catherine put this uncomfortable thought at the back of her mind and tried to forget it as she dressed herself for the night. Her nightgown was of cotton and covered her even more than her day dress did since it had a high neck, a collar and was tied demurely under her chin with a drawstring.

But she was naked beneath it and she was going to share her bed with a man who attracted her strongly, but of whom she knew nothing: not even whether he was married.

He was also a man who was somewhere outside in the streets, or rather the inns and stews of Amsterdam. Was he pleasuring another woman because she had forbidden him to pleasure her? The thought of him with a woman distressed her when she finally entered the bed and pulled the sheets up to her chin. She had already decided that she would not lie down or go to sleep until he returned. She wanted to be fully conscious when he did.

Time passed. Occasionally in the distance she

heard the sound of merrymaking. A woman laughed once, beneath her window. A man's voice said something to her, she laughed again and they moved away. Drunken singing in the distance came nearer and nearer. Catherine found that her eyes were closing, and that sleep was claiming her; it had been a long day. Resolutely she fought to stay awake.

The drunken singing was now just outside the inn. Then, thankfully, it stopped. The candle was beginning to gutter: it was as weary as she was. Footsteps on the stairs had her sitting up again. They reached the door and she heard it open, and a man's voice cursing as opening it seemed to prove difficult. It was Tom and Geordie. Geordie began to sing again in a tuneless voice until Tom shushed him.

They both fell into the room, flushed with drink and God knows what else. Tom, swaying and smiling foolishly at her, mumbled, "There's a good wife, Geordie, awake and waiting for me to come home. Do you go to bed, and leave us to celebrate my return."

"Don't want to go to bed," moaned Geordie, "want another drink."

"There's no more to be had tonight."

If Geordie was a miserable drunk, then Tom was evidently a cheerful one. He pushed Geordie, still complaining, into his ante-room and shut the door on him, before beginning to tear off his clothes.

Unwillingly fascinated, Catherine watched him strip for a moment, before saying in an acid-sweet voice, "Forgive me for asking but, during this merry evening's drinking, did you manage to find anything out about William Grahame?"

Tom shook a bleary head and winked at her. He threw his breeches on to a chair—which left him standing there only in his shirt. "Alas, no, woman, and a fine night we made of it while trying to catch our bird. All's to do again. And now your hard-working spouse has come for his reward."

So saying, he staggered to the bed, heaved the bolster out of it and himself inside it, and took Catherine in his arms, giving her a smacking, beery kiss before she fully understood what he was at.

Horrified, for in her wildest reveries she had never thought to find herself in bed with a happy, drunken man, who was stroking and caressing her, Catherine realised that the time had truly come when she needed to fight him off if she were to retain her maidenhead. This proved difficult, for he seemed to possess as many arms and legs as the proverbial sea monster, and no sooner had she pushed off one arm, than he trapped her legs with his.

Impossibly, Catherine found herself wanting to laugh; Tom's erratic and drunken good humour was beginning to have its effect on him for when, now thoroughly roused, he tried to kiss her, his aim was wildly off, and he embraced her pillow instead. Which had him saying despairingly to her, desire subsiding a little, "For God's sake, hold still, wife, and let me at you, you and the room are going around together."

"You shall not have me tonight," Catherine told him, recovering her common sense again, "nor ever—and certainly not in this condition."

He gave a low sigh when she spoke and she suddenly realised that, being as drunk as he was, his desire might outrun his ability to perform—at least she hoped so—but when he finally struggled himself on top of her, even that hope seemed a desperate one.

"Thass better," he mumbled happily, aiming a kiss at her, which this time found its target on her lips. Oh, how betraying the body is! Catherine thought, when the mind is no longer controlling it, for she could not prevent herself from kissing him back. Far from repelling her, his state of cheerful drunkenness made him seem vulnerable since it had silenced his caustic tongue.

"So soft, so warm," he sighed, holding her loosely in his arms, "what a comfortable woman you are, wife." Smiling down at her, he laid his spinning head in the crook of her shoulder, and heaving a great sigh of "nice," fell asleep as sweetly and swiftly as any babe.

To go in one moment from being on the point of

half-willing ravishment, to holding a sleeping and heavy man quiescent in her arms in the next, was strangely enough an anticlimax so stunning that Catherine, of all things, found herself disappointed. Her whole body was throbbing and thrumming in the oddest way—and the desire to cry was as strong as the desire to laugh.

She shifted Tom's weight so that he rolled away from her to lie on his side of the bed. Dead to the world, he showed no signs of waking up. Catherine restored the bolster to its proper place between them, and blew out the candle, which was on the point of expiring anyway.

Before she did so, she could not help looking at Tom. He was now lying in a posture of complete abandon. His shirt was rucked up above his knees showing long, strong legs and beautiful narrow feet—the ones with which she had recently struggled. His shirt strings had loosened and it had fallen open to the waist to reveal a massive chest decorated with whorls of red-gold hair.

His head lay on one strong arm and his relaxed face wore an expression of complete and happy contentment, as though he had truly succeeded in having his way with her. Catherine wondered what he was doing in his dreams.

Altogether he was—half-naked—as splendid a specimen of manhood as you might hope to see.

Lying awake in the dark, Catherine was asking herself a question. Do I regret that the drink overwhelmed him before he could have his way with me? She could not call it ravishment, for after the first few moments she had never truly tried to fight him off.

And if so, is it because I would prefer him to take me when he is in his senses rather than as tonight, when he is half out of them?

Either way, she could not find an answer.

Chapter Ten

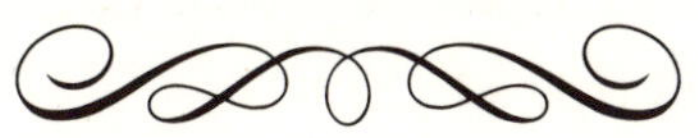

His head throbbing as though the devil were trying to beat a tattoo on it, Tom Trenchard woke up to find himself in a strange bed in a strange town. Memory was lost to him as he flung out an arm to encounter...a bolster!

"What the devil!" Heaving himself up, his head hurting and his stomach revolting against any movement, he looked down to find Catherine sound asleep on the other side of the bolster.

Memory—or rather part of it—returned. Enough to have him feeling a sickness that had nothing to do with drink. For all that he could remember was falling gleefully upon her—and after that, nothing. Great God, had he drunk so much that he had ravished a woman who had consistently held him off, and then had no memory of having done so?

He had always prided himself on having more conscience than most of his sovereign's courtiers where women were concerned—or his sovereign himself. It had always been his boast that any woman who lay with him did so willingly. Oh, he had the right to sweet talk her into agreement, but not to force her. He gave a groan that hurt his head. Had he, in his drunken folly, allowed the desire he felt for Catherine to drive him on to do the unthinkable?

He gave another groan and dropped his aching head into his cupped hands. For was it not the frustration her constant presence was causing him that had set him drinking like a madman the night before to try to forget her?

He felt Catherine stir. What would she say to him? What could he say to her? If only he were Rochester or Sedley, the task would be easy enough. For both regarded all women as prey, but he had never been able to bring himself to be quite as hard as that. Which was one reason why he had never married.

He groaned again.

"Tom?" queried a worried voice from the other side of the bolster.

For very shame he must answer. He turned his poor head, oh so gently, in order to look at her, and winced as he did so.

"You look ill," she told him, and then, kindly, "Shall I wake Geordie and send him for a restorative?"

"Good God, no." Unwisely, Tom shook his head,

before turning it away again. "He'll be in no better case than I am, and will probably need restoring himself."

"Oh, how stupid I am. I hadn't thought of that."

Through blear and red-rimmed eyes, Tom looked her full in the face for the first time.

"Catherine," he began. "About last night..." He stopped, not knowing how to go on. For a woman whom he thought he had ravished not many hours earlier, she seemed remarkably composed. Perhaps she hadn't minded, had changed her mind about lying with him. This little seed of hope had him asking her, "You feel well this morning?"

Catherine looked at him, puzzled a little by his odd manner, which, now that she thought of it, matched his sad condition; eyes bleary, blue shadows under his eyes, his face yellow, and a hangdog manner very unlike his usual cheerful brashness. Whatever was the matter with him? He had been a cheerful drunk last night. But this morning, now that he was sober, he was as dismal as Geordie had been.

And then, as she met his worried eyes, understanding flooded in. The only drunken man she had known well had been her father after her mother's death. And one of his symptoms the morning after had been what he called his "forgettory'. He frequently forgot everything that had passed in the later stages of a night spent in drinking.

What more likely than that Tom remembered nothing after he had leaped into bed with her, and had lost all knowledge of what had passed before he fell asleep. His owlish, worried look was most likely caused by his worrying over whether he had finally had his way with her against her will.

"About last night," he began again. "I didn't… frighten you, did I?" His expression was a pleading one.

She was right. He *had* forgotten. She would punish him a little both for forgetting what he had done, and for starting to do it—and failing.

"Frighten me? Oh, no. Why should I have been frightened?" And then the devil seized her tongue and spoke with it. "Why should I be frightened when you asked me to marry you? That flatters a woman, not frightens her."

"Marry you!" Had he been so far gone in drink as to say anything so foolish, even in the act of persuading her to lie with him?

"Yes, marry me. You said, most distinctly, that you would marry me if I lay with you. Surely you haven't forgotten?"

Tom licked his lips. What the devil should he do now? He had wanted to bed Catherine, not to marry her, even though she had begun to intrigue him more and more and rouse strange longings in him. And now, by all the devils in hell he had gained what he wished—apparently with the help of a spurious proposal of marriage—and gained no benefit at all from it because he couldn't remember a thing!

For once the sophistical and sophisticated courtier who was one of the leading lights of Charles II's entourage was rendered speechless.

"I must have been mad as well as drunk," he muttered at last.

Must he, indeed! What a fine compliment to pay a single young woman whose maidenhead he thought he had enjoyed, to tell her that he was mad to wish to marry her! He deserved to be teased. Catherine decided to prolong Tom's torments a little longer.

Her enjoyment was given spice by the contrary fact that, whilst she was teasing him, she wanted to kiss him and tell him that all was well. Through no access of virtue of his own, quite the contrary, she was still untouched. But if the thought of marrying her was so abhorrent, then he deserved to be punished.

"You were so happy afterwards," she told him, "that you spoke of our wedding being celebrated as soon as we returned to England, under the auspices of Sir Thomas Gower, who had indirectly caused to bring it about."

"I did?" groaned Tom. The feeling that drink had driven him mad grew stronger, as did another feeling. Well, if he had promised her marriage and she had given in to him, then his conscience informed him that he ought to marry her. He had never, ever, proposed such a thing before.

As he worried over this like a dog worrying over a large and strange bone, trying to decide whether to chew on it or not, he looked across at Catherine to discover that she had both hands over her mouth, trying to smother the laughter that his tormented expression was provoking.

What the devil was she laughing at? Enlightenment dawned. He leaned over the bolster to grab her to him.

"What game are you playing with me, wife?" and he kissed her. Not as he had done the night before, but gently and ruefully.

Held against him, her soft cheek rubbing against his rough unshaven one, Catherine said into his neck, "Oh, Tom, I cannot go on deceiving you. Nothing happened last night. True, you did get into bed with me and tried to lie with me as a husband lies with his wife, but before you did so drink overcame you and you fell asleep. Not a very flattering thing to happen, I do assure you. Particularly now that you seem to have forgotten everything that passed."

Tom held on to her for a moment before letting go of her. Was this strange feeling that overcame him when he did so regret that he had not offered her marriage? It had him muttering, "I am sorry that I behaved so badly as to try to take you against your will. That is not my way. All I can remember is walking through the door, seeing you…and falling on you. After that, nothing."

He looked wryly down at his shirt. "I suppose that I must have undressed myself, unless you or Geordie helped me."

Catherine was enduring some strange feelings of her own, for she could have continued with the lie and perhaps blackmailed him into marriage. Whether he would have allowed her to do so was quite another thing, and a thing she would not like to have tested.

No, it was all a joke, in which for once she had turned the tables on Tom for a change. "No," she told him, "you stripped yourself. Geordie was too far gone to help himself, let alone you, and I was too…"

"Transfixed," offered Tom helpfully. He was beginning to recover his usual comic sang-froid now that the dread word marriage was to be forgotten.

"Scarcely," riposted Catherine in her best Will Wagstaffe manner, "for if I had been transfixed, we should be discussing our wedding vows by now!"

She was well pleased with this swift reply and decided to write the exchange down as soon as she had a private moment that would allow her to turn into Will Wagstaffe.

Tom's shout of laughter at her naughty jest had him

holding his poor abused head, and brought Geordie through the door to stare at their amusement.

"You wanted something, master?" he asked mournfully.

"Yes, ale and water at the double, and for all three of us. And some dry bread for you and me, and cheese with it for the mistress."

"I'm glad some on us is happy this morning," grumbled Geordie as he went to do Tom's bidding, "seeing as how my head's banging like the bells of St Martin's in the Fields during the Great Fire."

Whether it was her teasing of him or the ale which Geordie brought him which did the trick, Tom was soon his normal cheerful self again. He took himself off into Geordie's ante-room to dress, leaving Catherine some privacy. He held what he called a council of war once they were all decent.

"I cannot see myself," he told Catherine with a cheeky grin, "staggering in and out of every alehouse in Amsterdam trying to find Grahame. I am alike to die of a syncope brought on by drink before the month is out."

"Then how shall we manage to find him in a city of a hundred thousand people?" asked Catherine anxiously, for Amsterdam was not only the richest city in Europe, it was also one of the most populous.

"Never fear, dear wife," said Tom, putting his forefinger beside his nose like a trickster from Alsatia in London where the rogues and vagabonds lived.

"Before we left England, Sir Thomas Gower gave me the name of a Dutch merchant in Amsterdam, one Hendrick Van Sluys, who has passed on some useful information to us in exchange for Sir Thomas preventing two of his cargo ships being impounded and their contents sold when they were compelled to put into Portsmouth in a storm. He said that I was only to use him if we were at *point non plus.* Time has gone by and we have now reached that destination!

"I propose that we put on our finest clothes and pay him a visit. He lives but a short distance from here on the Herengracht. We shall present ourselves as merchants—and then decide how to play him when we have discovered his true kidney—as the London cullies would say."

So it was that once again, splendidly accoutred, Tom and Catherine, Geordie in attendance, stood outside the door of a fine house, in Amsterdam this time, not Antwerp.

"If you begin by posing as a merchant," Catherine had said before they left the inn, "will Master Van Sluys not be surprised that you are calling at his home, not his place of business, and that you are bringing your wife with you?"

"Not at all," replied Tom, who was busy trying to

tie his lace cravat, and who was debating whether to ask Catherine to help him. "Mijnheer Van Sluys's place of business *is* his home. His cellars will be the storehouse of his merchandise.

"Sir Thomas Gower told me that he sells luxury goods of all kinds, glass and pottery being his specialisms. And his home will be full of treasures, too, because he has a portfolio of other interests, everything from cattle, land and dealings in the Stock Market. Dutch luxury is becoming notorious, and Sir Thomas told me that he is very wealthy.

"Your presence will not seem odd, for the Dutch allow their women far more freedom than we do. They are partners in their husbands' businesses and they form committees to run old peoples' homes and hospitals. The only area of life from which they are barred is that of government in any form."

"'Tis a pity that all women do not live in Holland," said Catherine pertly, "since their lot seems so much more preferable to our own. If I were to marry, my property would become my husband's to do with as he would, even though he had done nothing to earn it."

Tom gave up the unequal struggle with his cravat. "Do you tie this for me, wife," he told her, handing it to her, "and let us discuss the condition of women at a later date. I wish to call on Mijnheer Van Sluys today, not tomorrow!"

Sir Thomas Gower had been right about Van Sluys's wealth. Catherine had thought that Amos Shooter was living in extreme luxury, but it was as nothing to the splendour to which Hendrick Van Sluys was accustomed. She was also growing accustomed, after a different fashion, to Tom's extraordinary range of knowledge, far beyond that of your usual mercenary captain—which had at first surprised her.

Another surprise was that Van Sluys agreed to see them immediately when his servant took Tom's request for an audience to him. They waited in a lobby whose walls were hung with splendid maps of Dutch possessions in the Far East, as well as a bewildering variety of still lives, seascapes and landscapes.

"More cows," whispered Catherine irreverently to Tom. It had already become a shared joke with them that, after ships, nearly every Dutch and Flemish painting had a cow in it. Catherine had begun to count them, and had decided that her next play would contain a rich Dutchman who constantly boasted of his painted cows.

Presently the servant returned and, the house being long and thin because of the Dutch desire to save land, he led them through a series of the most splendidly furnished rooms with still more pictured cows in them, to a drawing room at the back that was the ultimate in splendour.

No less than twenty paintings hung on one wall, and three superb tapestries on another. Twelve leather-seated chairs were stationed around the room. A harpsichord stood in one corner. Marquetry tables with Chinese ivories on them stood about. Four armchairs faced a giant hearth, a wall of books behind them. A long sidetable held bottles, glasses and pewter dishes of sliced lemons and small round biscuits.

Through an open doorway could be seen an oak dining table large enough to seat twenty people, surrounded by twenty red velvet-covered chairs. The huge sideboard was of ebony and was loaded with Delftware and fine silver.

Mijnheer and Mevrouw Van Sluys were equally magnificent, both in their dress and their manner. He was large and majestic in sober black velvet; she was small and dainty in silver-blue satin. So magnificent were they that they quite eclipsed Tom and Catherine. This must be a mistake. Mijnheer Van Sluys would be sure to send them packing when he discovered what their true errand was. Such a grand gentleman could hardly be engaged in sordid transactions with English agents.

"Master Trenchard," said Van Sluys musingly after bidding them sit in the splendid armchairs. "A relation of Ned Trenchard, perhaps?"

"A distant cousin, no more," admitted Tom. "I am but a humble merchant."

"Ah, you would prefer to talk business! You will take a drink with me before we do so, will you not? Are you the kind of Englishman who only drinks ale? Or would you and your good lady prefer wine—as we do."

"Wine," said Tom. "We prefer the grape to the grain, do we not, wife?"

Catherine nodded, amused. Tom had certainly preferred ale last night! Perhaps that was why he was insisting on wine this morning.

"Well, very well," agreed Van Sluys, motioning to a footman to serve his guests and himself. A footman placed the lemons and biscuits reverently on one of the small tables together with plates, knives, forks, snowy-white damask napkins and four exquisitely chased wine glasses. The Dutch seemed to make a small ceremony of everything.

They began to talk business. Tom had primed Catherine beforehand and several times she smiled prettily and qualified what he had said.

"Oh, no more paintings. Dear. China sells far better. After all, we do have to eat, but looking at paintings is a diversion, nothing more, and once seen, often forgotten."

"A clever lady, your wife," commented Van Sluys approvingly. "Every good businessman should have one, eh, my dear," he ended, putting a hand on his own wife's arm.

They were committing themselves not only to the purchase of china and glass, but fine damask tablecloths and hangings.

"Later," Van Sluys said, after dishes of oysters and prawns had been brought in, together with a loaf of bread, and his footman had been sent away again, "we will go to the cellars, and you may show me what you prefer. You have no clerk with you to make an inventory?" Geordie was obviously no clerk, and was being entertained in Van Sluys's vast kitchen.

"My wife is my clerk, I need no other. And the secrets of business are best kept in the family, eh?"

"It does my heart good to meet so sensible a member of your country," said Van Sluys enthusiastically. "You Englishmen are usually not clever enough to use the talents of your women to best advantage. Why pay a clerk when you have one in your bed?"

"You have had a deal of business with Englishmen, *Mijnheer?*"

"Indeed, indeed. Very much." He winked. "I like the English—unlike those who rule us and are not wise enough to see that we need your help to keep out the French and those who would enslave us."

"Well said, sir. And did you tell Sir Thomas Gower that?"

Dead silence followed. Catherine, watching Van Sluys carefully as Tom had instructed her, saw the faintest flutter of his eyelids, the sudden stillness of his hands and the firming of his mouth when Tom mentioned Gower's name. The brute power of the man, concealed by his fine manners and his elegant home, briefly shone through the veneer of charming civilisation that he offered the world.

"You know Sir Thomas?" he asked, after slowly spearing an oyster, squeezing lemon on it, and swallowing it carefully.

"Intimately," said Tom. "Intimately." His own eyes were as hard as Van Sluys's had become and were focussed on his face. His wife said nothing, but she too, Catherine saw, shared in the tension which had suddenly gripped her husband.

"What do you want of me, Master Trenchard? Besides glass and other trumperies. You do wish to buy them—or is that a blind?"

"No blind." And if Tom was surprised by his quarry's bluntness—which he was—he gave no sign of it. "And what I want is simple enough. I need to know where to find William Grahame."

Tension visibly ebbed out of Van Sluys. "And that is all? I can easily tell you where Grahame lodges, and shall do so before you leave. But you said two things, and that is only one."

Tom smiled. He was beginning to enjoy himself. He thought that Van Sluys was more shaken by his sudden transformation from simple merchant to an

English agent than he ought to be. Time to turn the mental thumbscrews.

"I mistook," he smiled artlessly. "Three things. The second may also be simple. Do you know aught of Giles Newman?"

"Only that he is dead. I am told that he tried blackmail—and paid for it. Something you should remember, Master Trenchard. Next?"

Catherine could not but admire Van Sluys's coolness under fire. And Tom's as he directed the fire.

"What do you know of your country's dispositions that your friend and benefactor, Sir Thomas Gower, might like to know?"

Van Sluys was not in the least put out.

"Oho, so you *are* his intimate. One sees that well. I know nothing that the whole world does not know. That we intend to drive you from the seas. Except..." and he paused tantalisingly.

"Except?" Tom repeated.

"Except that William Grahame knows as much as I do, and I would prefer him to tell you what we know, rather than speak of it here. Here I am a simple merchant."

Tom looked round the splendid room, paid for by the wealth of the East Indies and Holland's gift for trade and commerce.

"Simple!" scoffed Tom derisively, Catherine echoing him internally.

"As simple as you are, Master Trenchard. No more and no less." He smiled engagingly, looking Tom up and down. "You see, Master Trenchard, a man of power can always recognise another, and I suspected what you were from the moment that you and your pretty wife entered this room. Does she know you, Master Trenchard? And do you know her? But let us leave that, and finish our business. Later we shall dine, and toast our two agreements."

"So, I ask you again, wife, for I have come to value your judgement—what did you make of Hendrick Van Sluys?" It was late afternoon and they had not long returned from dining with Van Sluys and his wife after they had inspected his vast and crammed storerooms.

Catherine pondered a moment before answering. "Why, I thought that he was a cheerful rogue—unlike either Amos Shooter or William Grahame." She stopped, wondering whether to continue, for what she might say of Amos Shooter could possibly distress Tom. After all, they had once been companions in arms.

As usual Tom missed little. Slight though her hesitation had been, he had seen it. "Go on," he told her. "You have not finished."

"No. I think that I do not trust either Van Sluys or

Amos Shooter overmuch, but of the two I would trust Amos Shooter the less."

"Why?" Tom was being provoking and knew it. He was leaning against the wall, facing her where she sat and was twirling a small parchment windmill, a child's toy that he had brought from a stall set up not far from the inn. "Is it because Van Sluys was more cheerful and has the prettier face?"

"You are pleased to mock," returned Catherine stiffly, "and I confess that I have little enough evidence on which to make such a judgement, but there is something about them both on which I cannot lay a finger but which leads me to believe that what I have said is true."

Tom bent down and handed her the windmill after setting its miniature sails spinning.

"And again," he said, his own face so near to her that she could see plainly see the red-gold hairs of his beard along the lines of his strong chin, "we are in agreement. And I cannot give you any good reasons for my judgement that Amos is less trustworthy, either. It is a feeling, no more, but to such feelings I have often owed my life when others around me have lost theirs. I think, sweeting, that your instincts are sound."

He finished his sentence with a light kiss on the corner of her mouth before propping up the wall again.

Catherine had already noticed that he called her

wife when he was teasing or provoking her, and sweeting when he was praising or trying to seduce her.

"Geordie tells me," he continued, "that they keep a good kitchen for their servants—unlike some whose riches are reserved for the drawing room. He has also discovered that Van Sluys is a burgomaster and is therefore a Regent, a member of one of the ruling families in Amsterdam. Which makes his dabblings in treason more interesting."

He paused, waiting for Catherine to comment. She held up the little windmill and set it spinning again, before obliging him.

"I suppose that he is playing both ends against the middle. That is, he believes that the French are more of a danger to Holland than we are, so he seeks to ensure that any victory the Dutch might achieve over us will not be so great that it might make us a weak ally in the future. Also, by telling Grahame to pass information to us, he is not personally committing treason by telling us himself."

"Oh, bravo," exclaimed Tom. "And tomorrow you shall visit Grahame and find out what Van Sluys thinks is important enough to hand over to Sir Thomas Gower."

"I!" exclaimed Catherine, startled into losing her usual composure. "On my own, without you?"

"Oh, you may take Geordie with you, and if aught went wrong he would protect you. Do not be deceived by his complaining and miserable exterior. Geordie's skill with a small sword is remarkable. Besides, he has taken a liking to you, believes that I am overharsh with you, and from thinking that I ought to seduce you on the spot, now thinks that I ought not to seduce you at all! Quite a chaperon is our Geordie."

"Which does not explain why you wish me to go alone. Why so?"

"Because William Grahame will be less wary with you than with me. Charm him. Allow him to think you foolish and that you might not even remember correctly what he tells you. More than that, I think that he might believe you over the matter of his pardon, rather than me."

Catherine played with the little windmill again, her face troubled.

"Believe me, sweeting, I would not ask you to do this thing if it were not that I think that you will manage him better than I could. Remember what Van Sluys said about the Dutch trusting and using their women, particularly their wives."

He came over to her and took the windmill from her to lay it gently on the big bed before he knelt beside her. "I trust you, sweeting, and I vow that I would not send you into danger."

Tom cursed himself inwardly, even as he spoke, remembering poor dead Giles Newman. They were playing a dangerous game, but he, Gower and Arlington had coldbloodedly decided to use Catherine against Grahame because it was known that he could easily be influenced by the charms of a pretty woman.

But he had not met her then, and as he took her hand to kiss it, he was blessed—or was it cursed?—by a sensation he had never thought to experience. He suddenly knew that, of all inconvenient things, he had fallen in love with her. He swore to himself that he would follow her and Geordie, and watch Grahame's lair as carefully as he could so that she might not come to any harm.

All that he wanted to do was to protect her, to keep her from danger, to lap her in silk, to lie her in his bed, and…and… But he had sworn an oath to Gower and Arlington and he had to keep to it, as she did, for there was the matter of her brother whom they had used to blackmail her into going on this venture. A matter of which he was beginning to feel ashamed.

He had fallen so strangely silent that Catherine looked into his hard, suffering face and said gently, "What is is, Tom?"

"Nothing," he said roughly, and crushed her to him, not to try to make love to her, but to hold her safe. "Nothing, and believe this, I shall not allow any harm to come to you, this I swear."

Oh, if only he could go back in time, to London, to

that night at the Duke of York's Theatre, he would—knowing and loving her as he now did—have gone back to Gower and told him that she was not suitable, that they would have to find another wench.

For this wench had become too dear to him for him to want to risk her. And when and how that had come to pass he did not know.

Chapter Eleven

"So, wife, you know what you have to say and do. Geordie shall be your footman and I shall follow you at a suitable distance and keep watch outside Grahame's lodgings. Between us we shall do our utmost to protect you."

Remembering Giles Newman's sad fate, Catherine nodded her thanks. Well but not ostentatiously dressed, Geordie behind her, she set off towards the far side of the Buttermarket where the New Church, Amsterdam's pride, stood. It was mid-morning and the huge square was full of people. A boy rolling a hoop dashed by her, and she also had to dodge an advancing coach, a great clumsy thing carrying one of the Regents and his fat wife.

On one side of the square an impromptu stage had been erected and a group of players were performing on it, watched by a crowd of well-dressed burghers. Catherine regretted not having the time to stop and watch them, but she needed to press on. She dodged a sledge on rollers, piled high with parcels, being vigorously pushed along by a stout young man—only to be nearly knocked over by yet another boy vigorously chasing a hoop.

Looking wistfully back towards the stage, she was surprised to see Amos Shooter standing before it. He was not watching the players but was talking earnestly to a large man in country clothing.

What was he doing here? He had said nothing to her or Tom about a visit to Amsterdam. She must be mistaken. After all, she was only seeing him at a distance, and when she looked again to try to make sure whether the man *was* Amos or not, he, and the fellow with him, had disappeared.

This odd sighting of a man she thought to be many miles away disturbed Catherine, but she said nothing to Geordie, and walked silently on through the rich and bustling scene, richer indeed than any she had ever seen before.

It was only when she was out of the square and making her way down a back street by a minor canal that the almost universal prosperity of central Amsterdam disappeared. She was suddenly confronted by beggars in rags, some apologetic, some bullying, but all were pushed away from her, cursing, by Geordie's staff.

The house in a side alley where Grahame

lodged was similar in design to Van Sluys's superb home, but on a smaller, dingier scale. The landlady who answered the door took them up to his room by a flight of steep stairs smelling of recently cooked food.

William Grahame betrayed no surprise on seeing her. He welcomed her in with a smile and offered them both a seat. Geordie refused in his usual put-upon whine, and took up a standing position, with his back to the door of Grahame's small living room.

"Mistress Trenchard, I vow that I did not expect to see you here in Amsterdam, but now that I do you are a sight to please any man's eyes." He looked around. "Your husband is not with you?"

"No, alas, he has a megrim today so I have come with our servant Geordie. He particularly asked me to give you his good wishes and to tell you that we have had a letter from London regarding your proposed offer."

Catherine coughed prettily behind her hand and added, "We called on you in Antwerp and found that you had already left for Amsterdam. Despite suffering from an attack of ague, my husband insisted on leaving Antwerp at once in order to tell you the good news—and he has sent me here on my own so as to waste as little time as possible."

She offered him Belinda Bellamour's best blushing smile and William Grahame blossomed before it, forgetting as he did so, to ask how she and Tom had known where to find him.

"Exceedingly kind of you, Mistress Trenchard—and of your husband, of course."

"Of course, sir," and Catherine blushed again. "You would wish to know what the despatch from London said?"

"Indeed—at your leisure, mistress. The walk from the Herengracht is not a short one." He was aware at once that by saying this last he might have given something away—for someone must have told him that they were lodging just off it since Catherine herself had not said where she and Tom were staying. Such an admission meant that either they were being watched, or someone to whom they had spoken had passed on the news to him.

Looking at Catherine, Grahame decided that she was too innocent a newcomer to the dangerous game she was playing to pick up such a slight reference. She appeared so young and charming that he underestimated her age, believing her to be barely twenty when she was almost twenty-five.

Grahame was wrong to believe that Catherine was as naïve as she seemed. Well used to all the nuances of speech both by being an actress and also by writing plays where such ploys were often used, Catherine had grasped immediately the inner meaning of what Grahame had said. She betrayed no sign of this when she answered him.

"Quite so, sir, but I am used to walking long distance in London and made nothing of this. I still have my breath. My husband told me to inform you that our masters have agreed to give you an unconditional pardon, but dare not send either the pardon or an open letter to you saying so. Such a move would be unwise, and the letter we received was, of course, in code.

"But we have the power to assure you that London will play fair with you—if you will play fair by us by giving us the information about the Dutch fleet's intentions of which you spoke in Antwerp."

"To you, mistress, or to your husband?" He looked across at Geordie. "And will your servant be present when such high and mighty secrets are passed to you?"

Catherine turned to say to Geordie, "Oh, I'm sure that my faithful footman will consent to leave the room—so long as he is in such earshot that while he may not hear exactly what we say, he will be aware that nothing untoward is taking place between us."

She almost felt Geordie bridle at the mere idea of leaving her alone with Grahame, but she was sure that it was a necessary ploy. She shook her head prettily at him. "Oh, Geordie, I am sure that I am perfectly safe with Master Grahame. Especially if you are near."

"I shall go no further than the other side of this open door," he growled, indicating the one behind him.

"If Master Grahame agrees to that, as I am sure he will, then you will agree, I trust, that you are still able to protect me from there—although from what danger, I cannot imagine."

Belinda Bellamour's smile was for both of them. And both men fell before it—although it would be more true to say that Geordie had already fallen, and that Grahame was about to do so. But their intentions towards her were quite different.

The moment that the door was left ajar with Geordie behind it, William Grahame rose from his chair on the other side of the room to come to sit near her. "For we must not be overheard by anyone," he murmured urgently.

"No, indeed, Master Grahame." Seeing that he proposed to move even nearer to her, she told him hurriedly, but keeping her voice honey-sweet, "I can hear you quite well if you remain where you are. I would not have my servant think wrong things about us whilst we are alone. I am sure you understand, sir, that a young wife must guard her reputation at all times—as you guard your secrets!"

He nodded, and then said, his voice very low, "I am still a little troubled that London might not play fair with me."

"Never say, sir, that you doubt my word."

Catherine primmed her mouth and put on an expression of great and earnest concern. "I lay my hand upon my heart, and assure you that Sir Thomas Gower himself, even before we left London, swore to me that your services to the State he serves were so great that your reward would be equally great. In the face of this, and the letter I carry with me, would you call me false or a liar?"

William Grahame would have done well to do both since not a word that Catherine had just uttered was true. The ring of righteous indignation in her voice owed everything to her career on the stage of the Duke's Theatre and nothing to honesty. Only the knowledge of the number of Dutch and Englishmen whom the man before her had callously sent to their deaths was making her so double-faced. She owed him nothing—especially since Tom had told her that he believed that Grahame might also have killed Giles Newman.

Moved, Grahame put out a hand to take hers. He knew very well that what Gower had told Catherine before she began her mission might have been a blind, designed to influence her, as well as him. But her patent sincerity affected him.

"Of course I believe you, my dear," he told her, still holding her hand in his, and looking into her beautiful violet eyes. "And to prove what I say, I will tell you what I have learned of the Dutch Navy's intentions.

"They plan a frontal attack on your naval base at Sheerness. They intend to sail up the Medway and destroy it, and Chatham, and the ships at anchor there, leaving England crippled and unable to fight at sea. This would be an almost mortal blow, coming on top of the financial damage caused by the plague and the Great Fire of London last year."

Catherine withdrew her hand sharply and stared at him. "Are you sure of this? That is as bold a stroke as I have ever heard of. Can I believe you?"

Nothing that Tom, Gower or Arlington had told her when they had briefed her before they left London had suggested that the Dutch would attempt anything quite so daring.

"Believe me, Mistress Trenchard, that is their battle plan. And I have more information about what the Dutch wish to gain in the peace talks at Breda. Information that would help England to negotiate a better bargain than they might have hoped for—seeing that this war has not gone their way since their victories in the plague year."

All this was even better than she and Tom had hoped. Now, if only Grahame would give her the information about the Dutch War aims that he believed to be so valuable, they might notify London of it at once—and then set out for home themselves, their mission safely over. Rob would be freed and she could take up her life again.

And say farewell to Tom Trenchard, a little voice said. Do I really want that? She tried to ignore the voice, to concentrate instead on persuading Grahame to give her this last vital piece of information.

"If what you have to say of Breda is so important, sir, then why not tell me of it now?"

"What! And give away both my bargaining counters? Nay, mistress. Send the first to London, and then you must bring me a letter containing my pardon. And come alone, if you please, without that tall oaf, your husband, who is not worthy of you, as I hope to prove when you visit me. And leave your servant behind, too.

"And after that, why, after that, I will give you what you wish—having gained from you what *I* wish." He placed his hand suggestively on her knee, pressed it, and winked at her.

Every hair on Catherine's body rose. *She* had only one wish. To push his desecrating hand from her knee and tell him to keep his damned information if the price of it was her virtue.

But the memory of Rob's predicament held her still and steady. She and Tom had promised to deliver Grahame, and Grahame's information, to Gower and his cohorts in London and she would try to keep her promise.

So she smiled Belinda's seductive smile at Grahame again. Only her talent for acting made it possible for her to pretend that what he was demanding from her as the price of his information was one that she was willing to pay.

"I hear you," she told him through stiff lips, "and when I have the further letter that you require I will bring it to you."

"Oh," he said softly, "I am sure you will. We understand each other, you and I." In proof of this mistaken belief, he placed his large hand on her breast and squeezed it. "An earnest of what is to come," he told her.

Catherine stood up, and removed his offensive hand. "Not now, dear William, not now. My servant is but a step away and will doubtless be thinking that you are giving me the entire plans of the Dutch government regarding not only the navy, but also their intentions towards the Spice Islands and their regaining of New Amsterdam! I am sure that we do not want him to report to my husband that our rapprochement is more than a business one."

"What a clever doxy you are," was Grahame's only, and admiring, reply.

Catherine made him no further answer but called to Geordie, "You can come in now. Our business here is over, and so we may go home and tell your poor ailing master of our success. The news should have him out of his bed and well again!"

* * *

"He suggested what?" Tom's voice rose to a drill sergeant's roar. "And Geordie not even in the room with you!" From venting his fury on Catherine, he now turned it on his servant. "Damn you, Geordie, didn't I tell you to stay with her at all times. Do you never do as you are bid?"

Geordie stuck out his lower lip and glared back at Tom. Catherine rode to his rescue. "And damn you, Tom Trenchard, for railing at poor Geordie when he was only doing *my* bidding."

They had returned to the inn to report on their meeting with William Grahame. Tom, after first congratulating Catherine for persuading Grahame to pass on the plans of the Dutch Navy, was now half-mad with rage on learning that the price of further information was that Catherine should agree to be Grahame's mistress!

Her intervention on Geordie's behalf did her no good at all; it merely served to fuel his anger the more.

"Your bidding, mistress, was it? *You* sent him out of the room in order to sell your body to Grahame." When Catherine tried to reply, to explain, he crossed the room to grasp her by the elbows and stare into her face. His own was suffused with blood. Catherine suddenly knew what he looked like in battle, and an awesome sight it was.

"No," he cried, shaking her, "I'll not have it. I'll not be cuckolded."

Silence followed this remarkable statement.

Geordie gave a cackle and Catherine said numbly, "Hardly that, surely. I am not your wife. What's more, I know quite well that your plan, aye and that of Sir Thomas Gower, was that I should play the whore with Grahame if that were necessary to gain the information he holds. So why are you complaining now? Why reproach me when I am merely following orders—to save Rob."

Tom stared down at her, to see that for all her brave words to him, fear of him was written on her face. The moment she had told him of her final conversation with Grahame, he had suddenly run mad with rage and jealousy. And the devil of it was that everything she had just said was true. She was not his wife, they *were* using her as bait, and he had no right, no right at all, to speak to her and Geordie as he had done.

But the thought of her in Grahame's arms, doing with him what she would not do with Tom Trenchard, had unmanned him quite. He suddenly knew why Othello in old Will Shakespeare's play had murdered his wife. The saying from The Song of Solomon, that jealousy is as cruel as the grave, took him by the throat to remind him what horrors he might be tempted to commit if he allowed his passions to run away with him.

As gently as he could he let go of her and stood back. Not only Catherine let out a sigh of relief, but Geordie also. Tom would never know that his servant had been ready to attack him if he attacked Catherine.

"Forgive me," he said humbly, which had Geordie staring at him. Tom Trenchard humble! Here was a turn up! "I should not have spoken as I did, but you cannot..."

Catherine did not allow him to finish. "Of course not. Even to save Rob." She shuddered. "How can I say that? I do not know what I might, or might not, do to save someone I loved."

"Nor do any of us." Tom's voice was as shaky as hers. "Let me recover my good sense. We can then discuss quietly what we *are* to do. Did Grahame give you any hint of what he might have to tell us? Or of whom he is dealing with in Amsterdam?"

Catherine shook her head, happier now that Tom was his usual controlled self again. For the last few minutes she had watched him, fascinated, as he had rivalled Betterton himself in giving vent to his rage. Betterton's stage rants were famous.

"There was one odd thing, though. I thought that I saw Amos Shooter when I was crossing the Buttermarket, before the play actors' stage. I could not be sure that it was he."

Tom looked at Geordie. "Did you see aught of Shooter?"

"Nay, master. I was too busy guarding the mistress—as you had bid me," he finished soulfully.

Tom ignored this piece of impudence. "I came through the Buttermarket in your wake, but I saw nothing of him. Which does not mean that he might not have been there. You have sharp eyes, sweeting."

There! She was forgiven. She was sweeting again, neither wife nor you.

To mollify him she said quietly, "As for Grahame, I was too busy holding him off at the end—whilst seeming to lead him on—to try to coax further information out of him. Nor, I think, did he wish to give it."

Tom thought for a moment before saying, "You did well, very well. What we must do next is encipher this information and send it to London tomorrow by the morning's post. For the rest, we must avoid suspicion by going about our business and loudly lamenting that old Noll Cromwell's successors are not ruling England."

"And if the letter comes back with no more concessions for Grahame, what then?" Catherine's voice was anxious and Tom put a consoling arm around her shoulders.

"Why then, we shall devise a plan. Do not fear, sweeting, whatever they would have you do, those who sit on their backsides in London, and leave the dirty work to us, you shall not sell yourself to Grahame, my word on't."

How warm it was, how safe to be held thus, to see Geordie grinning approvingly at them, so that the danger that they were running disappeared for a moment from her consciousness. She was alive as she had never been before.

Catherine remembered something that Betterton had once said to her about his experiences in the Great Plague: "One is never so truly alive as when one faces death at any moment." She had never thought that there might come a day when she would be in a position to test the truth of this observation!

Chapter Twelve

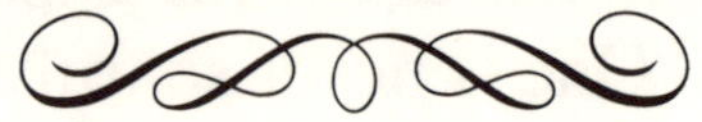

"Now what do you make of this?"

Sir Thomas Gower tossed across the table to m'lord Arlington a decoded copy of the letter containing the news of the plan to raid Sheerness. He was seated at the head of a long table in the Navy Office. Sam Pepys was there to take the minutes. He was flanked by Buckingham and Lord Clifford. George Villiers, Duke of Buckingham, was in one of his flighty moods and yawned ostentatiously as Arlington silently read the document through twice.

"I must apologise for springing this matter upon you without warning," Gower said, "but it reached me only last night and the matter is urgent."

"Truly so," agreed Arlington, handing the letter to Buckingham to read, "if we can give any credence to what is written here."

Buckingham tossed it across the table to Sam Pepys. "Read us what it says," he commanded. "I've a woundy sore head and have no mind to decipher some clerk's cramped script!" Although in many ways the cleverest of the men around the table, he was capricious to a degree.

Pepys did as he was bid and read out Catherine and Tom's letter, informing them that Grahame had handed over details of the Dutch plan to raid Sheerness and sail up the Medway.

Dead silence followed before Clifford spoke.

"We are expected to believe this?"

His tone was so sceptical that Sam Pepys looked up in surprise. He alone of the men there thought that the letter told the truth. But he was only their secretary and consequently held his tongue.

Clifford picked up the letter and waved it about. "Was your fellow in Holland drunk that he concocted such a cobweb of moon madness? He doubtless seeks to earn his money by sending you a tale that would sound well on the boards of the theatre rather than in the halls where statesmen need to make decisions."

Arlington nodded. "I trust our man in Holland," he said slowly, not telling them that "our man" was an intimate of them all. He would say and do nothing to put Stair Cameron in danger, and he knew only too well that Buckingham had a reputation for being indiscreet. "But I agree with you that this plan is fanciful, to say the least."

"A pity that the Duke cannot be with us," said Sam Pepys as tactfully as he could. He was referring to the Duke of York, the King's brother, who was an efficient naval commander. "His opinion would have been invaluable."

"As it is," said Clifford, ignoring Pepys's contribution, "I submit that no action need be taken and that we allow this letter to lie on the table. Even the Dutch are not so harebrained as to dare all on such a risky venture."

Several heads nodded. Of all the great men present, only Sir Thomas Gower frowned. Like Arlington, he trusted Stair Cameron and he thought that what he had written to them had been sent in good faith, but like the others he also thought that it was most likely a trick by Grahame to gain the pardon he wanted.

"And for the rest? The second matter promised?" he asked.

"I propose that we send Grahame renewed assurances of a pardon in exchange for further information, although judging by this it may be worthless," suggested Clifford. "We can determine what to do about that when we have examined it."

And so it was agreed.

Afterwards Arlington, frowning, said to Sir Thomas, "It would not be like Stair Cameron to send us nonsense, but I am also of the opinion that this information is worthless.

"Nevertheless, we will do as Clifford suggested and give Grahame another chance to pass on something useful. Which means that Stair and the woman are not to be sent word to return home until after they have forwarded to us Grahame's second offering."

Sir Thomas agreed. They walked out of the room, leaving the letter on the table, where later, at Sam Pepys's bidding, a minor clerk filed it away, to be lost in the State Archives for the next three hundred years.

So far Tom and Catherine had dared all for nothing.

Unaware that London had dismissed their hard-earned information as worthless, Master Tom Trenchard and his wife were discussing more urgent matters.

After the first few nights, both of them had become accustomed to sleeping with the bolster between them. That was not to say that Catherine was not uncomfortably aware of Tom's large presence so close to her. Worse, he frequently walked through her dreams, jolting her awake whenever, in the dream, he approached too near her—which was often.

She wondered how well Tom was coping with sleeping so near to her. Matters were helped—if that were the right word—by his not coming to bed until some time after she had retired.

He and Geordie usually ended the evening in the

taproom. Tom played a wicked game of chess and was constantly being challenged by the other patrons of the inn. She was often asleep when he finally climbed into bed, and he and Geordie were considerate enough to make as little noise as possible so as not to disturb her.

In the morning, Catherine usually awoke to find him gone. He washed himself at the pump in the yard behind the inn: she had been warned never to go there before breakfast since he was only one of many men making themselves ready for the day, parading around half-naked—or so Geordie had told her.

She was not to know that Tom's sleep was as disturbed as hers was. If he woke during the night to hear her steady breathing, he had to use all his self-control not to push the bolster aside and treat her as lustily as a healthy man should treat a desirable woman.

What kept Tom from falling on her was his growing respect for her as the days flew by, and the unfortunate fact that not only was he in love with her, but that he also loved her. He did not want any harm to come to her, and he was daily more and more amazed at the turmoil of mixed feelings that she roused in him.

Perhaps it was that that made him clumsy when he walked upstairs on the night of the day on which Grahame had sent word to Catherine that he was ready to pass on his latest, and most important, piece of news.

Tom had just played a hard and lengthy game of chess that he had won—a great relief to Geordie, who had staked his week's pay on him—and was more tired than usual. For once he lit a candle, but still managed to stumble as he climbed up the high steps into bed. He fell forward heavily on to the curst bolster.

Forgetting Catherine's presence and decorum generally, he roared in exasperation, "Oh, hell and all the devils preserve me from bolsters!" With that, he hurled the bolster to the floor.

The noise of his anger woke Catherine. Startled, wrenched from a dream of Tom and herself walking happily by the Amstel River, she sat up, alarmed.

"What's that?" she asked, having no idea what Tom had actually said, only that he had said something. "Is anything wrong?"

"Very wrong. It's this damned bolster. I've ridden us of it," Tom announced proudly. "We shall be more comfortable without it."

"What!" Catherine leapt out of bed and ran round to his side of it, to pick up the bolster and hold it to her as though it were a shield. "No such thing! We agreed."

"Well, I'm tired of the agreement. I disown it. The Dutch aren't the only people who can play skittles with agreements. Down with all bolsters and up with comfort in bed, I say!"

"And I say I shan't get into bed again until you agree that the bolster shall lie between us."

Tom lay back lazily on his high pillows. Standing there in the half dark, the candlelight illuminating her, Catherine looked more beautiful than ever. Her black hair was down, her violet eyes were flashing, and the white linen of her nightrail with its deep lace-edged collar gave her the appearance of an angel in an old painting. Only the halo was missing.

"Lovely though you look, my sweeting," he told her cheerfully, "I shall not agree to your terms. By all means keep the bolster—and spend the night on the floor."

Catherine looked at him, and her treacherous heart fluttered in her breast. In Van Sluys's superb home, she had seen an old Italian painting of the god Apollo lying on a cloud, his arm around a nymph no more remarkable in her perfection than he was in his.

Tom Trenchard, unshaven, muscular, his body golden in the candlight, his red-gold hair about his shoulders, might have been the model the artist had chosen for his image of masculine beauty. Never mind that his face was neither as soft, nor as pretty, as the god's, his body was a perfect match.

Anguished, her own body trying to deny its primitive instincts that would have had her jumping into bed to lie as close to him as she could, Catherine said stiffly, "You are no gentleman, sir, to suggest any such thing."

"I have never claimed to be one," returned Tom

naughtily, "so that makes no matter. Your choice, sweeting, your choice. The bed without the bolster, or the floor with it. Your choice, always your choice. I know what mine would be."

Catherine's temper was up. She stamped on the floor. "You are a bully, Thomas Trenchard, a bully, a very Mohawk. Have you no shame, to leave me on the floor whilst you lie on the bed?"

"*I* am not leaving you on the floor." Tom was sweetly reasonable, a grin on his face. "*You* are choosing the floor. I refuse to take the blame for your decisions."

Catherine wanted to fling the bolster at him, to wipe the grin from his face. "It is no choice at all, and well you know it. It is there to protect me."

"You'll be even better protected on the floor, for I shall not be there," Tom pointed out. "Which should be some comfort to you—if not much."

Before Catherine could reply—she was being rendered speechless by his impudence—the door to Geordie's ante-room opened and he put a weary face around it. "Cut the cackle, will you? Some of us want to get a bit of sleep, even if you two don't. Give me the bloody bolster if that's what's causing all the noise, my pillow ain't comfortable."

This was really the last straw! Angered beyond reason, Catherine spun round and flung the bolster at Geordie. Catching it and clutching it to his breast, he whined cheerfully at her, "Thankee, mistress. And a good night to the pair of ye now that's settled." He closed the door gently behind him.

What had she done? Now if she lay on the floor she had not even the bolster to ease her tired body. Stricken, Catherine made the mistake of looking at Tom. He was, as she might have expected, laughing at her.

"You! You!" she raged, walking to the bed, her hand raised. It was, though she did not yet know it, another mistake.

Tom began to sit up as she approached. "Me what? Catherine, my sweeting? I didn't throw the bolster at Geordie. *You* did."

She must hit him, she must. Frustration, anger, lust, nay, the desire to love him and be loved by him, all fuelled by the nights that they had spent with the denying bolster between them, had Catherine bending over him, threatening she knew not what.

Tom did not threaten, he acted. A wicked look upon his face, he leaned forward, quick as a snake striking, or a leopard pouncing on its prey, and scooped her up bodily so that she landed in the bed beside him.

But not for long. For now he turned her on to her back so that he might look down at her, as she panted with rage beneath him. Until he laid his mouth on hers and, quick as a flash, rage vanished and she melted beneath him…

Oh, the wasted days and nights when they had been apart! Tom had her nightrail off in a flash and she was pulling at his. Afterwards, Catherine was to think how strange it was, and yet how right, that she knew exactly what to do when they began to make love, as though she had been loving him all her life. His hands roved her body and hers roved his. Her hand stroked the golden down on his breast and his stroked her breasts, so small and yet so perfect.

Tom had always before admired buxom, large-breasted wenches, so how was it that Catherine's delicate perfection of form and feature so entranced him that even in passion's thrall he held back to treat her as gently and carefully as he could?

Tenderly he stroked her face and the long elegant lines of her body, which were even more lovely than he had imagined them to be when he had watched her move, fully clothed, about their room.

Catherine moaned and sighed beneath him. His lightest touch set her on fire where roughness would have repelled her. His very worship of her, the gentle brushing of his lips on her mouth, the cleft in her chin, the hollow of her throat, her breasts, the slight mound of her stomach, as he wandered lower and lower, had her writhing beneath him, crying for fulfilment.

Nor was this one-way traffic, for Tom, too, was roused beyond belief by the ease with which he brought her to fulfilment. The few weeks they had spent together, so close and yet so far away—the bolster being a symbol of everything that had kept them apart—only served to add to the fever in the blood now that the symbol had gone. Tom's hurling the bolster out of the bed, followed by Catherine throwing it at Geordie, had freed them both.

And then, as they came closer and closer and Catherine's legs, of their own accord, clasped him, the fever they shared grew and mounted. Until at the last, when she fully opened herself to him, Tom achieved what he had always wanted since he had first seen her as Belinda Bellamour, dancing on the London stage. He became Catherine's lover in every sense of the word.

Only to discover that he held in his arms that rare thing in the London of King Charles II, a beautiful young virgin, who gasped and cried as he entered her. But it was too late for remorse, for even as his brain told him that he must stop, his body achieved the most powerful fulfilment he had ever known. Tender consideration had brought him a pleasure that lusty carelessness had never conferred.

His love was shuddering and crying in his arms. And whether her cries were of pain or pleasure, Catherine hardly knew. But when he tried to draw away from her, to ease her pain, she only wound her arms around him the more tightly.

"No! no!" she panted. "Stay with me. Ah, God, I never thought such pleasure existed."

"But, sweeting—" and now the word was a very caress, not a mockery, and accompanied by the gentlest kiss "—I have hurt you. Oh, I should have known, but how could I?"

How could he, indeed? Innocence was such a rare commodity that men, aye, and some women, too, mocked at the mere idea that it could exist. But it did, and beneath him lay the living proof. And he had violated it.

"You should have told me," he said gravely, lifting his weight from her, but leaving them still united.

Mischief rode on the face that looked up at him. "Would you have believed me had I done so?"

His half-laugh in reply was rueful. "Aye, you have me there, sweetheart. I constantly jeered at your virtue, believing that, like most women, you had none. And now I have robbed you of it."

Catherine shook her head. "No, I cannot have that. I was your most willing partner. You could not have seduced me on your own. It takes two to make love—and you never needed to force me. Strange it was that from the moment I flung the bolster at Geordie I was lost."

Her words, and her loving face as she said them, had the strongest effect on Tom. He grew inside her, which would never do. To love her again, so soon after robbing her of her maidenhead, would be truly to hurt her. He must play the man and let her go, not play the selfish cur and think only of his pleasure.

Even as Tom decided this, he suffered the strongest pain of all. For was she not bound on the morrow to visit Grahame? Grahame, who thought that she was not virtuous and was his for the taking. The anguish he had suffered when she had told him of Grahame's proposed bargain had him by the throat again, and now it was doubly hateful to think of her lying with him.

He could not allow it, he could not—and he would not. When he had agreed that she should be recruited as the bait that might be necessary to achieve their mission, he had believed that she was any man's for the taking—or the paying.

And now he knew better.

He released her, so that they might lie side by side. He held her so that she rested on his shoulder, and he kissed the top of her head in lieu of kissing anything else. Even that small token of his love had his body protesting that it wanted more. He rebuked it.

After a moment he said, very slowly, "Catherine, I do not think that I can allow you to visit Grahame tomorrow."

So soon after their loving Catherine did not want to contradict him, but she must. They had their mission to fulfil and Rob's life might depend upon it. "Surely I must go," she said, "not to do so would be to break the promise I made back in London."

Passion ringing in his voice, Tom shook his head. "No, I forbid it. For he will not give you the information he has promised us unless you lie with him. That I am sure of. I know his kidney. And that you must not do. For your own sweet sake, you cannot become his mistress."

He did not say, And for my sake, too, for I cannot bear to think of another man touching you. You are mine, and you are precious to me. I have never felt this way about a woman before. I have taken my pleasure where I found it, and never heeded the morrow. When this mission is over, and pray God it may be so soon, I shall take you back to London with me.

Even now Tom could not quite bring himself to think of marrying Catherine. The habit of years still held him in its bonds, and although day by day these bonds were weakening, they had not yet broken.

He could not move her. Duty was more than a word to Catherine, as honour was. It was something by which she had always lived. Her father had believed in both and had lost all because of it. "No, not all," he had said once. "For I have never compromised my honour, nor broken my word, and that is more precious to me than land and money."

Holding her tightly to him, petting her rather than

making love to her, for he was fearful of hurting her any more, Tom at last gave way.

She finally said the one thing that could make him agree that she should meet Grahame. "I shall not lie with him, Tom. This I promise you."

"But if he refuses to pass on his information without that?"

"Then I must accept that I shall have failed—but, at least, I shall have tried. Besides, we have already sent the most vital news of all to London. They should be ready for the Dutch when they come. They cannot ask for much more than that."

Tom nodded thoughtfully. "We can always tell them that Grahame was tricking us and had little more to give."

"Oh, Tom, that would be a lie," said Catherine gravely.

"But a lie in a good cause. Sleep now, sweeting. We must be ready for the morrow."

Sleep they did, in one another's arms, leaving the candle to gutter low, giving light to Geordie when, after silence had fallen in the next room, curious, he entered to see them lying there, entwined.

"And about bloody time too," he muttered as the candle expired and he returned to his own lonely bed.

Catherine insisted on following Grahame's instructions to the letter. She had awoken the next morning, a trifle sore, but happy beyond belief. She had no regrets over her lovemaking with Tom, and was resigned to the fact that he might have no intention of marrying her. That would be to believe in fairy stories and Catherine was, above all things, a realist.

She would never marry now if she could not have Tom, and what roving soldier and adventurer would wish to be hampered by an actress wife? True love would mean that she must grant him his freedom, however much it might cost her. And she had had her perfect night with her lover, which was more than many women ever had.

As for the possibility of a child, we would not worry about that until her courses were due and did not arrive—and not much after that. It was commonplace for actresses to bear bastard children, and she would be commonplace. Nor need she fear that she might not be able to support a child. She could always write some more plays, and perhaps even the story of the fairy Morgana in King Arthur's time, an idea of which she had already spoken to a London bookseller.

Armoured in love—however brief the time of loving might be—Catherine walked across Amsterdam again, Geordie behind her, Tom trailing them in the distance. Geordie was to wait for her outside Graham's lodgings, and Tom would keep watch on Geordie. It was all rather like a child's game, she thought. But then, her life since Rob had been arrested seemed to have turned into a rather nasty child's game.

But at least the game had brought her Tom. She would live for the day, and count each happy moment and paste it into her book of memories, which she kept in her head, not on paper.

The landlady gazed at her sourly when she answered the knock on her door.

"What, another visitor for him?" and she jerked her thumb towards the stairs. "I'm not taking you up, and that's flat. You're the third he's had this morning. First there was a shabby little dwarf, next a showy gentleman in fine clothing—we don't see many of those round here—and now you. His door's always open—and don't trouble me when you leave. I've more to do than wait on him," and she flounced off, leaving Catherine to mount the stairs alone.

She knocked on Grahame's door twice before she realised that he was either out, or was not going to answer. But the church clock had sounded the hour of twelve as she had crossed the Buttermarket and Grahame had insisted that she come as soon after mid-day as she could manage.

Catherine was tempted to return to the inn, and tell Tom that Grahame had not been at home after all, despite his message. That being so, they could forget the whole sorry business and go home.

Something stopped her. The landlady had said his door was open. If it were not, then he had gone out. If it were, she would go in after knocking again. Perhaps he had not heard her, was dozing on his bed.

Further pounding on his door produced no answer. Catherine turned the iron ring on it that served as a handle—and it opened.

She walked in, gently calling Grahame's name as she did so. The room was empty. It was also in a dreadful mess. Books had been swept from their shelves; crockery from a dresser lay in shards on the floor. Every drawer had been wrenched from a tallboy and their contents strewn about the floor. A cupboard door hung open, and papers from it had been thrown over the smashed crockery and glass from the dresser.

Afterwards, Catherine was to wish that she had left at once, but curiosity and shock held her stock still. She looked around her, was about to bend to pick up a paper from the floor when the half-open door to Grahame's bedroom swung fully open and he came through it.

It would be more accurate to say that he staggered through it. His face was grey and a thin trickle of blood was running from his mouth. He had something clutched in his right hand. For a moment he steadied himself to stare at her before he fell forward on to the floor at her feet, still clutching the paper.

Catherine put both hands to her mouth to stifle a scream. Given what she and Tom were engaged in, she must not be found here with a dying man. She was sure that Grahame was dying, especially when she saw the dagger sticking out of his back. The blood from the wound it had caused had covered the whole back of his body and was still running slowly down to soak his breeches and his stockings.

She had never liked him, but sheer pity had her kneeling beside him on the floor in order to help him. She baulked at pulling the dagger from his back. But before she could as much as touch him, which she afterwards thought was just as well, because had she done so she would have been covered in his blood, he turned his head as it lay on the floor and croaked at her, "Mistress, you came." She could scarcely understand what he said.

Catherine nodded, said numbly and pointlessly, "Yes. I promised."

His head still turned towards her, agony on his face, he writhed, trying to raise his body, the effort causing him to gasp in agony.

"No, no," Catherine exclaimed fiercely. "Try to lie still."

He shook his ghastly head at her and finally succeeded in wriggling his right arm and the hand that held the paper towards her, saying something unintelligible. Catherine thought that it might be "For you."

Light dawned. He *was* trying to give her the paper. In her shock and distress she had not been thinking clearly.

She bent to take it from him, murmuring, "Lie still and I will fetch a doctor for you."

This time his words were clear, "No, no, too late. Go!"

Before she could contradict him, beg him to hold on until help came—even though reason told Catherine that he was right—Grahame's head fell sideways. A torrent of blood gushed from his mouth, and he lay still.

Death had claimed him.

Catherine never knew how long she knelt there. It seemed hours at the time, but Geordie and Tom later told her that very little time at all had passed between the moment that she entered the house, and the moment that she left it. She wanted to hold him, to close his staring eyes, to move him away from the broken crockery and the soiled papers amongst which he lay.

Self-preservation said no. There must be no blood on her if she should chance to meet his sullen landlady on her way out. He was dead. He might even have earned his death, but no man should die like that, and to leave him warred against all her better instincts. But there were Tom and Geordie to think of, as well as herself, and the paper to take away, which he had been so determined to give her.

She rose to her feet, and tried to control her shaking hands as she stowed the paper in the bag she was carrying. Grahame had seemed to think that it was important. Now there were only the stairs to negotiate, the landlady to avoid, so that she might be far away before the shock she was experiencing overcame her.

Carefully, Catherine picked her way on shaky legs out of the ruined room, leaving behind its ruined owner. She walked silently down the stairs and out of the front door to where Geordie was waiting for her.

He was about to make a light remark on the lines of "Well, that was quick, mistress, and no mistake," when he saw her ashen face, her white lips and her shaking hands.

"What is it, mistress? What's happened? I'll kill him for you if he's hurt you!"

Catherine shook her head, and smiled a ghastly smile. "Too late, Geordie, too late. Find Tom and let us go home, and there I will tell you all. But quick about it, we must not be found here."

Chapter Thirteen

"A dwarf and a well-dressed man, eh? Van Sluys, perhaps? We'll discuss that later."

After they had returned to the inn, Tom had given Catherine a glass of brandy, and made her lie on the bed before she told them what had happened in Grahame's room. Geordie had already reassured Tom that she had not been molested by Grahame. Tom had asked her to tell them everything that had happened in as much detail as she could remember.

Catherine drank a little more brandy. Tom said, "I shan't interrupt you again. Go on." She had already informed him when he had joined them in the Buttermarket that Grahame was dead, but had given him no details.

She told her dreadful story lucidly and well, much better than any junior officer had ever reported his tale to him, Tom noted.

Finally, she reached the point where Grahame had

given her the paper. She stopped to fetch it out of her bag and handed it to Tom.

"He was absolutely determined to give it to me, even though he was dying. I think that he was attacked in his bedroom, left for dead, heard me arrive and then, somehow, revived sufficiently and briefly to stagger in and live long enough to pass it on. It's in some sort of code, not ours. After that he died," she ended, taking another swig of the brandy.

The drink was making everything seem distant and far away, as it had done on the packet when they were at sea. It was as though what had passed had happened to someone else, and not to her.

Tom was examining the paper. She said hazily, "It must be important, but it's not very useful if we don't know the key to the code, is it?"

He gave her a wolfish grin. "But I think we do. A moment." He crossed the room to where his trunks stood against the wall, sorted through one of them and came back with Giles Newsman's prayer book.

"I didn't tell you at the time," Tom said, "but reading through it I found this paragraph near the beginning which had apparently been used as the basis of a cipher. Suppose we try to decipher this letter using Newman's code? We lose nothing if we can't, and gain everything if we can."

Catherine sighed lazily, "Oh, Tom, I'm too drowsy

to be able to decipher a letter. You shouldn't have given me so much brandy. All I want to do is sleep."

He came over to the bed, sat by her, put an arm around her and kissed her. "No need to worry, my brave girl. Try to rest. Today I'll be the clerk. If I'm right about the code, we must send a letter to London tomorrow, telling them what we have discovered—if we have discovered anything useful, that is."

"Who could have killed him, Tom? And why?"

"Not the dwarf, I think. He may have given Grahame the letter. The better bet is the richly dressed man. That could be Van Sluys, but I wouldn't have thought that he was the kind to do his own dirty work. Of course, the murderer might have broken in after the rich gentleman left. Whoever it was, was almost certainly looking for the letter. I wonder how Grahame hid it from him. We shall never know."

"Shuppose it were Amos Shooter, Tom." Catherine was so sleepy that she had begun to slur her words.

Tom considered. "We don't rule anyone out. It might be someone we don't know, who thought Grahame a danger to him. We also have to ponder on why Grahame should have gone to such lengths to give you an enciphered letter when he couldn't know whether we possessed the key to it. Unless…" and he paused.

"Unlesh what?"

"Unlesh, my schweeting," said Tom, tenderly mocking her, after kissing her cheek, which was now rosy again, "he was somehow sure that I was the stranger who went to Newman's rooms after his death and recovered the book with the key in it."

"Thatsh a jump in logic, Tom," Catherine told him. She yawned prettily. "May we discush this later? I'm going to shleep now." Which she did as sweetly as a young woman could, and Tom, kissing her as she closed her eyes, prayed that Grahame would not walk through her dreams.

The key to the code *was* in Newman's book. Tom deciphered Grahame's letter while Catherine slept, which she did until early evening, when she awoke with a yawn to find that Tom had now begun to write the letter to London, passing on Grahame's information.

Halfway through the afternoon he had run out of ink. He pondered for a moment whether or not to send Geordie to a stationer's to buy some more. He decided not to go himself because he did not wish to leave Catherine in case she awoke distressed and needing comfort.

An idea struck him. Catherine had on one occasion fetched a stoppered bottle of ink from the trunk she had brought with her. She would surely not object to him using it, seeing how important it was that the information in Grahame's letter should reach London as soon as possible.

He opened the trunk. Like everything connected with Catherine, it was in perfect order. Lying above her carefully packed clothing was the large leather box from which she had lifted the ink bottle. He opened that too and found that the bottle was held steady by straps fixed to the side of the box so that it should not fall over.

The box also contained two quill pens, a penknife to sharpen them with, a small glass bottle containing sand to dry the ink, and a great sheaf of paper, much written on.

Tom had not set out with any intention of prying into Catherine's private belongings—and so he had intended to tell her when she woke up. But he was only human and the sheaf of paper intrigued him. What was it that she was busy writing—presumably when he occasionally left her at night and in the day? More than that, why had she taken such great care never to be seen working by either himself or Geordie?

He now had a reasonable excuse to examine her papers, for their contents might concern the mission they were engaged on. Was she somehow secretly sending information about their mission to the agents of their enemies? And was that why everybody seemed to be beforehand with them?

The idea seemed far-fetched, but Tom, as he had told Catherine earlier, had more than once saved his own life by not dismissing far-fetched ideas and taking nothing on trust.

He looked across at the bed. She was sleeping so sweetly, a smile on her face, that he felt a cur for mistrusting her. Nevertheless, it was his duty to check what she had been doing. He picked up the papers and began to read them.

Catherine had obviously written at speed, but her hand was a clear and clerkly one and Tom was soon astonished to find that he was reading the text of a play. Even more astonished to find on the first page that the leading character was the self-same Lackwit whom he had seen Betterton impersonating on the stage of the Duke's Theatre.

He riffled rapidly through the thick sheaf of paper. There was no doubt that he was reading the work of one Will Wagstaffe, of whom he had so often joked and who was none other than the pretty woman who was sleeping in his bed.

Any final doubts he had vanished when he reached the last of the handwritten pages on which Catherine had scrawled proposals for the play's title, crossing all of them out except the last one which read, *The Braggart, or, Lackwit Married.*

Could it really be true? Could the witty and impudent Will Wagstaffe, whose bawdy jokes he had so enjoyed, really be his supposed wife, Catherine Wood, known also as Cleone Dubois?

Had she yet another name to add to the two that she already possessed? He read through the first page again, and as he did so her voice was in his head, reading the lines to him.

It was the self-same voice with which she had sparred and jousted with him, silencing him, or spurring him on to fresh heights of impudence himself, so that they had often ended by laughing together, drunk with their own wit.

Another thing. Was there no end to her? She had shown herself to be uncomplaining, untiring, brave and resourceful, so why be surprised at this new revelation? Were not these the characteristics that would enable her to write her plays, call herself Wagstaffe and persuade Betterton to put them on? The characteristics that were enabling her not only to survive, but to keep her brother whilst he studied for the law.

Tom carefully put back the ink bottle, the bottle of sand, and the papers, trying to remember exactly how they had been arranged, before closing the trunk. She must not know that he had discovered her secret. Thinking that, he remembered how she had replied with a double tongue when she had answered his question about whether she had known Will Wagstaffe. "I know no such he."

Of course she didn't. He was a she.

Tom laughed soundlessly, poked his head around

the door into the ante-room where Geordie was having an afternoon nap, woke him up and sent him out to buy ink and a new quill pen so that he might finish his work.

Thus it was that Catherine awoke to find him smiling at her, and putting the finishing touches on his letter to London. A pot of tea, cups, plates and some little Dutch cakes—they called them cookies—were neatly arranged on the table before him.

"Awake at last, sweeting. See what Geordie has brought for us. He told the landlady that you had a megrim, and this is what she produced to cure it. Tea is a restorative for everything, she told Geordie."

"Aye," agreed Geordie, "but you look better already, mistress."

"I feel better," returned Catherine, rising and walking over to sit opposite Tom and the tea. "What did Grahame's letter have to tell us?"

"Something important, my dear wife. But do drink your tea before I tell you. I wouldn't like you to disappoint Geordie and the landlady by leaving it."

The tea did act as a restorative. The events of midday began to fade a little from Catherine's mind. The cookies were excellent, and the three of them emptied the plate at "double quick time", Geordie's words.

Tom picked up the letter, and the one he had written to send to London. "The letter tells us that, in their negotiations at Breda, the Dutch do not wish to cede us any concessions in the Spice Islands in the Far East. They wish to retain their monopoly there.

"On the other hand, they have little interest in the settlements in North America that we conquered and took from them, renaming New Amsterdam New York. They see little profit or future in them. They will thus try to persuade us that the New World settlements are what *they* really want, and that the Spice Islands are secondary in the belief that we shall then think that they know something about the New World that we don't, and that this will change our minds about wanting the Spice Islands, and make us bid for North America instead.

"Now I know that our own government thinks that the trading future of the world—and thus of England—lies in developing the vast resources of the New World and the trade routes to them. But if the Dutch realise this, they might haggle with us, and if we can make them believe that they have won the diplomatic game by our—very reluctantly—accepting the North American territories, and relinquishing any claim to the Spice Islands, they will think that they have tricked us into doing what they want."

Catherine put her hands to her head. "Oh, dear, that sounds very complicated, but I think I grasp what you are saying. That the Dutch will think that they have gained everything if they keep the

Spice Islands in the Far East, and will let us have most of what we want at Breda, thinking that they have bested us.

"In other words, usually the old saying is, The bird in the hand is worth more than two in the bush, but you are arguing that the Spice Islands, the bird in the Dutch hand, will in the long run be worth *less* than the birds in the English bush, that is North American and New York."

"Exactly, you clever girl. After this fashion are negotiations won and lost. This will be invaluable news for our people in Breda. Nearly as much so as the news of the plans of the Dutch fleet."

Catherine wondered briefly how Tom came to know so much about so many arcane matters, but dismissed the thought. "And you have written of this to London?"

Tom waved his letter at her triumphantly. "No need for you to trouble yourself over the matter, dear wife. It is already enciphered and we shall post it tomorrow. Our mission is over. After that we shall pack our bags and depart for home. Van Sluys has sent word that our goods are already on their way to England. You may soon see your brother free again."

Over, it was over. Catherine should have felt delighted to learn this, especially after the horrors of the morning, but strangely the strongest feelings of anti-climax stole over her.

"And Grahame," she asked, "what of him? I suppose now that it does not matter who killed him?"

"Not if we are to go home immediately. We shall, I hope, leave our enemies behind. Believe me, the latest news that the French are drawing nearer and nearer to the Dutch borders will make them wish to arrange a peace with us as quickly as possible."

Home! After the horrors of the morning it had never seemed more attractive. As to what would happen between Tom and herself when they reached there—well, she would think about that then.

Alas, on the following day, just when they were about to pack, a courier arrived with a letter from London addressed to Master Tom Trenchard. He was a servant of Sir Thomas Gower's and the message, he said, was urgent. It was also untimely. Had they been able to leave an hour earlier he would have missed them, and they would have been safely on their way to catch a packet for England.

As it was, Tom read the letter with a glum face, thanked the courier before paying him and dismissing him and telling Geordie and Catherine its unwelcome news.

"It says that London is sending two envoys to meet us here. They should arrive within the next forty-eight hours and we are to cease all operations until then. They are not satisfied that the information we sent them about the intentions of the Dutch Fleet is accurate, and they wish to talk with us and then question Grahame themselves—"

"Aye," interrupted Geordie rudely. "They may visit him in Hell and take up residence there themselves! Is this what we risked our lives for, master? Not to be believed by them as sits at home on their fat backsides!"

Catherine felt the same. Last night, in bed, she and Tom had celebrated not only a mission safely accomplished, but their return home as well and now it seemed that they were not to leave after all and London considered their mission a failure.

"I don't like it," Tom said suddenly. "We are putting you at risk, sweeting." He picked up the letter. "Sir Francis Herrold and James Vaux. I don't know the second and I don't like the first. Let's make for the harbour and take ship."

Catherine said through numb lips, "I have no wish to stay, either, but might they not argue that by leaving after we received their instructions I have broken my word to them, and therefore Rob's life is still forfeit."

Tom swore an ugly oath. "Damn them, yes. If only we'd already left and consequently never received the letter... But 'if onlys' butter no parsnips. You're right. We must stay and hope that nothing goes awry because of Grahame's death."

"The mistress could leave with me," offered Geordie. "And you could deal with the two popinjays yourself."

Sadly Catherine shook her head. "No, Geordie. I made a promise and gained Rob's life in return. I cannot break it, and thereby put him at risk."

And so it was settled. "They may not take long to arrive," Tom told Catherine when Geordie had gone to inform the landlord that they would not be leaving Amsterdam today after all, "and until they do you must not leave the inn, nor must we do anything to arouse suspicion."

He put an arm around her and drew her to him, to kiss her tenderly on the cheek. "Never fear, sweeting. I am here to protect you, and to take care of you in the future also. I cannot allow any harm to come to you now, when I have just found you. Besides, luck may be with us—it has been so far."

Tom tried not to think that luck might change. Catherine was so soft and sweet in his arms, as no woman had ever been before. He wanted to tease her about being Will Wagstaffe, but this was not the right time, nor did he wish her to know yet that he had rummaged among her private belongings. Later, when they had returned to England and safety, they would have time enough to get to know one another.

Nor was he alone in hoping this. Held in the circle of Tom's arms, Catherine tried to tell herself that all would be well, but from the bitter experience of her changing youth she knew that—like the little windmill that Tom had given her—time's whirligig spun so quickly that from one day to the next nothing was sure.

Chapter Fourteen

"Waiting is one of the most damnable things there is." Tom was standing at one of the windows of the inn early one morning, looking out into the yard at the back, which was occupied at the moment by a large coach.

He swung round to smile at Catherine who was sitting in one of their room's most comfortable chairs, engaged in stitching a rose on a small piece of canvas. He had brought it home for her three days ago, together with the wool, to occupy her time, for she had said that she was not used to idleness. She wasn't idle in his absence, for she was nearing the end of writing *The Braggart* and was determined to finish it before she left Holland.

The picture that she presented, her head bent over her work, was a touchingly domestic one, fit to be recorded in one of the many paintings in Holland being commissioned by the rich bourgeoisie to celebrate their comfortable life. He was minded to buy some of them himself when this wretched business was safely over.

A week had gone by since the letter keeping them here had arrived. A week in which nothing more had been heard of Grahame and Catherine was beginning to feel safe.

She and Tom had been living as husband and wife, and were still at the stage when they could hardly bear to be separated, when to be with one another was to want to touch and be touched. Only Geordie's possible interruptions during the day stopped them from behaving like a nymph and satyr let loose in Amsterdam.

The nights were for celebration, and if at first Catherine had regretted their enforced stay, now she was beginning to enjoy it. For she had Tom, and how long she might have him was unknown, so *carpe diem*, "Seize the day", was her motto.

She smiled as Tom idly kissed the top of her head. "I must go out," he told her. "It's the only way to discover what is happening in the great world. The French are marching north, 'tis said, and they are still talking at Breda—but going nowhere. Our news might remedy that."

They had agreed that Tom must not stay in their rooms all day, even if Catherine did. She was not well, Tom told the landlord. The landlady asked if she were breeding, and Tom replied, "Mayhap," with a significant smile.

The notion that Catherine might be breeding pleased him mightily. He had never thought much of owning a small Tom before, but now he found that the idea held him entranced.

"Will you miss me when I'm gone, Mistress Trenchard?" he asked her, going down on one knee beside her, taking the embroidery from her hand and beginning to kiss her. From there it was but a short step to pulling down the bodice of her dress and beginning to kiss the treasures beneath. But when Catherine would have loosened the strings of his breeches, Tom stayed her hand.

"Not now, sweeting, Geordie will soon be back." His voice was thick with desire denied and he buried his head in her lap so that she could stroke his waving red-gold hair. "You said, Catherine," he told her, his voice muffled, "that you could not believe that such pleasure existed, and for all my wicked life before I met you, I have never felt such pleasure as you have given me. If I should give you a bairn in return, would you be unhappy?"

"Never, never." Catherine's denial was as passionate as she could make it. "I can think of nothing better than to have your child."

He dropped his head again, and groaned, "Ah, you do me too much honour, sweeting. I am not worthy."

Which was nothing less than the truth. He thought with distaste of the manners of Charles II's court and the sheer savagery with which the courtiers pursued pleasure. He had been one of them, but never again, he swore to himself, never again.

I am growing too old, I have found a woman to love, and I want a child, undamaged by the carelessness of loving. He knew only too well that promiscuous love brought disease in its train, and he had never been quite as reckless as many of his fellows, but reckless enough.

"We shall soon be home," he said and, forgetting his pose of poor mercenary captain become merchant, added, "I shall dress you in silks, we shall eat lark's tongues, and make love on a bed of flowers in a wood I know."

Catherine stroked his head again, saying gently, "You turn poet, sir. Rochester shall have a rival, and Etheredge, too," for she thought that his extravagances were mere imaginative licence, not the truth.

"Soon, soon," he said, rising. "This I promise you," but did not say what he promised, for Geordie's step was on the stair, and he had come to take turns in guarding her.

"I shall not be long gone," Tom assured her as he put on his plumed grey hat and his short leather jacket. "When I return, you shall come downstairs with me and give me another game of chess," for he had been teaching her to play and had found her an apt pupil.

He kissed her goodbye, passionately. Catherine, stroking the cheek he had caressed, walked to the window to watch him cross the empty inn yard, before picking up her stitchery again. In his little ante-room, Geordie was whistling tunelessly and cleaning Tom's new boots, bought in Amsterdam's market. Shortly he would go downstairs to arrange for their mid-day cold collation to be waiting for them there when Tom returned.

Catherine felt mindlessly happy after the fashion of those who have been well and truly loved the night before. So happy that she was beginning to fall into a light sleep over her work when she heard the tramp of booted feet on the stairs.

The feet stopped outside the door, and someone rapped smartly on it, shouting. "Open, in the name of the law!"

Geordie shot out of his room to open it and stand before Catherine, for there was nowhere where she might hide. She held on to her embroidery as though it were a talisman when three men entered, one of them obviously an important official.

"Mistress Catherine Trenchard?" he questioned her.

Useless to deny, for the landlord, who stood behind the men, jaws agape, must have told him her name. Geordie, undaunted by such authority so blatantly displayed, for all three men wore breastplates and helms as though they had come to arrest a nest of dangerous criminals, said defiantly, "What the devil are you doin' here? My mistress is a peaceable lady, as you may well see."

Number One waved him aside. "Mistress Trenchard I have come to arrest you for the murder last week of one William Grahame in the city of Amsterdam, and to take you to the Town Hall for questioning and from thence to prison."

"No, you ain't," bellowed Geordie. "I'll not have it!"

Number One negligently threw him against the wall, took Catherine by the arm, and handed her over to the two men behind him. "Another word from you, my man, and I'll take you in with her."

Catherine said swiftly as Geordie squared up to the man again, "No, Geordie, no. You cannot help me this way. Wait here and tell Tom when he returns what has happened. He will know what to do."

Geordie nodded sullenly, howling after them as they marched Catherine down the stairs, her embroidery still clutched in her hand, "Look after her, damn you, she's as good a lady as ever breathed, that she is."

Which might have relieved his feelings a little but had no effect on Catherine's captors as they matched her through the streets to the Town Hall.

* * *

Tom returned to the inn carrying yet another present for Catherine, a posy of spring flowers brought from the flower market, which was situated by a bridge over one of the canals. He was enjoying the thought of the pleasure on her face when he bounded upstairs. It occurred to him that never before had he behaved like a boy carrying fairings to his first sweetheart. He couldn't even remember having a first sweetheart.

But he had a sweetheart now.

He knew instantly that something was wrong when he walked through the door. Geordie was standing opposite to him, his face even more miserable than usual. There was no sign of Catherine. He put the posy down on the small table by the bed and said hoarsely, "Spit it out, man. What's to do?" Somehow he knew that the worst had happened.

Geordie didn't prevaricate. That was not his way. "The watch came and took her to the Town Hall for Grahame's murder."

"Damnation! I thought that by now we were safe." He made for the door, his head on fire, tears in his eyes—to do he knew not what. Geordie, insubordinate, caught him by the shoulder. "Not that, master. Think before you act. You cannot help her if you end up in prison too. Not like you to be an impetuous fool—sir!"

Tom's rage and despair subsided a little. "True, very true. I suppose the landlady talked and there are not so many strangers in Amsterdam that they were not able to track her down. Did they ask for me?"

"No, nor took note of me, neither. I thought that strange, master, but mayhap they believe it to be a quarrel between a man and a woman he tried to force to be his doxy. Remember that the landlady never saw you, and I only went in with the mistress once."

Tom nodded. "Belike they think that she killed him with his own dagger. They would scarce believe that she had gone there as a British agent."

He turned his suffering face away from Geordie, struck his clenched fist against the closed door and swore a violent oath. "I told her that I would protect her always. A poor protector I turned out to be! There is only one way out of this and that is to find out who did kill Grahame and turn him over to the authorities.

"Do you scour the alehouses, dens and stews around the harbour, and I will go to Van Sluys to see if there be any help or information to be found there. Ask about a dwarf—and I shall question Van Sluys, who might or might not be the richly dressed gentleman.

"After that I shall go to the Town Hall to find out what is happening to her—and try not to get arrested myself. That way I could do nothing to help her."

He picked up his hat, which he had gaily tossed upon the bed, and tried to avoid looking at the posy of flowers with which he had thought to please her.

The worst had happened and he was in hell, who had so recently been in heaven.

Van Sluys was in, and received Tom in the room where they had dined. He listened to his story and inclined his head in sympathy.

"Alas, I have no direct help I can offer you, *mijnheer,* would that I had. Of the small network of agents who work in Amsterdam I knew only Grahame. That is common practice, for the less one knows of others, or they of you, the less they can betray you.

"As for your wife, as Regent I can enquire about her, vouch that she is of good character and try to see that she is justly treated. But the case against her is a strong one, as you must see. Your best plan is to try to discover who did murder Grahame—which may be difficult.

"One thing I can tell you. Amos Shooter is in Amsterdam. He is not to be trusted, and will bear watching. You say your man is scouring the drinking dens for information. That, too, might prove fruitful. I wish you luck."

And that was all. Tom thanked him and left. He was not sure that Van Sluys was being wholly truthful with him, but he believed that he might try to help Catherine. And so he would tell her when he saw her. For that was his next errand, and one that would cost him dear. He had never thought to love a woman so much that the loss of her had him nigh running mad—and that was, as the old philosophers truly said, to give a hostage to fortune.

"Yes, I visited Master Grahame, sir, but no, I did not kill him, and that is all I can tell you, but it is the truth."

Catherine was being questioned by a magistrate who was the exact opposite of the one in Antwerp. He was burly, brutal in face and figure, and was possessed of a hard dogged manner. He was leaning across the table to question her, his cruel eyes avid.

"The landlady, as you have seen, swore that you were his last visitor, which leaves you, madame, in the position of being his most likely murderer."

"But sir," ventured Catherine, trying to keep her wits about her, "you also know that I visited Master Grahame around noon, and the landlady did not find him dead until six of the clock. Any number of persons might have secretly visited him during that time."

The magistrate smiled. "Oh, you may be sure that the landlady would have heard anyone who came in. She has the ears of an owl and the sight of an eagle where preserving the respectability of her home is concerned. No, you were the last to visit him."

Catherine and Tom had already decided that, if it came to her being questioned, she would claim to have left Grahame alive. To tell the truth, that she had found him dying, would never be believed—since she had informed neither the landlady, nor the authorities, of his death. Those two facts alone, would, in their eyes, seal her guilt.

"Come, mistress, tell us the truth. Why did you visit him, and did he, as the landlady thinks, for he had a bad reputation with women and many visited him, try to assault you? If the last, then your guilt is not so great and will be thus considered at your trial."

"I *am* telling the truth: I did not kill Master Grahame. I visited him to give him news of his relatives in England. He was growing unhappy in his exile."

Well, at least the first sentence and the last were the truth. The one in the middle wasn't. But I can hardly confess that I am here as an agent dealing with another agent, and both of us engaged in activity designed to damage the country Grahame was living in, thought Catherine wryly.

"Now why do I not believe you, mistress?" said the magistrate softly. "For I do not."

Catherine's brave front almost cracked. "I would wish to see my husband, sir. He will be greatly troubled by my arrest."

"Indeed, madame. Perhaps you might care to explain why you visited Grahame twice, and on neither occasion did he accompany you. Why was that?"

"He is trying to make his way as a merchant and he had other appointments on the days of my visits."

"Twice, madame, twice? Go to. I wonder if he knew what you were doing. He may visit you, that is if he wishes to see you after your involvement with Grahame, but only in the presence of a tipstaff. Take her to the cells, and leave her there to contemplate her sins and then she may tell us the truth."

The cell was a bare room, with stone walls, a straw bed, and a chair. A wash basin stood on a stand, a pail beneath it. Light came from two slits in the thick walls. Fetters were attached to the wall, for unruly prisoners, no doubt. Her guards made no attempt to chain her, simply locked her in.

Once alone, Catherine put her head in her hands and tried not to cry. She could see no way out—except that Tom, ever resourceful, might think of one. She found that she was still clutching her stitchery but, with no wool and little light it was of no comfort to her. A Bible stood by the wash basin and she began to read that to try to find some solace in it.

How long she sat there before they brought Tom to her, she did not know. For a bare second when he entered his face told its own picture of shock at her capture.

Ignoring the cold stare of the guard who stood at

the open door he took her in his arms, murmuring, "Forgive me, my dear heart, for not protecting you better, and allowing you to be dragged to this dreadful place. When you are out of it I shall protect you always, be sure of that.

"All I can say now is that Geordie and I are trying our best to discover who did murder Grahame so that you may be freed as soon as possible. I visited Van Sluys this afternoon and he has promised to intervene on your behalf. Oh, I blame myself for this—for bringing you to Holland at all!"

"Foolish Tom," said Catherine tenderly, "for you did not bring me here, I was sent by others more powerful than either of us. And had they not coerced us into going on this mission we should never have met, and never have loved."

"My darling, it is like you to try to comfort me when it is I who should be comforting you. What a brave gentleman you are, Mr Wagstaffe! No wonder you write such remarkable plays. God send you may be freed from this place to write many more."

These betraying words flew out before Tom could stop himself. Catherine stepped back out of the circle of his arms.

"You know! How do you know?"

"Forgive me, sweeting," he said, taking her little hand and kissing it, "but I looked in your trunk for the ink you carry and I naughtily examined your papers—to discover that I loved a bright genius. I have been intrigued by the man who wags the shaft, or shakes the spear, ever since I saw you as Belinda. I never thought that he was a she who would be my love and that I should tell her that I knew her secret in a Dutch prison."

"'We know what we are, but we know not what we may be,'" Catherine returned, kissing his hand, and damn the watching guards, "as Master Shakespeare wrote in *Hamlet.* I played in it once, and shall ne'er forget it."

"Forgive me for spying on you, my brave heart." He had never thought to ask forgiveness of a woman before.

"Of course I forgive you. I am sure that what you did was not deliberate. Besides, I should not have liked you to have run out of ink!"

To think that she could jest so bravely when she was in such danger.

"Time's up," snarled the guard suddenly. He took Tom by the shoulder to lead him away.

Tom shook off the man's hand and said hoarsely, "I shall come to see you tomorrow. With better news, I hope."

"Give my love to Geordie, too," Catherine called after him.

"What, has your wife cuckolded you with another

as well as Grahame?" chuckled the guard coarsely. And never knew how near he came to death, as Tom restrained himself from doing that to him which would have had him in prison, to be tried alongside Catherine. He must remain free to help her.

Chapter Fifteen

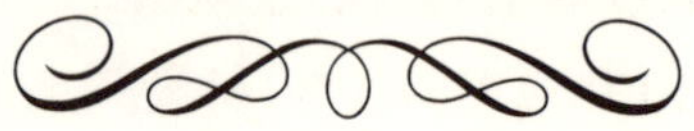

Neither Tom nor Geordie's investigations that afternoon or evening bore any fruit. They discovered nothing that might lead them to Grahame's murderer.

"Tomorrow," said Tom morosely as they wandered home nigh upon midnight. "We'll try again tomorrow."

They had heard further news of the French advance towards the Dutch border, which had Tom hoping that a truce between Holland and England might soon be declared. Such a development would be sure to help Catherine. May was about to pass into June, and the negotiations were still continuing.

Morning saw him sending Geordie out for further explorations. He stayed behind to write a letter to London, telling them of Catherine's arrest and asking what had happened to the envoys whose supposed arrival had placed her in such danger by their late arrival.

He was halfway through enciphering it when there was a commotion in the yard outside as a fine coach rolled in. Such a commotion that Tom went to the window to see what was about.

It was the envoys from England arriving at last—and in some state. First came Sir Francis Herrold, overdressed as usual, and full of wind and importance. Accompanying him was his toady, James Vaux, who would be Herrold's echo, Tom was sure. He cursed them both. Without their intervention, he and Catherine would now be safe in London.

He told them so when they came in, curled, prinked and pompous as though they were still at Whitehall, both ambitious for advancement. Herrold he had always disliked and the feeling was returned ever since Tom had succeeded with a Maid of Honour who had refused Herrold's clumsy advances.

"I wonder that you came at all, seeing that you have taken so long," he began. "And what is so important that you were sent to instruct me? God knows, I need no instructions from you, Herrold."

"I might have expected this from you, Cameron," returned Sir Francis Herrold, looking disdainfully round the small room, letting his greedy stare rest on the big bed that dominated it. "London thought that you might need help, seeing that you have taken so long, and all that you have sent us is a rigmarole about a supposed Dutch invasion that would not have deceived a child.

"When we received your latest letter about the Dutch intentions at Breda, Sir Thomas Gower was of the mind that you had found something definite at long last. My instructions from him are that you pack your doxy off home at once—her work having been done—and that you set off for Breda this very day with Vaux here, there to turn yourself into a gentleman again—if that be possible—and do your duty in the negotiations. I shall look after your doxy."

Red rage held Tom in thrall. His doxy, indeed! Pack her off home, indeed! Like a bale of soiled goods! The desire to take Herrold by the throat, to squeeze the life out of him and throw the body out of the window to join Newman and Grahame's was so strong that it took all his will-power to resist it.

"Damn you, Herrold, for your foul tongue," he began. "Know that my doxy, as you call her, has proved as good as any man on this accursed expedition. And for her pains she is languishing in a Dutch gaol on a charge of killing Grahame, of which she is totally innocent. And, for your information, I shall not travel a yard with you, to Breda, or anywhere else until she is out of the prison into which her devotion to duty has landed her."

"Bedded her, did you?" sneered Herrold. "So hot

for her you cannot wait to bed her again—" He got no further, for with an enraged roar Tom sprang on him and took him by the throat.

James Vaux, who had so far remained silent, protested feebly, "Steady on, Cameron, you'll do him a mischief."

"I should have done him one long ago," roared Tom, but sanity returning, he reluctantly let go of his victim, and stood back.

"Your face looks prettier coloured purple, Herrold," he growled. "You can be off, both of you. You heard me. I don't leave here without the lady."

"Be damned to that," snarled Herrold. "I have my orders, and so have you. Sir Thomas foresaw this. He told me to tell you that if you refused to go to Breda, or to allow her to return home without you, then we should hand her over to the Dutch as a spy.

"Seeing that she has already landed herself in gaol, I shall make no attempt to free her unless you travel with Vaux to Breda. I shall remain here to arrange her release and send her back to England before travelling to Breda myself."

"And be damned to you," Tom returned without thinking. "I shall go the gaol myself and tell them…" He stopped.

"That you are English agents? Come, come, what would that do but condemn you both to hang, when if you do it my way, she will be freed today, for I can give them the name of the man who killed Grahame. She will be safe in England and you will be safe in Breda, with no suspicion attaching to either of you."

He would kill Herrold one day for this filthy piece of blackmail, he most surely would, and have it out with Gower and Arlington for their high-handed treatment of Catherine. But for the present the swine had him on the rack. He was helpless, and Herrold knew it. If he could be believed, Catherine would only be saved if he went to Breda. And there was another thing.

"Who killed Grahame—and how do you know?"

"Amos Shooter killed Grahame. He has been playing everyone off against everyone else. He has spent his wife's fortune, and is in desperate need of money. As to how we know, you must ask Sir Thomas yourself. Since he is as close-mouthed as ever, I doubt whether he will oblige you."

James Vaux said in his pleasant and reasonable voice, "Come, Stair. Surely you can see that this arrangement is in the best interest of both of you."

"I promised to visit her today," returned Tom. "At least allow me to delay my journey until I have seen her."

Herrold was delighted to be able to say, "Those are not my instructions, Cameron. You are to leave at once—or the doxy is thrown to the wolves."

Geordie! Where was Geordie when he was wanted? He should have been back long ago. "I shall wait until my servant, Geordie Charlton, returns. He can accompany Catherine home." At least he could do that for her: see that she had a protector on her long and difficult journey back to London.

Herrold sighed. "By no means. You are to leave at once. I can pass on your instructions to your man if he does not return before you are ready to go. But make all speed, man, we waste time."

They had him by the throat and there was nothing for it but to follow orders. He could not help Catherine by staying.

"I shall delay long enough to write a letter to her, explaining why I am leaving her alone in Amsterdam, and you will do me the honour of delivering it," Tom said. He hated to have to beg anything from the swine before him, but he had no alternative. "And if Geordie does not return before I leave for Breda, you will be sure to tell him to look after Catherine for me."

"Of course," said Herrold, gracious in victory. "By all means, write your letter. Vaux's man will help you to pack." He gazed patronisingly round the room. "Not that you appear to have much of value with you!"

Tom resisted the impulse to strangle him. Instead he sat down and wrote his first love letter to Catherine; the first, indeed, that he had ever written to anyone. He poured his heart and soul into it, telling her how much he loved her, and how wretched he felt at having to go to Breda without her.

"But I know that Geordie will look after you, and, God willing, we shall meet again soon, never to part." He sealed it carefully and handed it over to Herrold with a heavy heart.

"I shall be sure to see that your doxy receives this, Cameron. I have to say that I never thought to find you in such a pother about an actress who doubles as a whore. More like you to enjoy the night with her and be off."

Oh, he was well aware that he had Tom on a chain as though he were a dancing bear, and could not resist jerking the chain. That he would pay for this one day soon, was the only thing that kept Tom from despairing altogether. He would make sure that his revenge was sweet when he took it. The knowledge that Catherine would wait in vain for him to visit her would haunt him all the way to Breda.

"And you will give her this purse. It has enough money in it to provide her and Geordie with an easy passage home."

"You may depend upon it, Cameron," Herrold said and, taking it from Tom, he placed the purse on the table beside the bed.

While Tom was downstairs settling his account with the landlord before he and Vaux set off, Herrold took Vaux on one side. He gave him brisk orders, enjoying his power over his friend. And then he took Tom's letter to Catherine from his coat pocket where he had stowed it, after promising Tom on his honour as a gentleman that he would give it to her as soon as she was released from prison.

He held it up in the air, saying regretfully, "No time to read it, alas, before he returns," and then slowly, laughing as he did so, he tore it to pieces, before tossing it into the small fire which burned in the grate.

"You promised to deliver it, Francis, on your honour," wailed Vaux, as the fire reduced Tom's letter to ashes.

"Honour! To Cameron, to a wench any man might have for a small fee? Who will doubtless lie with me tonight if I make it worth her while. Come, come, my friend, you know better than that."

He saw Vaux begin to hesitate, leaned forward and said to him, quite jovially, "Inform him of what I have done, Jem, my lad, and I shall tell the world of your little adventures with the pretty boys in Southwark. So, mum's the word, and all's well."

Vaux closed his mouth and shrugged resignedly. Cameron would have to take his chances if the wench thought that he had deserted her.

A thought that echoed Herrold's own, as he watched the coach containing his victim roll out of the inn's courtyard on its way to Breda. Next to deal with Cameron's man: another pleasure awaiting him.

* * *

Geordie had had a hard morning. He had been patiently wandering through the stews of Amsterdam searching for anything that might lead them to Grahame's murderer. He had told Tom that it might be a dangerous occupation, and so it proved.

At a stinking grog shop near the poor end of the harbour he had asked after a dwarf who might know one William Grahame. The landlord had professed no knowledge of any such dwarf. A dirty seaman had sidled up to him as he had left muttering hoarsely that he knew of a dwarf who lived nearby—a whole family of them, he had leered, refugees from one of the travelling fairs that toured Europe.

"Turned away for drunkenness and lechery," he had offered piously. "Give me a groat, master, and I'll take you to them."

All this in broken English. Geordie reluctantly handed over the groat and followed the seaman down a squalid alley, tripping over ropes and odds and ends of broken ships' chandlery. At the far end of it the seaman whistled, and the next thing that Geordie knew was that he was propped up against the wall of the alley, his money gone, and a dirty great headache blurring his sight.

He had no notion of how long he had been unconscious as he staggered back to the inn for succour, hoping that his failure would not distress his master overmuch.

But he found no master there. In the room that Tom and Catherine had occupied, he found a stone-faced gentleman in fine clothes who stared at him as though he were a cockroach who had lost his way from the cellars.

"One Geordie Charlton, I presume?" asked Sir Stoneface. He had a right nasty expression.

"Aye, that I am. Where's Master Trenchard?"

"Gone. I don't know where. Took off with a friend of his and mine who came for him from London."

Geordie stared malevolently at him. "And who the devil be you, when you're at home?"

Sir Stoneface rose negligently to his feet. He was wearing red-heeled shoes and stank of some fancy perfume. "Show a little respect for your betters, my man," he drawled, "or I'll have my footmen trash you."

"And where's Master Tom? Did he leave me a message?"

"Nothing. Just a couple of groats for your pains."

Geordie clutched his aching head. This was not like his master, not at all. But the whole world knew how capricious were the great ones who ruled it.

"And Mistress Trenchard? Where be she? Never say he left her behind."

"That's the usual way of dealing with doxies, my

man, as you should know. She's in Amsterdam gaol still—until I free her and pack her off home. And now, be off with you."

There was something wrong here, very wrong. But whether it was Master Tom or Sir Stoneface who was wrong, Geordie did not know. His head hurt him so much that it was difficult for him to do any hard thinking.

Sir Francis picked up a fat purse from the table by the bed. He opened it and took two coins from it.

"Your master left you two groats, I'll make it four, so long as you take yourself off forthwith. You understand me?"

"Aye, sir, that I do."

Geordie took the groats. He thought of Tom and Catherine and their loving. Of how Tom had always been true to him, and he didn't like this one bit. To be turned off with such a trifling sum after all the years he and Master Tom had spent together! He would not go away, not he. He would haunt the inn, try to discover what Sir Stoneface was up to, and replenish his empty purse by some means or other—fair or foul.

And keep a watch for poor Mistress Catherine when she was freed from gaol. From what Sir Stoneface had hinted, she might be in need of a protector.

Catherine was waiting for Tom. She had been taken before the magistrate again that morning after being given bread and water for her breakfast. He had questioned her sternly, but he had not been able to shake her. Her sincerity in denying that she had murdered Grahame was so patent that the magistrate was beginning to doubt her guilt.

On the other hand, she could not prove that she had not done so, and until then he must hold her. His men were making enquiries about Grahame, but had found no one who would confess to as much as knowing his name, let alone him. He sent her back to her cell.

And still Tom did not come. But she did not repine, for was there not the afternoon to look forward to? After mid-day, one of the guards brought her some gruel and a slice of coarse yellow bread to eat with it. She was drinking the soup when he returned to say, "That magistrate wishes to see you immediately. Leave that."

Hungry though she was, Catherine did as she was bid, and he led her back to the room where the magistrate had twice interrogated her. As usual, he was seated behind his big table.

Opposite to him, in one of the big armchairs that the Dutch favoured, was a fine gentleman, sour-faced and thin-lipped, who stared at her, stripping all her clothing from her as he did so. Catherine found herself hating him on sight and wondered what he had to do with her. She was soon to find out.

"This is Sir Francis Herrold from England," the magistrate said. "He is on his way to the diplomatic mission at Breda, but he also brings good news for you."

Sir Francis Herrold. Catherine found his name familiar. She said nothing. He rose and bowed to her, she curtsied back at him; she could do no less.

"Sit, mistress, sit," said the magistrate, his manner to her as polite as it had been peremptory. "Sir Francis has brought us proof that the murderer of William Grahame is one Amos Shooter, who has been spying for every state in Europe in turn. He was the fine gentleman seen by the landlady that morning before you arrived.

"We believe that he returned later, by a back staircase, and killed Grahame so that he should not betray his treachery. Only the French invasion of the Austrian Netherlands saved him from arrest in Antwerp. He fled to Holland in the confusion caused by the French attack in order to ply his wicked trade here."

He paused. "Sir Francis has told us that he was bankrupt, having wasted his wife's fortune and his own. We are trying to find him in order to arrest him. This news, mistress, means that we will release you immediately, and apologise for having detained you. Sir Francis will be only too happy to escort you to your lodgings."

Sir Francis inclined his head at this, and said coolly, "My pleasure, mistress."

Catherine wished that she liked the look of him more, for was he not her saviour? "Thank you, Sir Francis," she managed to say, and then, "Tom, my husband. Is he not with you?"

"Alas, no," replied Sir Francis, sadly, "but all shall be made known to you when you return to the inn where you have been living. We may go now, *mijnheer?*"

"Indeed, indeed." The magistrate rose and bowed them both out. He evidently considered Sir Francis a great man, and the coach he had arrived in, the liveried servants who accompanied him, all bore out that belief.

As though to emphasise her lowly station, Sir Francis was handed in to the coach by an obsequious footman before the same honour was offered Catherine. His air of consequence, his fine clothes, his silver-topped cane, and his lordly manners were overwhelming. He scarcely deigned to acknowledge the magistrate's farewells.

Nor did he deign to speak to Catherine as the coach rumbled along. When they reached the inn, his footman handed her out after his master, and he preceded her mannerlessly up the stairs to their rooms.

Tom! She was going to see Tom. She had not known how much he had twined himself round her heart until she had been arrested and lost him. And Geordie, too, had become part of her life. She had gained a new family, who had so bitterly lost one.

But there was no Tom and no Geordie waiting for her. The big room was bare of them and their possessions. Tom's coat, his hat, his two trunks, and his nightrail flung carelessly across the bed, all, all of them, were gone. The door to Geordie's ante-room was open and he was not there.

She turned to Sir Francis, who had rudely seated himself in the chair that Tom had used—although she was still standing—spread her hands and asked, like a bewildered, bereft child, "Where are they, Tom and Geordie? Have they gone without leaving me a letter—or even a message?"

Astonishingly Sir Francis began to laugh. She stared at him, and said haughtily, although the rapid beating of her poor heart was making her breathless, "What amuses you, sir?"

"You," he choked at her, raising his lace handkerchief to his mouth. "Think you, that once your value to him was gone, both as to your performance in bed with him, and with Grahame, that Sir Alastair Cameron would trouble with such as you any further? You deceive yourself, mistress."

"Sir Alastair Cameron? What is he to me?"

"Come, come, mistress, do no try to cozen me! Surely you know with whom you have been living since you left England? You must know as well as I do that Tom Trenchard is none other than Sir Alastair—or rather Stair—Cameron, one of the King's favourites because he never asks him for money, and occasionally does his bidding on such little adventures as these, changing his name when he does so.

"It must have pleased him mightily to find such a willing little doxy as yourself to pass the time with. Which is probably why he sent that nonsensical despatch about the Dutch Navy's attack! No doubt he was thinking more about your shopworn charms than of the work he was sent to do! But all that is over for you now. You are to go home at once."

For one terrible moment Catherine thought that she was going to faint. Tom, her Tom, was Sir Alastair Cameron, who had made such a brouhaha and nuisance of himself when she had been playing Belinda in *The Braggart!* He was not a poverty-stricken mercenary of relatively low degree, but a rich and powerful magnate who had the ear of the King and his Secretary of State, Lord Arlington!

It was no wonder that he had abandoned her without a word and left her to the tender mercies of this cold-blooded fop who plainly saw her as prey! For had not Tom seen her as prey, too? He had not meant one of the loving words that he had showered on her over the last few days, not one. He had simply been passing the time agreeably with yet another easy conquest.

The room began to spin about her. Sir Francis Herrold was leaning forward and murmuring slyly, "You need not go home at once, my dear, we could pass a pleasant few days together, here in Amsterdam, and you could earn yourself a nice little fee. I warrant that Stair Cameron has not given you anything for the odd tumble in his bed."

He moved towards her, his face aglow with lechery. "We can begin now, if you so wish."

"No," Catherine said, recovering herself, pushing back the awful faintness and putting her hands out to fend him off. "No, never, and if you come any nearer to me and try to force me, I shall go downstairs and tell the landlord what you are trying to do. They treat women more kindly here in Holland than they do at home, and it would go ill with you if you were to assault me."

She had her hand on the door knob, for he had been foolish enough to leave the way to the door open. He glared at her, and growled haughtily, "A stupid doxy, then. Well, well, you may have your way. Pack your bags and I shall pay for your passage home, but nothing more, if you refuse to earn it."

Could Sir Thomas Gower have meant this to happen to her? Could Tom? Could the man she had thought she knew have left her in prison to be insulted and mocked by a fellow courtier? Could he have agreed that she should be turned away, to find her way home alone and virtually penniless, with not even a word of thanks for work well done?

Instead, she had been offered only a sneering comment that what the three of them had discovered, and sent to London at great risk, was worthless. The feeling of faintness overwhelmed her again, and again she pushed it back. She would not be overset by this, she would not.

And where was Tom? Where had he gone? Without a word, and why should she be surprised that he had abandoned her? After all, had she not half-expected such an ending to their short idyll? She had had her pleasure with him, and he with her, and if she had been foolish enough to fall in love with him, that was her fault, not his.

But she could not forget that he had held her in his arms and promised to take care of her always. And always had turned out to be a few short days, and when, as this unpleasant man had said, her usefulness to him was over, he had left her behind and passed on to his next adventure, his next woman.

"And Geordie?" she asked, for Geordie had become her friend, too. "What of Geordie?"

"The ill-favoured servant? Why, he was turned away too—after being liberally paid. But this is none of your business, mistress. Come, prepare to leave, the packet departs on the evening tide and the sooner you are back in London, the happier we shall all be."

Mechanically Catherine packed her trunk, and dressed herself for the journey whilst Sir Francis went downstairs to eat a hearty meal. She sat on the bed, numb. So, Tom had turned Geordie away as well. She would not have thought that of him—but, after all, she had never really known him, only the man he had pretended to be.

Sir Francis offered to have food sent up to her, but she refused it. She had not eaten properly since she had been arrested, but the thought of eating anything made her feel ill.

A footman came upstairs to carry her trunk down and take her to the coach. "I shall come with you to the packet," Sir Francis had said, speaking to her as though she were an under-servant, "to make sure that you board it. We have no mind to leave you plying your trade in the Netherlands. You can do that at home."

"I am an actress," Catherine told him, "not a whore," but he merely laughed at her.

He was true to his word and watched her go aboard, the footman carrying her trunk. The last she saw of Holland was of him watching the packet sail towards the open sea. Behind him the spires of Amsterdam's churches ran like a tall fence on the long skyline.

The slow tears slipped down her face until, the harbour behind her, a familiar voice said, "Do not cry, mistress, I have come to take you safely home since he will not."

It was Geordie.

It was Geordie who saw her trunk safely carried ashore when they reached England, who made her shelter from the rain on the packet when she stood helpless beneath it, since she seemed to have lost the power to look after herself. It was Geordie who arranged her journey back to London and Cob's Lane. All the drive and resolution with which Catherine had run her life since her parents' death had leached out of her since Tom—no, Sir Stair Cameron—had deserted her.

She had thought that she had found the other half of herself, that consequence of true love of which all the poets sang. The dream had beckoned and she had followed it gladly.

She had been wrong. Today she was weak, but tomorrow, oh yes, tomorrow, she would be strong and let no man who protested his love for her ever come near her again, for all men were tricksters. For the present she had Geordie. Geordie who had caught her when, at the sight of him, the world had turned around her, and faintness had overcome her at last.

He had sworn an oath, sat her down on the wet deck and fanned her face until she had recovered.

"Bear up, mistress! You have been a brave lass so far. Never say die."

"No, indeed," she said, looking up at his face, more miserable then ever at the sight of her distress, "but who would have thought that he would have abandoned us both? For he has abandoned you, has he not?"

Geordie squatted beside her, and nodded agreement. "Aye, and 'tis not like him at all. I have been with him man and boy and all he left for me was two groats and no message—nor any hint of where he has gone."

"Nor me, either, Geordie. We are partners in misery, are we not?"

"That we are. I would never have thought that Master Tom would serve me so. But who knows what the mighty of this world may do to us, so long as they get their own pleasure? Poor folk like us are nothing to them. I saw yon Stoneface fetch you from the gaol, and I followed you to the harbour. One of his servants told me that they were sending you home. They thought it a fine joke."

He did not tell Catherine that he had stolen the fellow's purse for his pains, and that it would help them to get safely home again.

"Master Tom?" Catherine heard him use the false name and wondered whether Geordie had been deceived over that as well. "Do you not know what his real name is?"

"A 'course I do. Sir Alastair Thomas Cameron Bart. His mother was a Trenchard. Called himself Tom Trenchard, he did, when he were a young lad in exile when we soldiered against the heathen for a living. Allus been Master Tom to me, he has."

Catherine gave a great sigh. "He's gone, Geordie, and he has done the greater wrong to you."

"Aye, and still I cannot believe it. We live and learn."

After that, nothing was said between them except on matters pertaining to the journey. Catherine felt too helpless to check Geordie when he told her that he intended to see her home. For once he did not appear to be enjoying his misery.

"I cannot pay you, Geordie," she told him as he carried her trunk into her small house in Cob's Lane. "I have been left virtually penniless. I need to go to the Duke's Theatre to earn somewhat to make an honest living."

"No need to worry about that, mistress. I have enough to keep me for some little time, and will, if you so agree, rent a room from you and serve as your footman until you are settled again."

Catherine's eyes filled with tears. She did not deny him, for until Rob returned home—if he returned home, that was, for what had so recently passed with Sir Francis Herrold had made her doubt

Sir Thomas Gower's honesty—she had no masculine protector in a cruel world.

"You are sure that you wish to do this, Geordie?"

"Oh, aye. Give me a home, it will."

And so it was agreed. And of all strange things, Catherine thought ruefully as she composed herself for sleep and a future without Tom, she had acquired not the master, but his man!

Chapter Sixteen

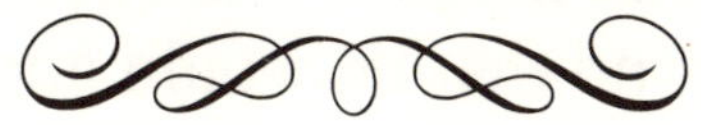

All the time that he was in Breda, richly dressed, one of the major figures in the discussions that were daily leading towards a hoped-for peace, Stair Cameron thought constantly of his lost love, wondering what she was doing.

Stair had spoken to Sir Francis Herrold when he finally arrived in Breda, asking him for news of Catherine. Herrold assured Stair that he had seen Catherine safely out of gaol and on to the packet. He did not tell him that he had turned Geordie away and kept the purse that Stair had left for them—nor that, through a bribed clerk in Breda, Stair's letters to Catherine were stolen and destroyed.

His revenge on Stair had taken long to ensure, but it was satisfyingly complete. He was too stupid to worry over what might happen if and when Stair discovered his duplicity.

Stair had expected Catherine to reply to his love

letter when she reached England, but no word came from her, which surprised him. He wrote several times to her at Cob's Lane, but nothing came back.

After a little time he began to worry that something untoward might have happened to her and Geordie. He consoled himself with the thought that, owing to the war, the post had become erratic, and made up his mind that he would apply for leave to return home as soon as he decently could…

May passed into June. Stair spoke to Arlington, who had arrived in Breda for a brief visit, asking that he be relieved of his duties and be allowed to go home as soon as possible.

"I have done the state some service," he argued. "What I learned from Grahame about Dutch demands for peace, and the information I passed from him to you about the raid on Sheerness…"

Arlington interrupted him, "Oh, you must know, Stair, that no one gave that business about the raid any credence. It was simply Grahame's daydream designed to get him a pardon—which, of course, we would never have granted him whatever he sent us. It was a piece of luck for us that Shooter disposed of him."

Stair gave him a deadly glance. "I offered him his pardon in good faith. I am sorry to hear that you were prepared to cheat him had he lived."

Arlington laughed. "Oh, come, Stair, you know that no one trusts anyone in this business! And you had your payment in the company of the little actress we provided for you, I trust."

Stair saw red again, but controlled himself. "She did the state some service, too. I hope you saw her well rewarded. And was it necessary for you to order Herrold to send her home so abruptly?"

"No doubt she was paid," returned Arlington, who had not the slightest idea whether Catherine had been rewarded or not. "And confess, you could scarcely have arrived at Breda masquerading as Trenchard with your little doxy in tow. We did you a favour."

"Hardly that, but no matter," said Stair drily, containing his anger at Arlington's light-minded references to Catherine. There was no point in making an enemy of a man who was more useful as a friend. "She will gain a better reward than money, I trust, when I return to England."

Arlington was too tactful to enquire what that would be. His old friend seemed a trifle hipped where his little doxy was concerned. And who could have foreseen that? He, too, decided that silence was always the best policy.

Nor did he have much to say two days later when the dreadful news from England was delivered to him by a grim-faced courier. It dealt a shattering blow to Arlington's hopes of defeating the Dutch and being able to lay down peace terms from a position of supremacy.

Stair was present when Arlington opened the despatch in the privacy of the offices assigned to them. George Downing, the British Ambassador to Holland, and the rest of the peace delegation were present, waiting for the day's orders.

Arlington's face lost its ruddy colour. He threw the paper down on to the table before him, and stood silent before them all, trying to regain his composure.

"The devil's in this war," he announced at last. "I have just been apprised of the gravest news a man could well receive. On June the twelfth, De Ruyter burned down Sheerness, sailed up the Medway and raided Chatham, destroying much of our fleet and capturing *The Royal Charles,* its pride."

He tried not to look at Stair as he spoke, knowing that he must be thinking sadly of the disbelief accorded to the accurate information which he and Catherine had sent back to England. Before Arlington could continue, he was interrupted by the sound of cheering in the street outside. The news had reached Holland and all Breda was rejoicing.

The advantage given to England in the peace negotiations by the French invasion of the Austrian Netherlands was destroyed by this humiliating defeat. The glum faces of everyone in the room told their own story.

"The only thing we may be able to salvage from this dismal business," Arlington said heavily, "is that we shall appear to add to our humiliation by ceding all our interests in the Pacific and accept instead the territories in North America in lieu of them. Territories that we want."

Heads nodded. The peace talks would soon end, and they could all go home, their tails between their legs.

Stair said nothing. He would not compound Arlington's misery by speaking of the lost opportunity to defeat the Dutch that he, and his advisers, had thrown away. At least this news meant that he would soon see Catherine again, although he wished that some means of bringing that about, other than a stunning defeat, had been necessary.

Once the others had left, he remained to speak alone to Arlington. "I would not say so in public," he announced hardily, "but if you had heeded the information we sent you, we would have been waiting for the Dutch when they arrived—and the consequent humiliating defeat would have been theirs.

"Because of that, I ask you again to allow me to return home at once. The talks will end soon, in any case, and you will not want my presence at them further, seeing that I am in possession of what you can only regard as the most unfortunate information!"

He smiled winningly. Arlington had spoken lightly of cheating Grahame and had intimated that blackmail and cheating were part of the rules of the game. That being so, he had no hesitation in blackmailing Arlington.

Let me go home, he was saying, or I will tell the world that you had news of Dutch intentions, and not only ignored it, but mocked at it and the senders!

He knew he had won by the wry expression on Arlington's face. He laughed abruptly. "We shall make a statesman of you yet, Stair. That was as well done as anything I have yet experienced. Your knife went between my ribs so sweetly, I hardly knew that I was injured. Yes, you may go home, to enjoy your little actress. Herrold seemed to think that you had enjoyed her already."

Stair smiled again. He would not tell Arlington that he would soon make Herrold pay for all the insults that he had heaped upon him in Amsterdam. He had been an honest soldier once, but had for the last few weeks played the dishonest diplomat and spy in his country's service.

But that was over now and when he got back to England—well, he would be an honest soldier again—and make Herrold pay his dues. Nor would he ever be a spy again: the experience had left a bad taste in his mouth.

But he was not able to leave as soon as he had

expected. The negotiations began to proceed at such a pace that Arlington begged him to remain until they ended. "I need your support, Stair," he argued, "against such as Herrold, who do not understand the long view, and I conceive it to be my duty to claim it and yours to give it. In any case, you would scarcely have time to take ship before the rest of us are ready to leave."

"You are demanding a great deal of me," Stair told him gravely, "and when and if the time comes when I need something from you, I shall not hesitate to ask it."

Arlington looked at him knowingly. Stair Cameron had changed, no doubt of it. It might not be anything more than the inevitable alteration brought about by time, giving men a gravitas and a responsibility that they had not possessed in early youth. Stair was in his middle thirties, a time when most men began to take stock of their lives.

But it might also be, improbably, the influence of his little doxy, for Stair had privately confessed to him that he wished to marry her and settle down.

In that he was unlike some such as George Villiers, Duke of Buckingham, Arlington conceded wryly, who remained a permanent youth even though he was now in his middle forties. But Stair Cameron was proving himself to be of a different kidney. He had been a useful member of the negotiating party, unlike

Herrold, whose open dislike of Stair warped his judgement, since he opposed automatically everything which Stair suggested, however wise and reasonable.

Stair had avoided Herrold and his crony Vaux whilst at Breda, but on their last evening before they left for home the entire delegation took the opportunity to drown the memory of the defeat at Sheerness by indulging in a wild drinking party.

In the middle of it James Vaux staggered up to Stair, who had remained comparatively sober, and sat down opposite to him. "Thought you were leavin' Breda early, Cameron."

"Hal Arlington asked me to stay on," Stair replied coolly. He had no wish to talk to Vaux, and rose to leave. Vaux leaned forward to seize him by the elbow, saying earnestly and drunkenly, "Was never happy with the way Frank Herrold treated your little doxy, Cameron. Want you to know that, whatever happens."

Stair pulled his elbow out of Vaux's restraining grip and said, surprised by Vaux's words, "Whatever happens, Vaux? Why, what could happen—to me and mine?"

Vaux opened his mouth to speak, but no words came out. An arm in scarlet satin took him by the elbow and lifted him to his feet.

"Take no note of poor Vaux here," murmured Sir Francis Herrold, pulling Vaux towards him. "He scarce knows what he is saying. 'Tis merely the drink talking, eh, Jem, my lad? Should know better than to take too much, always a mistake."

Stair watched him walk Vaux away, hissing into his ear. What had Vaux been about to say that Francis Herrold did not wish him to hear? Unease rode on his shoulders again. He had half a mind to pursue Herrold and try to discover the meaning of Vaux's drunken hints. The only thing that prevented him from doing so was the certainty that he would become so heavily involved with the man that his departure from Breda would be delayed.

No, best to let it go. Tomorrow he would be away, and he could scarce wait to see Catherine—and England—again.

"Thought I saw Amos Shooter in the Strand today, mistress. He's like a ghost haunting us—you were certain that you saw him in Amsterdam."

Catherine handed Geordie his dish of soup, before giving her brother his. On the day that the naval defeat at Sheerness had been cried in the streets, and the London mob had rioted, screaming for somone's blood, Rob had been released. He had arrived at Cob's Lane, unshaven and gaunt, swearing that, after his experiences in the Tower, he would never meddle in politics again.

"And a good thing too," Catherine had told him briskly, "for my life since I last saw you has scarce been a bed of roses." She gave him an edited version of her time in the Low Countries, speaking little of Tom and not telling Rob that he was, in reality, that noted courtier, Sir Alastair Cameron. Nor did she tell Rob that she had gone there to save him from hanging.

Fortunately, she had already warned Geordie to guard his tongue when Rob came home, for one of Rob's first remarks when he had been fed and watered was aimed at him.

"So, we seem to have acquired a footman. Where the devil has he come from? And can we really afford one?"

Catherine had risen to Geordie's defence, although he needed none, for Rob's doubtful reception of him had merely served to confirm his melancholy view of life.

"Tom Trenchard abandoned both of us, and Geordie was so kind to me after that, and saw me safely home that it would have been a brute thing for me to have turned him away as well. Besides, he's more of a lodger than a footman, seeing that for the first week I was back his rent kept me in food before I found work at the Duke's Theatre again."

Catherine had told neither Rob nor Geordie that Betterton had been delighted with *The Braggart, or, Lackwit Married,* which was currently in rehearsal and being advertised on bills about the town. She was already working on a new play.

Neither she nor Geordie had told Rob that the government had ignored the information that they had sent back from Holland, for neither of them wanted him to be spurred into unwise political action again.

Since then Rob and Geordie had become unlikely friends, occasionally grumbling at one another. Imprisonment had turned Rob into a silent man and he and Geordie were happily silent together. There were quite a number of secrets being kept in the little house, for Geordie did not tell either Rob or Catherine that he had followed Shooter to his lodgings and discovered that he was known there as Master Harris.

They had just begun to drink their soup when a knock came at the door. Rob flinched at the sound. Since the day of his arrest any sudden noise distressed him.

"Never fear," said Catherine gently. "They can scarcely be coming for you again."

Geordie reluctantly put down his spoon, and grumbled his way to the door. He opened it—and then shut it again immediately. Whoever was outside now beat a rapid tattoo on it.

"Who the devil was that?" Rob demanded.

"Someone you don't want to know," returned Geordie morosely, sitting down again.

Catherine was seized by a terrible suspicion. She

rose and pushed by Geordie who was attacking his soup with relish, and opened the front door.

She had been right to be suspicious, for it was Sir Alastair Cameron, also known as Tom Trenchard, who was standing there, a bewildered expression on his face. Before he had time to as much as utter a word, Catherine shut the door on him, saying smartly as she did so, "No pedlars wanted here today."

Rob, who had briefly seen a fine figure of a man standing outside who was certainly no pedlar, said impatiently, "What silly game are you two engaging in?" Before either Catherine or Geordie could stop him, he opened the door himself. This time an angry Stair Cameron, his eyes blazing, stepped into the room.

"What the devil are the pair of you playing at that you should refuse me entry?" he exclaimed in a deep voice. There he had been on the doorstep, dreaming of seeing Catherine again, and of the joy with which she would greet him, and instead she had shut the door in his face, and turned him away! And Geordie had been no better. He had been prepared for his man's usual litany of complaint at life, but not to be denied absolutely.

"That," said Catherine, staring him down, "we might ask of you, Sir Alastair Cameron! What the devil are *you* doing here, expecting to be welcomed after you turned the pair of us away in Amsterdam without so much as a word of farewell or any notion of where you might have gone?"

"And only four groats between us," grumbled Geordie, "and half of that given to me by your fancy friend; a fine reward after years of faithful service."

Catherine saw Tom—for she could not yet think of him as Stair, however hard she tried—turn his face away from them both for a second.

So *that* was what James Vaux had been trying to tell him. Herrold had destroyed his letter to Catherine, and stolen the money he had left for her and Geordie, leaving them penniless. Mingled shock and rage at such treachery combined to silence him—coupled with the belated knowledge that he should never have trusted the man.

Catherine interpreted his silence as guilt. "Oh, you may well look away from us, sir. My only wonder is that you have dared to come here at all."

"Just a moment, Catherine," said Rob, his face bewildered. "What in the world is going on? I thought you said that you were both in the Low Countries with an ex-soldier called Tom Trenchard. Now you have named this man as Sir Alastair Cameron. Were you there with two men?"

"Yes," said Catherine.

"No," said Geordie.

"Which?" cried Rob exasperated. "Which of you is telling the truth?"

"Both of us," announced Catherine. "For Tom Trenchard was the name I knew him by until Sir Francis Herrold enlightened me as to his true identity before I was packed off to England at short notice like an inconvenient parcel. And Tom Trenchard and Sir Stair Cameron are two very different beings."

"Enlightened you, did he?" said Stair in his best sardonic mode. "I could think of a better word for what Sir Francis Herrold did, but you would not like it."

"Why don't you leave us alone?" Catherine told him passionately. "Please go. You know where the door is."

"No!" exclaimed Rob, suddenly turning into a lawyer. "There's something damned odd going on here, and I want an explanation."

Stair thought, irrelevantly, that Catherine had never looked so lovely. Her eyes were shining, her cheeks were glowing, and fiery indignation informed every line of her body. His busy mind had quickly worked out what Sir Francis Herrold had done to the pair of them, and he could not blame Geordie for his indifference or Catherine for her anger.

He would appeal to her brother, who seemed to be a more commonsensical man than he might have thought him from his knowledge of the conduct that had landed Rob in the Tower.

"If we could all sit down together, and talk

quietly, without anger or passion, I can explain to you why you think that I betrayed you both. I assure you that I did not.

"In the meantime, you might offer me a glass of ale."

Catherine let the hurt feelings and the memory of betrayal, which the sight of him had revived again, subside a little. She saw that he had not come finely dressed as Sir Stair Cameron would have done, nor was he as plain and shabby as Tom Trenchard at his worst. He simply looked like a pleasant gentleman, not a courtier at all.

"Very well," she conceded grudgingly. "But tell me what I am to call you."

"Stair will do," he told her, smiling at her for the first time. "May I sit down?" Without waiting for permission other than a nod from Rob, who appeared fascinated by him, he pulled out the empty chair next to Geordie and accepted the tankard of ale that Rob had already poured for him.

"Your good health," he announced gravely, toasting the three of them.

Catherine let out an exasperated sigh in return. Geordie merely grunted. "We are waiting for your explanation, Sir Alastair," she said coldly.

"Stair," he said, grave again. "Tell me what happened when they let you out of gaol, Catherine, and you, Geordie, tell me how Sir Francis Herrold treated you when you finally returned."

"Sir Francis Herrold treated me as though I were the merest doxy who treads the London streets," Catherine told him bluntly. "He said that you had had your fill of me, and ordered me to leave by the next boat. He even took me to it as though I were his prisoner. He paid for my passage home in the packet, and that was that. I was left without any money to enable me to travel from the docks to Cob's Lane.

"I thank God that Geordie followed me to the harbour and then boarded the packet. He paid for me to reach home safely, and has been serving me ever since. He even kept me until I found work again since I had left Holland penniless. Are you surprised that we do not want to see you?"

And then, through the tears that she had never shed after he had abandoned her and which were threatening to fall at last, she choked, "Oh, Tom, I never thought that you would treat me after such a cruel fashion, never. To leave me without a kind word, or any message to comfort me on the lonely journey back to Cob's Lane."

"And if I told you that I never treated you so, what then?"

Catherine stared at him. "He said, that fine gentleman, Sir Francis Herrold said…"

Stair interrupted her, swearing an oath so dreadful that all three of them shuddered, and Geordie said reproachfully, "Master!"

"That fine gentleman must have destroyed the love letter that I left for you, explaining why I was leaving for Breda without saying goodbye to you after he and London blackmailed me into going there immediately by threatening your life if I did not. This I swear."

Catherine put her hands up to cover her face and began to cry at last. She hardly knew whether she was crying for sorrow or for joy.

Stair moved swiftly from his chair to kneel on the floor beside her, and put a loving arm around her. "No, do not cry, sweeting. You could not have known. Why should you not think that I was willing to desert you when the time came? Many would have done, but once I knew you and came to love you, I would not have hurt you for the world.

"I could not have believed that even Herrold would destroy my letter and lie to you so brutally. And what of my letters that I sent you from Holland? Did they never arrive either?"

Catherine put her hands into her lap. She was shivering. "No," she told him, her voice little more than a whisper. "No, nothing came. Oh, I hoped so much that you might relent and wish to see me again—and Geordie, too...who had been so kind to me, and so faithful to you."

He kissed her gently on the cheek, for a brief moment ignoring Geordie and Rob. "Oh, my dearest heart, I would have done anything to spare you this."

He lifted his head again. "And Geordie, too. You said that I had left you nothing but two groats for your pains, and turned you off into the bargain. When you returned to the inn, what did Sir Francis say and do? For besides the letter I left for Catherine, I also left a purse of money for you both so that you might get safely home."

"A purse of money!" and now it was Geordie who swore. "Tell me, master, was it left on the table beside the bed? For Sir Francis gave me his two groats from that. I thought that it was his purse."

"That was where he placed it after I gave it to him," Stair said.

This provoked an instant reaction of, "Oh, the villain! The vile sneaking villain! He lied to me and to the mistress. He stole your money and turned my mistress away without so much as a groat! I'll cut his throat for him, that I will!" from Geordie, who was so incensed that he made for the door straightaway.

"No," exclaimed Stair commandingly, his arms still around Catherine. "I'll not have you hang for the swine. In due course he'll gain his just reward for what he did to you both. This I promise you."

"If," announced Catherine spiritedly, "I had written of Sir Francis's villainy in a play, everyone would say that it was not possible!"

She shivered at the thought that what he had done might have parted her and Stair forever. She hugged him to her all the more tightly for having wronged him over the last few weeks when she had thought him a villain who had deserted her. To have him back again, cleared of all guilt, was like a dream come true and it was enough for her to grant him whatever he wished from her—whether it be marriage or no.

Rob, who had been listening closely to them, his eyes swivelling from one to the other, said in his new sober manner, "A question for you, Sir Alastair. What are your intentions towards my sister? As the man of the family I ought to know. Are they honourable?"

Three pairs of eyes surveyed him, bemused. Catherine because never before had Rob said anything half so commonsensical about anything. Stair because Rob's questions had put him squarely in the dock, and Geordie because he had never before heard any one question his master's behaviour to his face.

Stair rose slowly to his feet, leaving Catherine gazing up at him almost fearfully. During the three weeks that they had spent apart, his anguish at not hearing from her had told him how much he loved her. It had brought him squarely before the knowledge that he would not, could not, lose her. Nor, in honour, loving her so, he could not, must not, debauch her.

The man who had sworn that he would never marry was ready to marry the virtuous woman who had sacrificed her virtue only because she loved him. That he was sure of. At the age of twenty-four she had come to him virgin, having resisted all the temptations of a life in the theatre—that hotbed of immorality.

Because of that, even if he had not loved her, it was his duty to love her. But he did love her, and duty did not enter into it.

He was silent for so long that Rob said irritably, "Well, sir, well?"

"Well, very well," replied Stair almost absently, his eyes still on Catherine. He saw her lips quiver and knew by the empathy that lovers share that she was fearful that he was about to refuse her; that Rob had spoken out of turn.

He had never thought that he would ask a woman to marry him. Even if he had ever done so, he would never have thought that he would propose to her before an audience consisting of her brother, and his servant—who stood unwontedly quiet behind him.

Stair sank to his knees before his dear love, took her small hand in his and looked deep into her beautiful violet eyes, which were shining at him, assuring him of her love.

"My darling," he said, "my dearest heart, will you do me the honour of marrying me, of becoming Lady Cameron?"

Catherine took a long breath, and then asked anxiously, "You are sure that you really mean this, Tom…I mean, Stair? That you do not consider that you are compelled to marry me because of…" and she searched for a suitable word, ending with "…everything?"

"It is precisely because of 'everything' that I wish to marry you," Stair told her, gently kissing the palm of each of her hands. "I want you for your wit, your courage, and your steadfastness. Because I love you, and only you, and above all, perhaps, because I cannot think of a better way of having Master Will Wagstaffe in my bed to amuse me!"

"Will Wagstaffe!" exclaimed Rob. Stair noted at once that Robert Wood was no fool, he had picked up the allusion at once. "What does he mean by that, Catherine?"

Catherine coloured, released Stair's hand, and said reproachfully, "Oh, Tom—" for it was difficult to remember that he was really Stair "—you have given my secret away!"

"You cannot keep your secret forever," Stair told her, "particularly if you marry me, although I must remind you that you have not yet given me an answer to my question. Now that I have disposed of the 'everything' that troubled you, perhaps you will do so."

"Do you intend to allow me to continue to write plays for the theatre? Are you willing to play the Duke of Newcastle to my Duchess?"

Stair recognised at once this reference to Margaret, the Duke of Newcastle's wife, whose eccentricity consisted of writings plays and poems and expecting them to be published as a man's would be.

"I have not the slightest intention," he assured her, "of allowing myself or the world to be deprived of Master Wagstaffe's wit. The Duchess's does not hold a candle to it. But I fear that you must cease to be an actress. You will have no time to be one when you are my wife."

It was Rob's turn to sit down, clutching his head. "I am quite bemused," he announced, "first Tom Trenchard, the penniless adventurer, turns out to be Sir Alastair Cameron, whom even I know is one of the King's counsellors. Then he proposes marriage to my sister instead of making her his mistress, and finally my sister turns out to be Will Wagstaffe, whose plays are the talk of London. Either I am drunk—or run mad. Which?"

"Neither," Catherine said, "for I had to become Will Wagstaffe in order to earn us a living—being only an actress was not enough—and the rest seems to have followed. It will not trouble me to retire from acting—when I have finished my current contract with Betterton, that is."

Geordie said, "Make the most of it, Master Rob. For this is the eighth wonder of the world—that Master

Tom should marry. He always vowed he never would. Alas, I think that our adventuring days are over."

"Not quite," said Stair, laughing. "For Master Wagstaffe here has still not given me my answer, and there is another matter or two to settle. Come, mistress, yea or nay. Do not palter with me, my darling heart."

"Oh, Tom, I mean, Stair," sighed Catherine hanging her head and blushing, "you already know the answer, and this is the strangest proposal a woman could receive—being made before two other people."

"Only," said Stair, feasting his eyes on her, "because I wish to be absolutely certain that you are fully committed to me, before witnesses. There has been enough confusion between us already. And still you have not answered me."

"You know the answer. It is yes, it was always yes, and always will be. Will that do?"

"Splendidly so! I call upon all here present," Stair declaimed grandly, "to witness that Mistress Catherine Wood, who like me has more names than one—indeed, exceeds me by having three!—has consented to be my wife. Is not that so, sweeting?"

Catherine rose and curtsied. "Exactly so."

"Well said." Stair looked around the room, particularly at the table set for a meal that had not been eaten. "And as token," he announced, grave for once, "that you are now *my* family, let us break bread together."

Catherine was beginning to feel that she was living in one of old Will Shakespeare's plays, *All's Well That Ends Well,* except that her intuition told her that Stair—she really must learn to call him by his proper name—and Geordie seemed to have something else on their mind.

It was when she asked Stair, after their meal, whether he had discovered who had killed Giles Newman and William Grahame that she first became suspicious of him. "Oh," he told her airily, "about the only useful thing Sir Francis Herrold did was to inform me that Amos Shooter, who was playing a double—nay, a treble—game had disposed of them."

"Geordie thought that he saw Amos Shooter in London recently," Catherine said. "You remember that I thought that I saw him in the Buttermarket in Amsterdam.

"A much-travelled gentleman," remarked Stair, still airy, and left it at that.

"I am also beginning to think that it was he who betrayed us to the authorities in Antwerp," she added.

"Perhaps," Stair said, "but that is all over now, sweeting. Let us forget it," and he kissed the top of her head in lieu of anything more personal, seeing that they were now drinking coffee with Rob and Geordie.

Geordie was later to tell Stair that all that Rob needed to put him on the right path in life was a firm fatherly hand.

"Such as yours," said Stair.

"Aye, you may well laugh." Geordie was a trifle bitter. "But it is the truth."

"I am not laughing," Stair told him. "For you offered me a firm elder-brotherly hand—to some effect, I believe. If you can make Rob Wood less of a hothead, then that is all to the good. You will save me the trouble!"

He had evaded Catherine's questions about Amos Shooter for a good reason, and when she had also said to him in an earnest voice, "You won't try to punish Sir Francis Herrold for what he did to me and Geordie, will you, Stair? He didn't succeed in destroying what we had between us, and that is his real punishment," he never gave her a firm answer—which, of course, she immediately noticed.

No sooner was he alone with Geordie after Catherine had set off for the theatre and Rob had retired to his room to study, than he pursued the matter of Amos with him.

"You are sure that it was Shooter whom you saw in the Strand?"

"Quite sure, master. I followed him to his

lodgings. He is known there as James Harris and his wife is not with him."

"Gone back to her family, no doubt." There was something on Geordie's face that made Stair ask, "What is it, man? You look as pregnant as a woman nearing her term!"

"I wants to serve Shooter as he has served others, that's all, Master Tom. You've got your hands full with Sir Francis. Leave Shooter to me. No call for you to be suspected of dealing with two. Mum's the word, eh?" And he put his finger by his nose. "Less said the better, even between the pair on us."

Master and man looked at one another in perfect agreement. Stair said, "You're sure you want to take this on, Geordie?"

"Aye, master. He served the mistress a nasty turn, so he did, and he deserves what he's going to get for that alone." He hesitated and added, "You be careful with Sir Francis, I wouldn't want her to be hurt any more than she needs. She's a brave lady, that she is."

"I'll be careful, Geordie. Trust me, no heroics. And no comebacks from the authorities either."

To make sure of this, after bidding Catherine farewell—for they were remaining chaste until their marriage—he made his way back to Arlington's lodgings at Whitehall.

"A word with you," he said, and when Arlington bade him sit down and speak he told him of Sir

Francis Herrold's treachery to Catherine, and that she had agreed to become his wife.

"A remarkable lady," Arlington said at last, "if she can trap you into marriage! No, Stair, do not be angry with me. I respect the lady, too. If for no better reason than that, between you, you sent us the news that might have given us the beating of the Dutch—if we had heeded you. But you said that you wanted something from me?"

He waited for an answer. Stair said shortly, "I wish to deal with Sir Francis at once, and I don't wish to find myself in gaol before I even have time to marry. I shall not seek him out in the precincts of Whitehall, but corner him somewhere where duelling is not a crime—as it is in the King's neighbourhood. And I shall try not to kill him, but humiliate him, instead. I have no mind to be the centre of a scandal when I am about to be married."

"Very wise," approved Arlington. "You may rest assured that any punishment that you hand out to him for so mistreating your lady will not be looked ill upon. Believe me, he far exceeded his instructions when dealing with you and your lady. Neither Sir Thomas nor I gave him leave to blackmail you as he did. True, we wanted Mistress Wood to come home without you, but not after the cruel fashion which he arranged.

"I would not like you to think that I gave orders

that you—or she—should be dealt with so scurvily—or that I would ever be a party to betraying you to our enemies! Quite the contrary. As for Herrold, there are many of us who will be happy to see him humiliated—if that is what you succeed in doing. But wise of you to check with me, Stair, that such a move as you propose would be acceptable. You are growing cautious in your old age."

"A wife and the hope of a family in the not-so-distant future changes a man's character more than a little, I find. But I grow didactic. And I never was as rash as Rochester and the rest of The Merry Gang are. At least grant me that."

"And more, Stair, and more. I wish you luck—in all your enterprises."

Stair found Sir Francis Herrold, his toady, James Vaux, by his side, in the Great Coffee House, not far away from the Poultry and Cornhill, well away from the palace of Whitehall, and much frequented by those about the King and court. Sam Pepys, the Clerk to the Navy Board, was often there, and was present that night.

Sir Francis had drunk more than coffee. His face lit up when Stair walked in. "Ah, Cameron, you are back, then? And your doxy, is she back? Has she found a new keeper yet?" Discretion was never his middle name, and Stair blessed him for it. At least it would never be said that he had begun the quarrel.

"I have no doxy, Herrold. I assume that you believe all men are as loose as you in their habits or—" and he swung his gaze significantly towards James Vaux "—perhaps even more so."

"And what the devil do you mean by that, Cameron?" bellowed Sir Francis, ignoring James Vaux's hand pulling at his arm to try to quieten him.

"You must make what you will of it yourself," returned Stair negligently, "for I cannot tell what is going on in the lump of pig's swill that you call a brain!"

Sir Francis made to lunge across the table at his taunting enemy, who was only too happy that he had diverted Sir Francis's innuendos away from Catherine. He had no wish for her name to be flung about in public. Several of Sir Francis's court tried to hold him back. They were successful, but they could not make him hold his tongue.

"By God, Cameron, I'll call you out for that, damned if I don't."

"And damned if you do," returned Stair agreeably, in no whit troubled that the other man was the aggressor who might name his weapons. "Where shall we meet—and when?"

Sir Francis hesitated. He had meant merely to

provoke, not to find himself in a duel with a man whose courage and skill were a byword.

"Can't think, eh?" riposted Stair, amused that he had neatly trapped his man. "Now? At Leicester Field? My second shall be Buckhurst—if he so pleases," for that gentleman was lounging against the wall, amused by what was passing.

"With pleasure, Stair. Can't stand the man m'self. Few can. Do the world a favour by ridding it of him."

Several present who were not Herrold's toadies muttered their approval. Someone shouted, "Let's to Leicester Field and have done with it."

"A splendid notion," approved Stair, and nodded familiarly at Sir Francis. "Settle it now. With small swords, I suppose—although it is your choice. Vaux to be your second, I presume?"

Vaux's anguished face showed that Stair might presume, but Vaux could not approve. But neither he nor Herrold could back down without losing their place in society. Leicester Field it was to be, and presently. Herrold fancied himself with the small sword and agreed to that, as well.

"It's too dark to fight," was James Vaux's only—and desperate—contribution.

"Nonsense," said Stair pleasantly, "there'll be enough light to kill a man by, I'm sure." He had no intention of killing anyone, there would be too much trouble for the survivor afterwards, and he would tell Buckhurst to spare James Vaux, and hope that he would.

So it was decided. Leicester Field it was. A small crowd followed them, which grew larger when interested passers-by learned that four fine gents were about to have a set-to in the usual place for such activities.

Stair would have preferred to have finished Francis Herrold off for good and all, but wisdom said no. Wisdom also said short and sweet would be better than long and drawn out, which would have added more to Herrold's humiliation, but might not be wise. There was his future with Catherine to think of.

But humiliation it still was. Stair toyed with his enemy for a brief space before he finished the bout by inflicting on him the *coup de Jarnac* of which he had told Catherine. Herrold fell to the ground, moaning with pain, and unable to rise. The bout between the two seconds was brought to a close by Stair, who swung his sword up between Buckhurst and Vaux's. He had no wish to see Vaux dead, and Buckhurst was flighty enough to kill him for the fun of it.

"Damn you, Stair, I was just about to inflict the *coup de grâce* as you inflicted the *coup de Jarnac*." He laughed heartlessly at Herrold who was being held up by two of his servants. Stair handed his small sword to Geordie and walked over to where Herrold was sitting, his face drawn.

"Note this, Herrold." Stair's voice was as hard as he could make it, as hard as the soldier he had once been. "If I ever learn that you are insulting me and mine as you have done this evening, and lately in Holland, I shall finish off the task I began today. Next time I shall not cripple you, but kill you. Do you understand me?"

Herrold made no reply.

Stair repeated what he had said. "Yes, or no, Herrold?"

"Yes, Cameron, I understand you." The words were groaned out with difficulty.

"Good, and see that you continue to do so."

Stair turned away, vengeance having been done. Geordie handed him back his cloak and sword, and said softly. "Your task done, master, mine is yet to be fulfilled," and slid away into the growing dark.

Stair, with Buckhurst's arm through his—he had forgiven Stair for not allowing him to kill Vaux—walked back to Whitehall. He was sure that he had silenced Herrold for good and all since his downfall was already being cried in the streets by the many who had witnessed it.

He would never revile or insult Catherine again.

Geordie's target was Amos Shooter. He walked briskly to Shooter's lodgings; all his usual dallying was missing. He was in luck, Shooter was there. His appearance and his rooms were both a pale shadow of all that had surrounded him when he had been a wealthy merchant in Antwerp.

He stared suspiciously at Geordie. "What the devil do you want of me?" he demanded. "You are Tom Trenchard's man."

"No longer," replied Geordie, lying in his teeth. "We have had a right falling out, and I am hot to be no man's man. Also, I would wish to do him an injury, seeing that he has turned me off after many years of faithful service. So I have come to give you information."

"Why, what have you to give me?" Shooter was plainly still suspicious.

"You must know that my late master is high in the King's favour, and is privy to the secrets of state through his other friendship with Lord Arlington. Come, I hear that you, too, have lost all after such noble service to the state."

Geordie was careful not to say which state, for he was not quite sure of all of Shooter's many and varied treacheries.

"Aye, that I was and did their dirty work for them—only to be betrayed."

Geordie might have felt sorry for him had he not known of the trail of dead and ruined men Shooter had left behind him. Worse, he had put Catherine in danger and, after Tom Trenchard, Catherine was his guiding star. He had no relatives, few friends and Tom had rescued him from servitude when Tom had been a lad starting out in the world and Geordie had been a poor young man already scarred by life.

Shooter looked narrowly at him and sighed. The man before him might have something to tell him, and if he did not, or was trying to trick him, well then, he could be easily disposed of, like many before him.

"Speak on," he ordered grudgingly.

Geordie smiled cunningly at Shooter and said, "I shall require little from you other than a promise to pay me for my information. As a start, you may buy me a tankard of ale at the nearest tavern and after that I shall tell you my news."

For a moment Shooter hesitated. "Why not here, where we may be private?"

"Where more private than a noisy alehouse? We shall appear to be drinking companions, no more, no less. Best that I am not seen at your lodgings. Landladies have long tongues." He hesitated, before half-turning away, saying, "If you do not want my information, then I may as well try to sell it elsewhere."

His prey was desperate. He was alone, the agents of three governments were pursuing him because he knew too much, and he thought Geordie a sly fool because he was, like many before him, misled by his careless dress and his servile manner. A fool who would sell himself for a mere tankard of ale!

"Very well then, lead on. There is a tavern in the next street. We may reach it through an alley a few doors from here."

Excellent, thought Geordie with a grin. It was a dark night, with a pale sliver of moon. Exactly what he might have wished. He and Shooter reached the alley where Shooter, talking to a man he imagined to be a lesser villain than himself, was taken completely by surprise when Geordie caught him by the arm, swinging him round so that for a brief moment they were face to face.

Before Shooter could grasp what was happening to him, Geordie, in one subtle movement, slid his dagger into Shooter's ribs whilst murmuring, "This is for the mistress."

Shooter fell dying to the ground, and Geordie, transformed into a flying elf rather than a dawdling goblin, slipped out of the alley and made for Cob's Lane, Catherine and his supper, his vengeance accomplished.

"And where have you been?" Catherine asked him when he returned to Cob's Lane. "Misbehaving yourself with your master, I suppose." For Rob had come home not long before, telling her that it was already being cried about the streets, the coffee houses and the inns, that Sir Alastair Cameron and Sir

Francis Herrold had fought a duel at Leicester Field and that Sir Francis had been disabled for life.

To her amusement, Geordie performed his most artistic cringe. She shook her head at him. "Do not lie to me, I know that your master defied me by risking his life to punish Sir Francis for his treachery towards us. I suppose that you have been celebrating his naughtiness."

Something in Geordie's face made her suspicious of more than that. Oh, she trusted neither of them, they were a scaly pair of rogues and whether either of them would ever settle down into being good honest citizens she begged leave to doubt. She was not sure that she even wanted them to.

"No," she told him. "Say no more. I have no wish to know what the pair of you have got up to. I most certainly should not like it. Go to bed without supper, that shall be your punishment."

Catherine laughed ruefully to herself as Geordie scuttled out of the room and up the stairs. One thing was certain, life as Lady Cameron was never going to be dull! She took that thought to bed with her in lieu of Tom—no, Stair!

And as she drifted into sleep she knew that, once they were married, there would be many more nights for them, and all as joyous as those she had already spent with him in Amsterdam.

Epilogue

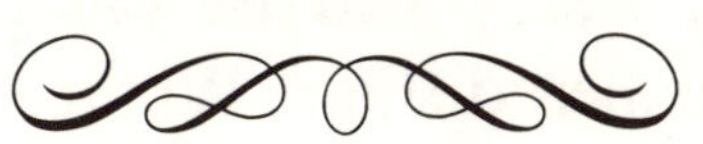

Two men from the court of King Charles II at Whitehall sat on the side of the stage of the Duke of York's Theatre in the summer of 1667. One of them was short and plump and was wearing a monstrous black curled wig. The other was tall and muscular, he was not wearing a wig, but his own waving red-gold hair. Neither of them were sporting masks.

They were watching a play called *The Braggart, or, Lackwit Married,* by one Will Wagstaffe, which was rapidly reaching its end. The chief actress, one Mistress Cleone Dubois playing Belinda, was on the stage being reconciled to her husband, Amoroso, after having discomfited Lackwit in no uncertain fashion.

Betterton, who was playing Lackwit, lay at the back of the stage, groaning, after being assaulted in a vital part of his anatomy by Belinda.

In a moment, the play over, they would all jump

to their feet, join hands and move to the front of the stage to accept the applause of the audience. *The Braggart* had been a riotous and bawdy success, and many were asking who the author was. The name of Wagstaffe was, all were agreed, a pseudonym.

"D'you still favour her legs, Stair, now that you are married to them? And are you going to join in the play?" whispered Black Wig to his companion, who on this visit to the theatre had behaved himself rather better than he had done in the spring.

"Yes to the first question and perhaps to the last," whispered Stair.

"Pity that, about the last," returned Arlington. "I rather enjoyed your part in the action when we came here in the spring. Has your inventiveness finally run out?"

"By no means," said Stair, who had not relished the sight of Catherine being kissed by another man, even if that man were simply a mummer, a mock hero pretending to be violently in love with a mock heroine. "As you will later discover."

"And shall I then discover who Will Wagstaffe is?"

"Ah, you must wait to learn that!"

Arlington fell silent. The play ended. The applause was lengthy—this was the first night and it was plain by the audience's enthusiasm that the play would run for at least a fortnight, making it a most notable success.

Catherine, standing between Betterton and Jack Hayes, the actor playing Amoroso, found that her eyes were filling with tears. Oh, it was not that she wished to continue as an actress, far from it. She had only become one in order to earn a living and the pains associated with being a female player had been greater than the pleasure.

She had spent a large part of her time avoiding forced seduction. Many thought actresses fair game—the equivalent of whores. No, her real dedication was given to becoming a playwright whose work would be ranked with the best.

She looked towards Stair, who had risen to his feet and was applauding her loudly. That look told him of her love. "No, no regrets," she had said to him earlier, for he was worried that she might regret having to leave the stage. She hoped that he had believed her.

Betterton released his hand from that of the woman on his right, and Catherine let go of Jack's. Together she and Betterton walked to the front of the stage. Applause broke out again.

At length Betterton raised his right hand and announced, "My friends, Mistress Cleone Dubois has something to say to you, but before she does so I have a piece of news for you. I have frequently been asked who Master Will Wagstaffe really is and I have always told you that I had not permission to give you his true name. But tonight I may do so for, my friends, Master Wagstaffe is none other than this same Mistress Cleone Dubois, who tells me she will write many more such as *The Braggart* to entertain you."

Astonishment reigned for a moment before renewed applause broke out. Stair tossed a posy in Catherine's direction, which she picked up and waved at the audience. Those few, like Arlington, who knew that they had been secretly married earlier that day, redoubled their enthusiasm, began to cheer, and to tell their neighbours the happy news.

Betterton raised his right hand again. "Pray silence for Mistress Dubois who will now speak her own, and the play's, Epilogue." He stood back to allow Catherine to hold the stage alone.

For the first time in her life stage fright threatened to overwhelm her. Before her was a sea of avid faces, alight with the knowledge that it was a woman who had written the comic masterpiece that they had just enjoyed.

Stair's voice broke her temporary trance. "Courage," he said, in his best mocking manner. "*Le diable est mort*—the devil is dead—so you need not fear him."

The spell of fear was, indeed, broken. Suddenly Catherine wanted to laugh instead. She gave the audience a vast curtsy before she spoke the Epilogue that she and Stair had written between them that very morning.

"Friends, I reject the buskins and the mask
In favour of another, harder, task.
For Hymen calls, the marriage god, no less,
His call so strong my answer must be yes.
Yet absent though I be, I shall not quite
Desert my other Muse, since my delight
Is still to comment on life's varied scene;
To write with passion, true and bold and keen,
More plays in which to celebrate our time
In words and music, dancing and in mime.
So now farewell, forget me not, I trust
'Til theatre, actors—and myself—are dust!"

Silence followed, and then more applause, led by Betterton. Stair, still applauding, moved across to her to see that her eyes were full of tears. "Weep not, sweeting," he murmured in her ear. "This is but the mime of which you spoke. Outside is the real world where we shall walk together."

And then he took her hand, and bowed, with Catherine beside him falling into the actress's farewell curtsy.

"Friends," he announced, his voice as resonant, and as powerful as the actors who had preceded him.

"I have but lent my wife to you for this night and for a few more. But rest assured that I will see that she keeps to the promise that she has just made you. Will Wagstaffe will write again. And now, I, too, will append mine own Epilogue to the play."

Amid cheering he began to do just that.

"An orange, a posy, a perfumed glove,
Were the three presents I gave to my love,
When on these very boards I first met my wife—
And that was the end of my bachelor life!"

He bowed as the cheering broke out again, and took Catherine by the hand, saying *"Adieu, adieu, adieu."* Walking backwards, he escorted her from the stage.

One of the King's courtiers had provided the audience with yet another night's entertainment. To make matters even better, this time the courtier had married his actress, not simply made her his mistress.

Stair did not allow Catherine to pause in the green room. Tonight was theirs, and neither the players nor the audience would share in it. Holding her tightly by the hand he led her through it, through the stage door, and into the street, to where their coach waited. Geordie, clad in a resplendent new livery, handed them in.

"Still no regrets?" he asked her as the Duke's Theatre fell behind them, for he was more than a little troubled that she might not have wished to end her career as an actress.

"None," said Catherine, whose dreams had come true that day, for was she not married to the man who had featured in them from the moment that they had met?

"Good," said Stair, leaning forward to kiss her as the coach drove into the night and into the future, where as man and wife they were to share in that contentment that many wish to achieve but few do, but whose magic beckons us all towards a distant dream.